WHO GUARDS
THE PRINCE?

WHO GUARDS THE PRINCE?

Reginald Hill

Pantheon Books, New York

The Library of Congress Cataloged the First Printing of this Title as
Follows:

Hill, Reginald.
Who guards the prince?
I. Title.
PR6058.1448w5   1982   823'.914   81-48225

ISBN 0-394-52077-7

ISBN 0-394-71337-0 (Pbk.)   AACR2

Manufactured in the United States of America

First American Paperback Edition

'*Who guards a Prince must other Oaths unspeak,*
Reck not of Friend, on Foe no Vengeance wreak.
Who guards a Prince must pawn his proper Life,
Orphan his Children, and Widow make of Wife.

These Debts denied, what then is his Reward?
Who guards a Prince, and fails, himself shall find no Guard.'

Morland's *Mottoes*

'These signs and tokens are of no small value; they speak a universal language and act as a passport to the attention and support of the initiated in all parts of the world. They cannot be lost so long as memory retains its power . . .

'The great effects which they have produced are established by the most incontestable facts of history. They have stayed the uplifted hand of the destroyer; they have softened the asperities of the tyrant; they have mitigated the horrors of captivity; they have subdued the rancours of malevolence . . .

'On the field of battle, in the solitude of the uncultivated forests, or in the busy haunts of the crowded city, they have made men of the most hostile feeling, and the most distant religions, and the most diversified conditions, rush to the aid of each other . . .'

Benjamin Franklin

Part One

SIGNS AND TOKENS

1

'These several points I solemnly swear to observe without evasion, equivocation, or mental reservation of any kind . . .'

The Entered Apprentice felt ridiculous and he felt frightened.

He felt ridiculous because his left trouser leg was rolled up above the knee, his left breast was bared, and he was wearing a slipper on his right foot.

He felt frightened because he had a noose round his neck, a blindfold round his eyes and a dagger at his throat.

The ceremony ground interminably on, till at last he heard the Præceptor's voice say, 'Having been kept for a considerable time in a state of darkness, what in your present situation is the predominant wish of your heart?'

His voice was hoarse as he croaked, 'Light.'

'Let that blessing be restored to the candidate.'

There was a single clap from several hands and, with a disproportionate sense of relief, he felt the blindfold being removed.

Once restored to normal vision, his sense of fear rapidly faded, but his sense of the ridiculous remained and he found himself looking for irony in the congratulations of his fellows, but finding none.

Last was the Tyler who had entered the room as quietly as ever.

'Is that it then?' said the Entered Apprentice.

The Tyler did not answer but looked at the Præceptor, who had joined them.

'Yes, it does all seem a little absurd, doesn't it?' murmured the Præceptor, 'I quite agree with what I see you are thinking.

Form without substance is as pointless as, say, substance without form.'

'No, no. Not at all,' said the Entered Apprentice, *fearful of being thought critical.*

The Præceptor smiled and said, 'Now, don't disappoint me. And we'll try not to disappoint you. Look, there's a bit of business you can help the Tyler with, if you would.'

'But of course.'

'Excellent,' said the Præceptor. 'I must be off in a minute. One of those television chat shows. So tedious, but I don't like to refuse. Step next door and the Tyler will put you into the picture. I'll just say my goodbyes and be on my way. Once again, welcome to our company.'

'I'm really honoured to have been invited to join,' said the Entered Apprentice *stiltedly.*

'Yes, I believe you are,' said the Præceptor. 'And I think I can honestly say that few of our members live to regret it. Goodbye now. And good luck.'

2

The tide was at the ebb.

It was the moment of the held breath and the stopped clock, in popular mythology the most likely time for the ill and the aged to release their hold on life and slip quietly away.

Dr Wainwright didn't believe the myth. Twenty years of general practice had taught him there was only one common denominator in his patients' times of death. They were usually bloody inconvenient.

But even his medical cynicism was not proof against the magic of the moment. Landward, the sea-front buildings were a black frieze against a smudgy pink sky. On the beach the last rays of the setting sun glanced palely off the wet sand. Stretching out before him to a shadowy and mysterious horizon, the sea lay perfectly still, gathering its strength for a renewed assault on the land.

The only movement and sound came from a small figure close by the water's edge. This was Lucy, his five-year-old daughter, and she was part of the magic. She was attacking the wet sand vigorously with her little spade, piling up one of the irregular mounds she called her castles. In a few moments the tide would turn and wash it away. Lucy would be distressed. But no amount of persuasion could get her to build further away from the water's edge.

'Daddy! Daddy!' she called shrilly. 'I've caught a fish.'

As if the girl's voice had broken a spell, a breeze sprang up in the darkening air and crazed the glassy surface of the sea.

The tide had turned.

'What have you got then?' asked Wainwright, moving forward. 'A shark, is it? Or a whale?'

He bent down over the little girl, expecting a piece of sea-weed or at most the shell of a crab.

But what she was holding up to him was more solid than that and had something of the shape of a fish though not the look of one.

'It was in the hole,' said Lucy proudly. 'I dug it up.'

Wainwright took the object from his daughter's little hand. It felt soft but tough. He held it close to his eyes in the darkling air and let out a quiet exclamation. Bending forward, he immersed it in the sea and agitated it to remove the clinging film of sand.

Then he examined it again.

'What is it, Daddy? What kind is it?' asked Lucy impatiently.

'I'm not sure, darling,' he answered, taking out his pocket handkerchief and wrapping it carefully round the object. He looked down at the hole from which it had come. Already the returning sea had filled it with water. Another couple of surges and it would disappear completely.

'Daddy, the water's going over my castle!' protested Lucy, her attention suddenly diverted. She began to try to shovel the sea backwards with her spade till Wainwright bent down and took it from her hand.

'I tell you what, dear,' he said, thrusting the spade into the sand till only the handle and a couple of inches of shaft remained visible. 'If we mark the spot like this, we can come back and repair your castle later.'

Now he picked a mark in the black silhouette of sea-front buildings, a high gable with a crooked chimney stack, and taking his daughter by the hand he set off towards it.

Lucy, not at all convinced of the wisdom of abandoning her spade, hung back, looking behind her. As the tide surged over the handle she cried out anxiously, and when her father showed no sign of slowing down she began to sob. But for once her tears had none of their usual softening effect and after a while she saved her energy and dried her eyes.

Wainwright hardly noticed. It took a great deal to distract his attention from his daughter, especially in distress. But what he was carrying in his pocket was distraction more than enough.

It was a tongue.

It was a human tongue.

And it had been torn with brute force from its owner's mouth.

3

Four miles inland the same breeze which sprang up on the turning tide sent fine white ash drifting over Detective-Inspector Douglas McHarg's sturdy brogues.

He didn't notice, but Chief Fire Officer Potter who stood alongside him coughed ostentatiously, though the ash got nowhere near his face. 'Have you seen enough, Inspector?' he asked in irritation. 'We've been here an hour and soon it's going to be too dark to see anything.'

The two men were standing in the burnt-out shell of a small cottage which had once housed the family of the miller who owned the old watermill against which it abutted. Derelict till the affluent late 'fifties, it had been refurbished as a country retreat, exchanging hands at progressively larger prices till it had been bought three years earlier by James Morrison, a freelance journalist, in one of his not too frequent periods of affluence.

Now, for Morrison, affluence and austerity alike were over. The white film on McHarg's shoes probably contained a fair percentage of what was left of the man.

The fire had started in the small living-room. Morrison, as was his wont, had been drinking long and hard in the local pub about a mile away – probably well after hours though naturally the landlord wasn't admitting this. He had returned home and continued the session privately, or so they surmised from the dissolved shards of what was probably a whisky bottle near the calcined bones of what was probably Jim Morrison.

'A cigarette end on a cushion stuffed with polyurethane foam,' CFO Potter explained once more. 'Him too bottled to notice; and once it started smouldering you'd get enough hydrogen cyanide to put him out in next to no time. After that, once the fire got hold, well, this place was timber-framed, with a thatched roof. An incendiary bomb in other words, just waiting for a drunk with matches.'

'We're standing on that drunk with matches,' grunted McHarg.

'All right!' exploded Potter. 'So we are. I'm sorry for the poor devil. But why have you dragged me out here again?'

McHarg didn't answer. He couldn't because he didn't know. But something about the memory of that morning, with the dawn chorus starting up all around regardless of, or perhaps deceived by, the heap of glowing embers still too hot to permit a close approach, had stuck with him all day and made him impulsively invite the Chief Fire Officer to confirm his report on the spot.

From the millhouse whose yard-thick stone walls had easily resisted the onslaughts of the flames, Police Constable Ian Arrowsmith who'd spent most of the day fending off rustic sightseers was watching the scene. With him was Ken Daly, a fireman who had driven Potter here.

'Come on!' muttered Daly impatiently as he watched the two figures in the gloaming. 'Get a bloody move on! I'm off duty in half an hour.'

Arrowsmith chuckled.

'Your boss won't leave here till HM's good and finished,' he said. 'So you'd best settle down and be patient.'

'Inspector McHarg, you mean?' said Daly. 'Why HM?'

'His Majesty,' said Arrowsmith. 'Not that anyone ever says that to his face. He used to be on the royal squad up at the Yard, evidently.'

'Queen's bodyguard, you mean?' asked Daly, interested.

'No. One of the Princes, young Arthur, I think. Something happened. God knows what. One story says he told the Prince or someone important to fuck off. Or mebbe they just missed some of the Crown Jewels! Whatever, he ended up down here in the sticks a couple of years ago. And he doesn't look likely to go higher than Inspector. But he still acts like he's bloody king. So, HM. It fits.'

'I wonder what he's dragged old Potter back here for?' said Daly.

Arrowsmith shrugged his ignorance and changed the subject.

'Bloody marvellous, this thing,' he said pointing to the water-wheel which stood still against the pressure of the racing stream. 'It's linked up to a small generator, you know. No candles needed here if there was a power cut. Must be nice to have money.'

'The poor bastard doesn't need candles now, not for light anyway,' said Daly. 'Why isn't it moving?'

'Your lot knocked it off this morning. I mean, there wasn't much point in generating electricity, was there? That's what holds it, that locking bar.'

'This?' said Daly, taking hold of a long metal lever. He eased it towards him, just to test the resistance. It was so well oiled and maintained, there was hardly any. With a series of clicks on the locking ratchet, the great shaft was freed and, slowly at first but with gathering speed, the wheel began to turn.

Attracted by the noise, Chief Fire Officer Potter turned towards the millhouse and bawled, 'Daly! What're you playing at? Turn that blasted thing off.'

'No,' said McHarg. 'Wait.'

He too turned to watch the rise and fall of the wheel silhouetted vaguely against the darkening sky. For perhaps a minute he watched and listened to the rhythmical splash of water against paddles, the gurgle of the stream and the more intermittent and irregular creaks and groans as the ancient timbers protested their never-ending task.

After a while McHarg smiled.

'Thank you, Mr Potter,' he said. 'Let's go.'

He strode towards his car, kicking up a cloud of ash, making Potter cough again, genuinely this time.

'Stupid bastard!' he muttered, including comprehensively Inspector McHarg, James Morrison, and himself for putting up with this uncommunicative, opinionated policeman.

He'd have found a lot of support for his antipathy, both in and out of the force. But when McHarg got back to the central police station in Sanderton, he found himself greeted with more than customary enthusiasm.

'Mr McHarg, sir,' said the desk sergeant, nodding towards the interview room from which the sound of voices came. 'I think DC Brownlow would welcome a bit of assistance.'

'What's up?'

'Nothing really. Well, it's one of our local GPs, you may know him, Wainwright. Something about digging up something on the beach. He says it's a man's tongue.'

4

His Royal Highness Prince Arthur, Duke of Wenlock, Colonel-in-Chief of the Welsh Light Infantry, and Laird of Gulvain, had been schooled by experts to keep his feelings to himself.

Even when his visit to East Anglia to open a new electricity generating plant fell so far behind schedule that the girls' pipe-band assembled to enrich his departure was almost invisible, though far from inaudible, in the fenny mists of evening, his young features showed no sign of impatience or boredom.

His personal detective, Inspector Dewhurst, showed much more concern at this unscheduled twilight, but the Prince ignored him till his equerry, Captain Edward Jopley, murmured a reminder that he was dining at Windsor along with the Canadian Commissioner. Only then, with every sign of genuine reluctance, did he climb into the waiting limousine. Captain Jopley got in beside him. And finally Dewhurst, never taking his eyes off the applauding spectators, slipped into the front passenger seat and said tersely, 'Drive!'

The car slid away, preceded and pursued by police outriders.

And now, only now, when the last child with the last Union Jack on the last pavement had been left behind and the flat, dark fields lying alongside the arterial road were flowing past did the Prince permit himself the luxury of a yawn.

'Mr Dewhurst looked a trifle ruffled at the end, I felt,' he said, having first made sure that the soundproofing glass panel was properly closed.

'Just worried about security, sir,' said Jopley. 'It got dark awfully quickly. It is his job, after all.'

'Of course it is, my dear chap. And very well he does it, too. But he's not exactly the laughing policeman, is he? You know, I sometimes miss old McHarg. Do you remember McHarg, Edward?'

'Indeed, sir. Not a great humorist either, I wouldn't have said. And at least Dewhurst's polite.'

'True,' said the Prince. 'About Dewhurst, I mean. But believe me, you could have some laughs with McHarg. Not polite, though. No, if he'd been as worried as poor Dewhurst about being behind our schedule, he'd have chucked me into the car an hour ago and if I'd complained he'd have told me it was nothing to do with me, but his artistic Scottish soul couldn't bear those girl pipers a minute longer!'

He chuckled reminiscently, a young man very much at ease with life. Jopley raised a wan smile which did not go unnoticed.

Prince Arthur regarded his equerry shrewdly. Edward Jopley was just turned thirty, a slim, upright man, meticulous about his personal appearance whether in or out of uniform. Now there was a slight but uncharacteristic slackening about his posture and a couple of strands of black hair had strayed unchecked across his brow.

'Edward,' said the Prince, 'are you all right? You're looking a bit peaky. I noticed earlier.'

Jopley made a conscious effort to pull himself together and said, 'No, really, I'm fine.'

But the Prince was not a man who took merely a token interest in those around him. Jopley had his job because he was unobtrusively efficient, extremely prudent, and the Prince liked and trusted him without ever feeling he could make such a close friend of him that their job relationship could be threatened. Now he applied his mind to the problem of the equerry's trouble with genuine concern.

'God, how crass of me,' he said suddenly. 'This news at lunchtime. Of course.'

They had caught the one o'clock news as they motored (late) from the generating plant to the civic luncheon. The Prince always liked to listen to the news ever since he'd made a jokey speech to a group of miners who had just heard (which he hadn't) of new proposals to close pits in their area.

'Edward, I'm sorry. That journalist, Morrison, the one who died, you were at school with him, weren't you? I remember your mentioning it once when you asked if he could travel on our plane. How awful for you. I'm sorry.'

Jopley nodded. 'Thank you, sir,' he said. 'We weren't very close, but I have to admit it was a shock.'

'A dreadful way to go. And hearing about it like that. I remember him vaguely. He seemed a very nice man. And bright too. Extremely original talent. I read some of his articles.'

'Yes, he was original all right,' said Jopley. 'Too much so for some people.'

Prince Arthur's mind was schooled to docket odd bits of information about people and something now popped up about Morrison and drink. He'd been pie-eyed at a press-conference . . . someone important . . . embarrassing questions . . . Jopley would probably remember but his present assessment was that his equerry should be weaned off the subject rather than urged into reminiscence.

'What you need is a good night's rest, Edward. Try to turn in early tonight.'

'I'm dining too, sir,' said Jopley, in a tone of slight reproof. 'Her Majesty is very insistent that I be present at all briefings.'

'Yes, of course,' said the Prince a little testily. Tonight's dinner was in part a preliminary to his imminent visit to Canada. He could have done without it. It had been a long day and a couple of chops on a tray in front of the telly would have suited him better. Besides, he'd spent more than a year at school in Canada in the not too distant past and felt he knew the country pretty well. Still, his was not to reason why, not yet awhile anyway . . .

'At least he's not like that Australian,' he added with a chuckle. 'The one that mixed port and brandy and stayed till four a.m. You can still make it to your mattress before midnight, Edward. Curl up with a good book. Or a bottle. Or something.'

Jopley smiled but did not answer and the Prince had to repress his curiosity, which had already brought him unpleasantly close to impertinence, as to the nature of Jopley's sex life.

Not that he could be any more open about his own. He closed his eyes and sighed. Had he been more intellectually inclined he might have puzzled over the problem of conventional morality. There had been a time when he was happy to choose discreetly but with no qualms of conscience from the many offers which were continually being put his way. But that was before he fell in love. So now, despite the fact that the object of his love was three thousand miles away and he hadn't seen her for six months and he had no idea how things at present stood between them, he refused all offers. The result was that the moment he allowed his vivid imagination to wander across the Atlantic he found himself in a state of acute and occasionally embarrassing sexual excitement.

He opened his eyes and shifted his position on the car seat.

'Canada,' he murmured. 'You know, Edward, I'm really looking forward to this trip. The fresh air, the ski-ing, hunting in those forests.'

'And old friends too,' said Jopley.

'That's right, Edward. Old friends too.'

The Prince sighed deeply. *Deirdre*, he thought. *Are you still an old friend? Or are you just an old friend?*

He said, 'It will do us both the world of good.'

5

Three thousand miles to the west Deirdre Connolly was helping the Granda open his birthday mail.

Every year brought an increasing load, but today, his ninetieth birthday, had seen all records broken and Old Pat Connolly wanted to enjoy every nuance of every greeting. Some of those postmarked Washington gave him special pleasure.

'Do you see this, Dree?' he cried in his light, high-pitched but still rapid and articulate voice. 'This fellow now, he'd rather be sending me a wreath than a card. *May you live another ninety*, he writes, God damn his hypocritical soul!'

Dree smiled mechanically. She was a little preoccupied. Normally she had first sight of all the mail that came to the house and was able to examine her own in privacy. Not that she usually had anything to conceal but today there was a possibility . . . she pushed the thought out of her mind but in the same instant Old Pat said, 'Now here's something for you, Dree.'

'Is there? Thanks, Granda,' she said, reaching for the envelope.

He didn't give it to her straightaway, but studied the printed exterior.

'Now what the devil can Emerson Corporation of Montreal have to do with you, girlie?' he asked. 'That's lumber and mining, is it not?'

She leaned forward so that her shoulder-length hair, dark red to the edge of blackness, fell across the pale oval of her face, and pretended to sort through the scatter of cards and letters.

'It's their marine division, I expect,' she said lightly.

'I'd been interested in a new dinghy design they were financing.'

'Boats again, is it?' he groaned. 'You'll end up getting yourself drowned. And don't we have enough good American firms without getting mixed up with these blasted Englishmen?'

'Canadian, Granda,' she corrected.

'Same thing,' he grunted. But he passed her the letter.

It was another hour before she would escape from her grandfather's study on the pretext of checking that all the catering arrangements for the celebration *ceilidh* were under way. She retreated to her bedroom and ripped open the envelope.

It contained nothing the Granda could not have seen. It merely thanked her for her esteemed enquiry and confirmed that arrangements for viewing were unchanged. But it brought the blood racing over the smooth curves of her cheeks as she looked, unseeing, out of her window across the long lawns which ran on all sides from Castlemaine House towards the shadow of the distant pine-woods which marked the inner perimeter of the Connolly estate.

The Connollys had not always lived in such style. When the first Patrick had arrived in the mid-nineteenth century he had settled his pregnant wife in one squalid room in a Boston dock-front tenement and thereafter devoted more of his time to supporting the Fenian Brotherhood than his own rapidly increasing family.

The second Patrick, however, while not disapproving his father's politics, had observed with envy how some Irish families had already established rich and powerful dynasties in Boston. Determined to be independent, he had moved inland to Springfield and set about establishing a small foundry to service the burgeoning New England armaments industry. For a long time the going was rough, but when the European war-clouds appeared distantly on the horizon, he had gone for broke and thrown all his resources, financial, physical and mental, into being ready.

When war came, the Connolly business boomed in every sense. The first Patrick died of old age and also of anger at the thought of Irish labour providing arms to help the hated English to victory. But his son was triumphant and with his new wealth eradicated the memory of the one-room Boston slum by returning to that city and purchasing a house on Beacon Street as a prelude to establishing his family by force of wealth in Boston Society. Not content with this, he had purchased the New Hampshire estate, which he had sentimentally re-named Castlemaine, and later on, a hunting lodge in North Maine which he had tried to name 'Killarney' but which his family simply called The Lodge.

Not that the old Irish nostalgia had died in them. His son, Patrick the Third, Dree's granda and now head of the family, was an even more astute businessman than his father and the family fortunes had burgeoned. But politically he was a throw-back to his own Fenian grandfather. The great adventure of his life had been his presence at the 1916 Dublin rising, and thereafter time and distance had only sharpened his detestation of all things English and he had given vast support in money and in arms to the Irish Republican movement in all its manifestations.

The next Patrick, Old Pat's only son and Dree's father, had looked set fair to carry the Connolly political attitudes into the highest councils of the land till his tragic death by drowning in a sailing accident off Cape Cod in the early 'sixties. His wife had died with him and their four children had come to live with Old Pat, first in Boston and then at Castlemaine as this became more and more the old man's main residence.

The eldest of the four, Patrick Xavier or PX, as he was universally known, looked set to scale the heights that his father had come so close to. Then in 1978 as a US Senator he had gone to Northern Ireland on a private fact-finding tour. While visiting Belfast he had paused to refresh himself with a pint of Guinness in a Catholic Club in the Creggan. In the store room under the bar an aluminium keg packed with one hundred pounds of gelignite exploded. And again there were tears of grief and anger at Castlemaine House.

But today, if Dree had anything to do with it, the house would be filled only with merriment. She knew it wouldn't be an easy task. Her two elder brothers and the Granda could find a thousand new ways of irritating each other, even, or especially, on a day like this. But their mutual irritation would be nothing to the explosion which would follow if one whiff of the secret she was nursing was picked up by Old Pat. She remembered the day of the great row six months before and shuddered. But even that memory couldn't stop her from feeling weak with joyful anticipation as she studied her calendar.

She'd better ring Goffman to check that the arrangements for the Lodge were perfectly understood, she decided.

But the bedside phone rang just as she reached for it. It was the gate man, nearly three miles away.

'Mr Christie's car just passed through, Miss Dree,' he said. 'And I think I can hear the chopper coming.'

'Thanks,' she said.

Christie was her eldest surviving brother. Assistant professor in the Department of Political Science at Boston University, he now lived in the Beacon Street house with his wife, Judith, and their four daughters. The other brother, Conal, was the family's new political hope and had flown up from Washington for the *ceilidh* to be met by the Connolly helicopter at the airport.

She went downstairs to tell her grandfather.

As she expected, she found him still in his study. Family occasions always found him at his most Irish and it was here that he kept his collection of mementoes of great men and the great struggle (most of them, so Conal cynically asserted, palpable fakes).

He was standing by the window, still an arrow-straight figure despite his age.

'Granda,' she said.

When he turned he had a gun in his hand, its muzzle

pointing straight at her. It was a Webley .45 revolver, very old but gleaming with the light oil rubbed into it every day.

'Dree,' he said. 'Did I ever show you this now?'

Not more than a thousand times, thought Dree. But she said affectionately, 'What's that, Granda?'

'It's the weapon of our great namesake of glorious memory, James Connolly. He carried it on that famous Easter Monday and when he was laid low with a bullet in the ankle, he gave it into my own hands. God rest his soul. Did you know that when those murdering English bastards killed him, they tied him to a chair for he could not stand? Did you know that? They're an evil people, Dree. Every last one of them. All tainted, all. From bottom to top, and the worst taint is at the top. You'd never forget that, Dree, would you now?'

Those piercing pale blue eyes fixed on her as though they would read her soul. She forced herself to keep calm and said, 'Christie and Conal are on their way, Granda.'

'Are they now? Good. There are things I want to discuss with them. And you too, Dree. Before the *ceilidh* begins.'

Dree's heart sank. That didn't sound good. The Granda's notion of a family discussion was usually a simple, direct statement of his intentions and desires, backed up by a weapon deadlier than the revolver he still held – control of the family wealth. Christie's salary at Boston U couldn't keep him at the level his wife Judith reckoned was her due. And as for Conal, he knew that his political ambitions would be somewhere over the rainbow without vast financial backing.

I'm the only one with real hope of financial independence, she told herself with sudden glee, then frowned, partly because the thought made all kinds of unmakable assumptions, and partly because of the pain that independence would cause this old man she so loved.

The noise of a helicopter's vanes was now audible.

Old Pat put the Webley on his desk.

'Let's see what these brothers of yours have to say for themselves,' he said.

Outside, the huge station wagon which Christie needed to transport his family was racing towards the house with the chopper keeping pace only a few feet overhead.

'What's that fool Patch playing at?' demanded Old Pat.

Patch was the helicopter pilot.

Deirdre said unhappily, 'I expect Conal's flying it. You know how he likes to goose Judith.'

'I told Patch that Conal wasn't to be allowed to touch the controls!' said the Granda angrily.

'Yes, but you didn't tell him how to stop Conal,' said Dree.

The station wagon drew up in front of the house and the chopper swung away towards the concrete pad round the side. The car doors burst open and four small girls ranging from seven to three debouched on to the drive and came racing towards the Granda, shrilling, 'Happy birthday!'

Their mother, Judith, followed them, looking angrily after the chopper and obviously complaining to her husband. Once close to the Granda, however, her expression changed to a wide smile and she embraced him affectionately.

Christie kissed his sister.

'How's it going, Dree?' he said. 'You all set to come back with us?'

She nodded and said, 'I'm fine, Christie. You look a bit tired.'

It was true. In fact at thirty-six, Christie Connolly was already beginning to look middle-aged. His flesh was spreading, his gingery hair receding. He had a broad loose face, strong-jawed but gentle-eyed. On more than one occasion the Granda had charged him with weakness because from the start he had shied away from the only two acceptable careers in the old man's eyes – practical politics or management of the Connolly business empire. But he had

had strength enough to resist every possible pressure and pursue his chosen academic career.

Now from the helicopter there came her other brother. Conal was only two years younger than Christie, but there might have been a decade in it. Slim, taut, restless, full of burning energy, he had the kind of dark good looks which ought to belong to the true-bred Irish hero. Tipped by many as a future (and not-too-distant future) presidential candidate, Senator Conal Connolly would have been the old man's pride and joy if he had been willing or able to conceal his amused indifference to the Granda's Irish extremism. He claimed there weren't enough votes in it to be worth the hassle, but Dree often suspected that this was his way of snarling defiance at the hand he relied on to feed him.

'Conal,' said Old Pat, impatiently pushing Judith and her gaggle of girls aside. 'Are you by yourself now? Where's Mary and my little Peggy then?'

'Hello, everyone. Happy birthday, Granda. Hello, Dree. Christie. Well, how are you-all, sister-in-law Judith?'

His parody of her South Carolina accent made Judith flush angrily once more. Dree said hastily, 'Nothing's wrong with Mary, is there, Con?'

'No. It's just that Peggy's got a heavy cold and we thought it best they should stay in New York and nurse it.'

'They're in New York?' said the Granda, alert.

'That's right. I'll be going down there after the celebration here. I mean, I can't miss the *other* St Patrick's day, can I?'

'That's wit for you, is it, Conal,' said Old Pat angrily. 'There was a time when a man needed more than a clever tongue to make a mark in the Senate.'

'Things change, Granda,' said Conal.

'They do indeed. I want to talk with you two in my study now. You as well, Dree.'

He turned round and marched into the house. Deirdre dug Conal in the side.

'For God's sake, Con!' she said. 'Can't you behave just for today?'

'For you, Dree, I'll try,' he said with a grin, putting his arm round her shoulder. It was strange, in terms of simple affection Christie won every time, but in terms of mood and temperament she had always felt closer to Conal.

The Granda was waiting for them in the study seated behind his desk. Conal rolled his eyes at the sight of the Webley which still lay there, but he said nothing. From an open drawer Old Pat produced a typewritten document which he tossed on to the desk next to the gun.

'Read this,' he commanded.

Conal picked it up and began to read with Christie peering over his shoulder. Dree watched. She felt sick. She had no idea what it was, but she felt a gut-burning certainty that it had something to do with her. From some distant part of the house came the sound of the *ceilidh* fiddler trying out his instrument. He ran up and down a few scales, then suddenly he broke into *The Wearing of the Green*.

'What the hell does this mean?' asked Conal through tight lips.

'You're a senator, your brother's a professor,' sneered Old Pat. 'You should be able to understand a little bit of legal jargon. But I'll put it simple, shall I? It's a will, a new will. To tell truth, it's just the same old will as before, leaving everything I have to you three. Only now I'm putting it all in trust. And there's conditions, that's what a trust means. And there's one main condition you should all take notice of. In the event your sister marries a Protestant of English blood, and especially one that's got any connection with those murdering bastards at Windsor, the trust is immediately cancelled and all the estate is to be divided equally between Holy Mother Church and certain patriotic associations dedicated to the liberation of Ireland!'

'You're crazy!' said Conal. 'It'll never stand up in court.'

'Maybe not,' said Old Pat. 'But when they get the smell of money in Rome, they don't shake off the scent easily, and if the will's to be broken, it could take thirty years and as many millions in the breaking. Do you have that time to spare, Con?'

Christie came in now, his face flushed with indignation.

'Granda, this is a cruel thing you're doing to Dree. Six months ago in this very room she told us she was finished with that Englishman for good, and I for one was not sorry. But for *her* sake. I said then that I thought Dree was good enough for a Prince but that *that* kind of life was not good enough for Dree. But this is different. This is an insane restriction you're trying to impose!'

'Insane, is it?' flashed the old man. 'You'll need to prove that, Christie. Perhaps in the meantime it'll teach you both to take better care of your sister.'

The three men were all looking at Dree now and she knew that they were recalling that last family conference six months before, and all that had led up to it.

No, not all. Only she could remember all.

She remembered now.

Her very first meeting with Prince Arthur, three years ago, had been prefaced by a family row.

There had been snow on the ground and in Boston the bright lights strung across the streets signalled the approach of Christmas. But there was to be another festive occasion that December which was even brighter in terms of social significance and glitter. This was the reception to be held at the State House in honour of the Prince's visit.

Naturally there was an invitation for the Connollys. Even more naturally, Old Pat had forbidden any of them to attend. None of his family was going to bow or curtsey to an English Prince!

Deirdre at twenty understood little of his reasoning. All she knew was that she was vastly disappointed, but after a brief flash of Celtic rage, she might well have accepted her disappointment. It was Conal who made an issue of it. He told the old man not to be a fool. Boston expected a Connolly presence at its great occasions. Politically, he personally ought to attend. And as for his sister, it would be a cruel thing to deprive her of such a night. Old Pat was reduced to a brooding silence which Conal took for consent. And when the great night came, Deirdre put on a simple gown of white silk and went to the State House adorned with that unselfconscious beauty which outdazzles all that the art of jeweller, couturier and coiffeur can offer.

It had been a magic evening. The Prince was clearly enjoying himself, smiling, talking, joking, laughing, and when the music started he took to the floor at once and seemed determined to dance with every woman in the room in turn.

Deirdre's turn came early on with a waltz, and thereafter the Prince's system seemed to break down. Ladies, tremulous with anticipation, began to tremble instead with resentment as he danced three in a row with *that Connolly chit*.

The photographers had a field day. The incredibly handsome young couple were the focus of all attention. But only one person other than the Prince had made any impression on Deirdre's mind.

No matter how much they whirled around the floor, over Arthur's shoulder she always seemed to see a solid, granite-faced man whose cold unblinking gaze seemed to touch her very skin.

'Who's that?' she whispered. 'The one who feels you with his eyes.'

'You mean Mr. McHarg,' laughed the Prince. 'My detective. He's just checking you for concealed weapons.'

He pressed her close in a spin and added, 'I can't detect any.'

'Me neither,' she answered. She felt deliriously happy.

It was a happiness which lasted till the Granda saw the papers next morning. Even Conal could not deflect his great wrath, and in the end it was Deirdre's tears which calmed him.

'It was only a dance, Granda,' she wept. 'I'll never see him again. So where's the harm?'

But she was wrong about not seeing him again, though she pleased Old Pat when an invitation came shortly afterwards to attend a farewell party for the Prince at the British Embassy in Washington by tearing it up before his face.

The following summer, she visited Europe with a party of friends, most of them enthusiastic sailors, and after a short stay in Ireland visiting ancestral shrines, she had gone on to join them for Cowes Week on the Isle of Wight.

And there her path and Arthur's crossed again.

They saw a lot of each other, but very rapidly by tacit mutual consent they fell into the habit of distancing themselves in the public view to keep the press fooled. She was naive enough to believe at first that this was for her sake. Only later as their intimacy grew did she realize how strong an opposition there would be in his family also to the connection.

'The thing is,' he explained, 'apart from the fact that your grandfather's almost run out of terms of abuse for my relatives, if I should happen to want to marry a practising Roman Catholic I'd have to renounce my right of succession. And you'd think I was the Great White Hope instead of being pretty lowly placed in a queue a mile long!'

It was the first mention of marriage. It was made in bed the first time they slept together. In the morning, Deirdre, who had a sharp sense of fun, heaved the mattress up and pretended to look for the princess-testing pea he'd placed there. But it was no fairytale world they lived in, and a happy-ever-after ending looked a long, long way away.

Miraculously, they kept their romance out of view of the media for two whole years. As minor royalty, Arthur was not subject to the intensity of scrutiny and pursuit endured by his mainstream cousins. But it still took skilful planning, trustworthy friends and a lot of luck.

But finally luck had run out. Perhaps on the Prince's side first. And perhaps his own family had arranged for the news to be leaked to Old Pat. From their point of view, it would have been a good move. His fury was terrible. He had lashed Deirdre with his tongue and when she was reduced to helpless tears, he had turned on her brothers. It had looked as if something would have to give beyond hope of repair – either Old Pat's heart or the fabric of the family. Only one thing had brought them back from the brink and that was Deirdre's screamed assurance that she was not seeing the Prince any more, that they had brought their relationship to a halt.

She was, to say the least, being Jesuitical. The truth of the matter was that she and Arthur had both hesitated at the brink of coming out into the open about their feelings. Both of them were too aware of the effect their marriage would have on their respective families to take the step easily. They had agreed not to see each other for six months before taking a final decision. A fairytale test, Arthur had called it. The period had just started when Old Pat had thrown his tantrum.

And now it was almost up.

But her half-year of quiet living at Castlemaine, her assurances that nothing was going on between her and the Prince, these had not altogether stilled the suspicions in the old man's mind. And now he had devised this new barrier to any resumption of the connection, by making her brothers' financial future dependent on her obedience.

Conal was right, of course. It was an act of insanity. And Christie was right too when he called it an act of cruelty. Suddenly she felt herself calmer and more self-assured than she'd done for weeks. This was above all an act of provocation and her Connolly blood did not take such things kindly.

She still did not know what decision she had reached about her relationship with Arthur. She had no idea how he now felt about her. All she knew was that she was going to see him again soon and that none of these three men, no matter how much she loved them, was going to deprive her of that.

She said: 'You must excuse me. There are arrangements to be checked.'

It was an almost deliberate ambiguity. Feeling very controlled, she went straight to her room and picked up the telephone. A few minutes later she was connected with old Henry Goffman who ran the general store in the small township of Summit a few miles down the valley from the Connolly Lodge in North Maine. He also acted as caretaker and supplier of the Lodge and anyone going up there always checked with him first to make sure no other member of the family had a prior booking.

'Mr Goffman,' said Dree, 'I just wanted to confirm that I'd be using the Lodge on March 17th. Probably a couple of nights, I don't know, but definitely the seventeenth. You'll see to that? OK. Thanks, Mr Goffman.'

When she rang off and rose from the bed on which she was sitting, she started as she saw Conal standing in the doorway.

'March 17th?' mused Conal to the air. 'That's St Pat's Day. Now what will the Granda say if you're not by his side in Boston at the celebrations of the greatest day of the year!'

'Nothing,' said Dree steadily. 'He's already announced he's going to stay quietly at Castlemaine this year.'

'Has he now? And you, Dree, will be visiting with Christie from tomorrow, I gather. Are Christie and his brood going to the Lodge too?'

'No. Just some friends,' said Dree.

'Is that so? Why, I may join you then,' he probed.

'It'll be a full house,' said Dree lightly. 'Besides, Con, won't you be parading up Fifth Avenue in your green suit, trying to keep a hold on the Mick vote?'

He laughed, but didn't answer the question. Instead he said, 'Dree, I came up to say, don't let yourself be upset by the Granda and his daft will. You know what he's like, everything's got to be played with full orchestra.'

'It doesn't bother me in the slightest,' she assured him.

'Tell me, Con: what's the real reason for Mary and Peggy not coming? It's not just a cold, is it?'

'Oh, but it is,' he said. 'It's that interesting condition, a cold in the marriage. Symptoms: irascibility, thirst, nausea, withdrawal. Prognosis: bad.'

'Oh, Con, I'm sorry,' she said sincerely. 'I'm really sorry.'

'I believe you,' he answered. 'I also believe there's a little bit of the politician in you too, Dree. You're a good changer-of-subjects, aren't you?'

'I don't know what you mean,' she said, pushing past him. 'But I do know I've got a *ceilidh* to arrange.'

Behind her she heard Conal's light, cynical laugh. Then his footsteps came after her down the stairs.

6

The weather had changed in twelve hours and now as the tide approached the ebb once more, there was very little of the previous evening's magic in the air. Squalls of salty spray blasted in from the sea and hissed against the hot metal of the swaying arc-lamps. Half-a-dozen figures clad in waterproof capes and rubber boots moved in and out to the shifting, ghastly light with the slowness of an underwater ballet. They followed the retreating waterline, probing the gelatinous sand with long spikes and occasionally summoning a colleague with a spade if some obstruction were encountered.

McHarg listened attentively to each cry but so far nothing had been unearthed which merited his attention. He and Dr Wainwright were seated in the relative warmth of a police Land-Rover parked as far down the beach as McHarg had felt able to go on the wet sand. The two men looked not dissimilar in the dimly lit interior of the vehicle. Both were stockily well-built with a breadth of shoulder not yet overtaken by width of waist. Both had a frost of grey hair at their sideboards and the skin beneath both sets of eyes was pouched and creased by too many disturbed nights, too many chronic worries.

The differences began in the detail of their faces. Wainwright's long pinched nose and hollow cheeks combined with wide, slightly twisted lips to produce an expression of world-weary pessimism, while McHarg's broad, blunt nose was set over a mouth sculpted to cry defiance, and framed by a jaw and a brow either of which looked as if it could be used to break ice in the Antarctic.

'This was my night off,' said Wainwright. 'I'm back on call in an hour.'

'Night off? What's that?' wondered McHarg. 'I was up at four yesterday morning paddling around in hot ash up to my ankles.'

'Police barbecue?'

'Ha. Human barbecue. Some poor sod in one of those timbered cottages up the river at Little Pailey. Pyres if you put a spark to them.'

'Arson?'

'Smoking when drunk, the fire chief says. A journalist.'

'It'd be warm at least,' said the doctor, taking another sip of coffee.

'He'll be dead, you reckon?' said McHarg a little later. 'This chap who lost his tongue.'

'Possibly. Depends what happened next. With proper medical treatment he might be OK. Left to himself, he'd probably choke on his own blood if the shock didn't kill him.'

'Let's hope the poor sod was dead when it happened,' said McHarg.

'It seems a rather pointless thing to do in that case,' said the doctor.

McHarg regarded him curiously. 'It seems rather pointless either way,' he said. But he added thoughtfully,

'Mind you, it rings a bell somehow. I don't know why, but it does. Odd.'

Wainwright glanced at his watch and shifted impatiently. 'What's the point of this anyway? You're hoping to find other bits of the poor sod?'

'It'll be over soon,' assured McHarg. 'Have some more coffee. When the tide turns, that's that. For tonight. You're sure it was a man, by the way?'

Wainwright shrugged. 'It was large enough, but your laboratory should be able to tell you that. I hope to God . . .' He let his voice tail away.

'Not long now,' said McHarg as cheerfully as he could manage. He reached under his seat and pulled out a briefcase.

'Fancy a sandwich?' he asked, extracting a Cellophane-wrapped package.

'What've you got?' said Wainwright.

McHarg prised apart two slices of impact-sealed bread and inspected the interior.

'Tongue,' he said.

'Oh Jesus!'

Suddenly there was a change in the cumbersome activity at the water's edge. The uniformed sergeant in charge turned towards the Land-Rover, and raised his hand above his head and made a circling motion.

'They've found something,' said McHarg. 'Sorry. We're going to get wet after all.'

The wind hit them like a wet pillow wielded by a giant. It seemed to gust from all quarters so you couldn't even lean into it as you walked. At least it's keeping off the vulgar curious, thought McHarg.

'What's up, Bert?' he asked the sergeant when they reached the huddle of glistening oilskins.

'We've found a spade, sir,' said the sergeant.

McHarg looked down. The suck and thrust of the tide had almost pulled the tiny implement out of its lodging place in the sodden sand and it lay askew, fragile and pathetic as a makeshift cross on a battlefield.

'This is your daughter's, Doctor?' asked McHarg.

Wainwright nodded.

McHarg bent down and picked up the spade.

'OK, Bert. Mark the spot so it stays marked. Take a couple of bearings too. And dig like buggery. You've got about a minute at the most. I want everything you find here, including the bloody sand!'

Leaving behind the group of policemen now feverishly shovelling the sand from the area marked by the spade into large plastic bags, McHarg and Wainwright walked back to the Land-Rover. As they neared it, a figure appeared in the theatrical glow of the headlights. McHarg recognized one of his DCs.

'What is it, Jimmy?' he asked.

'Super's here, sir,' said the man, jerking his head back towards the promenade. 'He'd like a word.'

'OK.'

They got into the Land-Rover and McHarg started it up, engaged the four-wheel drive and took it back towards the promenade in a slitheringly tight circle that had Wainwright cursing.

'Won't be a sec,' said McHarg as he brought the vehicle to a sharp halt behind the only other car in sight.

''Morning, Douglas,' said Chief Superintendent Tim Davison through the half-covered window. 'Is that Wainwright with you?'

'Yes, sir,' said McHarg, crouching down beside the car, partly for audibility but mainly for protection. He had tried the handle of the rear door but it was locked and Davison had made no attempt to open it for him.

'What do you make of him, Douglas?'

'Seems OK,' said McHarg, surprised. 'Down to earth. Reliable.'

'They've got to seem like that, I suppose,' said Davison.

He spoke in monotone and sounded slow and dull-witted. McHarg was not deceived.

'What's up, sir?'

'Some of them couldn't tell a tit from a tennis ball,' continued the Chief Superintendent. 'It's a cock-up, Douglas. That thing he found. Waste of time.'

'You mean it's not a tongue?' said McHarg in amazement.

'Oh, it's a tongue all right. I've had the lab report. But it's not human. Dog's. Some sort of big dog.'

'They're sure?'

'That's why they've got the letters after their names. I thought I'd let you know before you got too wet.'

'Thanks,' said McHarg, feeling his trouser legs clinging to his calves like a cold poultice.

'Look, Inspector, I've really got to get back home. That phone's going to start ringing in half an hour and I'll need a hot bath.'

It was Wainwright, grown impatient and come to hurry him along. In his hand he clutched Lucy's tiny spade.

McHarg glanced from Davison to the doctor. It didn't seem a time for introductions.

'Is something up?' asked Wainwright, sensitive to atmosphere. 'I can make my own way home.'

'No, no,' said McHarg. 'It's just that, well, no use beating around the bush. That tongue you found. We've had the lab report. It's a dog's.'

'It's *what*?'

'A dog's. The Chief Super's just told me. I'm sorry.'

He should be apologizing to *me*, thought McHarg. But it was clear Wainwright was in no mood for apologies.

'Are you crazy, or what?' he demanded.

'That's what they say at the lab,' replied McHarg defensively.

'What kind of morons do you employ down there? Retired lollipopmen?'

McHarg bent down to the car window again in search of support.

'Pass it to the RSPCA,' said Davison, winding the window up. He motioned to his driver and the car began to pull away.

'Stupid bastards!' exploded Wainwright.

'Look, I've said I'm sorry, though I don't know why I should be,' said McHarg, beginning to get angry. 'Let's get you home, shall we?'

'Oh, go to hell!' snapped Wainwright. Turning on his heel, he strode away, carrying the spade like a battle-axe.

McHarg watched him go, then returned to the Land-Rover. There were half-a-dozen very wet men on the beach and he didn't relish telling them that they had been wasting their time. It would be little consolation to them that he had been wasting his too.

And perversely, now that it didn't matter any longer, the mists of memory evaporated and suddenly he recalled with perfect clarity what it was that had made the grisly business seem somehow not totally unfamiliar.

It had been about two years earlier, the summer of Mavis's death.

It was a period McHarg did not care to remember, but his subconscious was cunning and frequently pushed small insignificant memories to the surface of his mind to lure him unawares into those gloomy depths.

And this was such a one. It was a memory of a television programme. McHarg was no television addict and now he didn't even own a set. His only period of concentrated viewing had been during those last few weeks when the cancer which had been his wife's slyly persistent companion for nearly a decade suddenly exploded into frenetic activity. A year earlier McHarg had resigned from Special Branch where his Royal Bodyguard duties could keep him away from home for six months at a time. There'd been lots of rumours about his reasons for resigning, but the truth was simple.

His only child, Flora, a student at East Anglia University, had told him with a coldness that should have been beyond her years but which he recognized as his own that his frequent absences leaving Mavis in their small London flat were helping to kill her mother. Flora herself had been on the point of going to America for an exchange term at Boston University. With the perversity of youth, on her return, instead of being delighted that McHarg had transferred to Sanderton CID, she was angry that he had chosen this small south coast town, which was nearly twice as far from her University as London.

But there'd been good reasons for choosing Sanderton. It was his old friend Tim Davison's patch and that had made the transfer easy. More importantly, Mavis had loved that part of the coast and made the choice herself, though Flora was always reluctant to accept this.

For nearly a year, her health had seemed to respond to the tonic of open countryside and fresh sea air. Then the decline had started and soon she could go out no further than the garden, and spent all her evenings in front of the flickering television screen with McHarg in an equal agony of spirit by her side.

And now the memory came, slyly opening the door on to all kinds of other memories.

With an effort of will he pushed them aside and concentrated on his recollections of the programme.

It had been the sight of the familiar portico of the Old Bailey which had caught his attention. The camera tracked in, mixed to the gloomy splendour of No 1 court and dwelt for a moment on the sharp, anxious features of the man in the dock. He moved his right hand wearily across his brow, as though to brush away sweat, then allowed the fingers to droop rather awkwardly over his left eye. Now the camera passed to the judge, seated high in full judicial regalia. A big close-up showed him speaking, but the words that McHarg heard were not the words on his lips. '... *these several points I solemnly swear to observe without evasion, equivocation, or mental reservation of any kind, under no less a penalty, on the violation of any of them, than that of having my throat cut across, my tongue torn out by the roots and buried in the sand of the sea at low water mark . . .'*

That was it! Yes. That was the memory that this daft business with the dog had triggered off.

Now the presenter's voice had come in. *'Did any memory of this, the first of many such extraordinary and extreme oaths a Freemason has to take to protect the secrecy and the interests of his fellows, pass through the mind of Mr Justice Bucknill when, in 1911, he observed the poisoner, Seddon, make a Masonic distress signal from the dock?*

'If it did, he did not let it sway him from his duty.'

The camera backtracked to show the judge wearing the black cap. His voice came up speaking the old words of the death sentence as the picture mixed to Seddon, who raised his right hand to his brow once more, then dropped it hopelessly to grip the edge of the dock.

The presenter resumed. *'Yet for many people, despite the good works, the open-handed charities, the neutral stance on politics and religion, Freemasonry still raises the question – what special privileges are available to members? How far does Masonic loyalty go?*

'How many times have Masonic distress signals been made – and answered?'

7

'You mean, the dog was a Freemason who talked?'

Chief Superintendent Davison regarded McHarg with a lopsided grin that a neurotic underling might have construed as a sneer. McHarg didn't. He wasn't neurotic and he'd known Davison too long. They had been friends and equals once in their early days with the Met. Now equals no longer, they remained friends as far as their differences in rank permitted.

'No, I don't mean that,' said McHarg. When McHarg didn't think something was amusing, there was a coldness in his look which sooner or later stilled laughter and erased lopsided grins.

'Where'd you get all this Freemason stuff?' asked Davison, almost sulkily.

'I remembered it. There was a television programme about it a couple of years ago. *The Master Builders*. One of those investigative documentaries. I checked at the library this morning. It's there in the oath. But I don't need to tell you this.'

'Because I'm a member of the Sanderton Lodge, you mean?' said Davison.

'It's a small town, sir,' said McHarg neutrally.

'And no secret either,' said Davison equably. 'Do you object?'

'What you do in your spare time's your own business,' said McHarg. 'If you start wandering round the office in a blindfold and an apron, I'll get worried.'

'Thanks, Douglas. I'll try not to worry you. So what's the tie-up? You remember some sensationalized TV programme which gets most of it wrong . . .'

'You did see it, then?'

' . . . and somehow make a connection between a Masonic ceremony and this poor bloody mongrel. I don't see it. What's bothering you?'

'Listen, man,' said McHarg, becoming more Scottish in his exasperation. 'I'm not saying there's any direct link. But something happened on that beach. Something nasty, however you look at it. Something that smacks of ritual and goes a bloody long way beyond whatever puerile mummery your mates indulge in down at the Lodge!'

'For God's sake, Douglas! Be careful what you say!' Davison had let himself be exasperated at last.

McHarg bared his teeth in a ferocious grin.

'Might affect my career? Too late, the virgin cried.'

The two men looked at each other. They had arrived here in Sanderton by different routes. But they both knew that while for Davison it was a staging post, for McHarg it was almost certainly the end of the line.

'Come on, Douglas,' said Davison wearily. 'There's no reason why you shouldn't get a leg-up still. But not if you play around with daft stuff like this. So drop it, will you? Leave it to the RSPCA. You're managing to do the work of two men as it is. And you're due up in London tomorrow for the Partington trial.'

'That shouldn't keep me long. I'm only the arresting officer. And I can drive back nights,' said McHarg.

'No way!' exclaimed Davison. 'You relax a bit, taste the good life. I don't want you back here till you're done. And don't imagine it's going to be easy. You did a damn sight more than arrest the bugger and he'll be pulling all the stops out on this one. He's got money and influence. It could drag on for ages.'

McHarg couldn't disagree. At the end of the 'sixties, Stanley Partington had been a bright young politician with a head for figures, widely tipped as a future Chancellor and thought by some to be capable of going all the way. His bluff good looks and ruddy complexion, which won him the nickname 'Sailor', made him a perfect media figure. By turns Minister of State and Opposition Spokesman on a whole variety of subjects, his star seemed to burn ever brighter.

But it was casting shadows too.

His name began to be associated with many of the financial scandals which were such a feature of business life in the 'seventies. Nothing definite, nothing proven, but in the end he resigned his parliamentary seat 'for health reasons', promising to return at the earliest opportunity. Two years later, as official interest grew in the dealings of one of his African companies, his health once more required that he should convalesce in a Swiss sanatorium. At just that time a fire had swept through his company headquarters in

London, totally destroying all records. Rumours of his personal involvement were rife. He successfully sued *Private Eye* for printing some of them, but two years later an official investigation into Partington, despite meeting obstructionism on a huge scale, was coming to a head.

McHarg knew only what he read and he certainly had had no idea that mild December evening just before last Christmas that the Commander of the Fraud Squad was pressing the case for an arrest warrant to be issued. The issue was in doubt, but it was going to be a close enough thing for alarm bells to start ringing.

And in McHarg's office, the phone rang too.

The voice wasn't very distinct, drunk rather than disguised he thought. And there'd been a lot of strange background noises. But the message came through loud and clear. 'Sailor' Partington was planning a little Christmas cruise in the *Atlas Rose*, a Weymouth 42 motor cruiser presently moored in Sanderton Marina.

That was it. Another man might have spent time contacting the Yard to see if this information was significant, or at least might have chatted to his own immediate superior.

McHarg pulled his coat on, climbed into his old Volvo and headed straight for the marina.

He was just in time. The boat was nosing its way from the moorings. McHarg stepped on board but made no attempt to interfere with Partington at the controls.

'Just keep going,' he invited.

A couple of hours later the cruiser returned. There'd been trouble with the engine, McHarg explained. They'd drifted around a bit till it was put right.

Curiously it was Partington, the experienced amateur sailor, who seemed to have suffered most. Grey-faced and retching, he had looked like a case for hospital but he'd been taken back to the station instead where McHarg formally arrested him. When the news reached the Yard there'd been mingled jubilation and consternation, the former from those who'd wanted a warrant to be issued, the latter from those who'd argued there wasn't yet enough evidence – and won the day.

There was more evidence now. From the boat McHarg produced a large quantity of money, various interesting papers and a signed statement which there was not a cat in hell's chance of getting admitted in court. But the newspapers were on to the arrest in a flash and now even the most reluctant of the top brass had to concede that the case should go forward which it was now doing, three months later.

'That reminds me,' said McHarg. 'Something curious. That business with the tongue put it out of my mind last night. You remember the tipoff I got about Partington? I think I know who gave it.'

'Do you now?' said Davison. 'And does he admit it?'

'Hardly. I think it was that poor sod who got himself burned to death yesterday morning,' said McHarg. 'That journalist, Morrison. There was a background noise to that phone call, sort of creaking, groaning, bubbling. I thought of something urban, an old boiler perhaps, or a laundry. But after I came away from that fire there was something going on in my mind, some kind of echo. I made Potter go out there again yesterday evening. He wasn't pleased.'

'I know,' said Davison drily. 'I've had him on the phone complaining.'

'And I thought I'd been mistaken,' continued McHarg. 'But just when I was ready to leave, the water-wheel started turning again. And that was it! I'm sure that phone call came from that cottage!'

'Or any other cottage or house near a mill wheel,' said Davison.

'True. But I might just do a bit of checking on friend Morrison's background when I'm up in town.'

'Oh, come on, Douglas!' said Davison. 'You're not crying "murder" now, surely! Potter was quite adamant about the cause of the fire.'

'Who said anything about murder?' said McHarg innocently. 'If Morrison, a journalist, knew enough to tip *me* off, I'm just interested to know who might have tipped *him* off, that's all.'

'For Christ's sake,' said Davison. 'You'll kill yourself sooner or later, Douglas. Haven't you got enough on your plate without chasing every little hare you start?'

McHarg stood up.

'What I do in my own time's my own business isn't it?' he asked neutrally.

'I wish I could believe you had some time of your own,' answered Davison. He glanced at his watch. 'I'm meeting Heather for lunch in the Atlanta. Why don't you join us?'

'No, thanks,' said McHarg. 'I don't eat at lunchtime.'

'A drink then. You do *drink*, don't you? Even at lunchtime.'

There was perhaps more sarcasm in his voice than he had intended. But not much.

McHarg looked at him coldly for a moment.

'Yes, I drink,' he said. 'You can buy me a drink if you like. Sir.'

Heather Davison, the Chief Super's wife, was already in the bar of the Atlanta Hotel. She greeted McHarg warmly. Since his wife's death, McHarg had contrived by simple lack of response first to weary, finally to alienate, nearly all the friends he and Mavis had shared. Heather Davison had persisted, however, and her reward was that two or three times in the past six months he had come round for supper and shown signs of enjoying it.

'Are you lunching with us?' she asked.

'Sorry, I can't,' said McHarg.

'He can do without *food*,' said Davison, placing a large Scotch before his subordinate. Heather shot him a sharp, disapproving glance.

'You're looking tired, Doug,' she said.

McHarg looked at her affectionately. She was an attractive woman with deep brown eyes and a warm smile.

'I was up pretty early,' he said.

'I know. So was Tim, but he doesn't look like you. You need that holiday. Are you all ready?'

'Ready?' he said blankly.

'Yes. Visa, traveller's cheques, air ticket. You're not planning to swim to Boston, are you?'

'He might walk on the water,' grunted her husband, sipping his sherry.

'Yes, I'm ready,' said McHarg. 'That doesn't mean I'll go, though.'

'Not go?' said Heather, astonished. 'But Flora – she'll be so disappointed.'

'Perhaps. She hasn't written for three months.'

He tried to keep the hurt out of his voice. He'd understood Flora's attitude at first. The end had come so quickly. When the terminal deterioration had set in, Flora had been in the middle of her final examinations. Mavis had pleaded with him not to contact her till they were finished. A couple of days would make no difference. McHarg was not a man given to weakness but weakly he had agreed.

It had seemed at first that Mavis was right. Then on the day that Flora finished her exams, Mavis had died. McHarg was by her bedside, clumsily arranging some flowers he had brought and telling her about his plans for the garden. And suddenly he had realized his words were falling into a silence deeper than the despair they were trying to conceal.

Time became meaningless thereafter.

Then suddenly she was there. Flora. His daughter. Shoulder-length hair, so richly black that it seemed to smoulder, as did the huge accusing eyes in the pale strong face.

'How long had you known?' she cried. '*How long?*'

'A few days. Three, four. It started and she said, your mother said . . .'

'*What?*'

'Not to tell you. Not to bother you. Not till your exams were over. She said it would be all right. She said . . .'

'*She* said? *She* said?'

'Yes,' said McHarg, perplexed. 'I didn't want to, but she made me promise. She thought . . . she seemed . . . your mother . . .'

'Liar! Liar! *Liar!* It was you. Always you! You didn't want . . . you didn't like . . . you . . .'

McHarg moved forward, hand outstretched.

His daughter turned and rushed out of the room, out of the house. Later she had returned, anger contained in a rigid case of cold, polite control. McHarg had made no attempt to break through it, believing that now time would be his friend.

But there had not been any time.

After the funeral Flora had said, casually, 'I think I'll take up that offer in the States.'

McHarg knew, mainly via his wife, that Flora had made an excellent impression during her term at Boston and there had been talk of a post-graduate place, part teaching, part research. They suspected there was a man involved, but Flora had made it clear she put being close to her mother first.

Now: 'There's nothing to keep me here,' she said.

McHarg had nodded, poker-faced, as at the start of an important interrogation. But had nothing to ask his own daughter.

That night he drank a full bottle of Scotch. He had seen her once more before she went.

And since she went he had not seen her at all.

They exchanged short infrequent letters, assuring each other of good health and reasonable weather. Flora made no mention of returning to England and it was Heather Davison who six months earlier had come up with the notion that McHarg should visit the States. Once proposed, she did not leave the idea alone till she'd got McHarg to admit to a desire to see his daughter again, or at least a flicker of interest strong enough to be called a desire by comparison with anything else in his life.

Unfortunately Flora's interest flickered even more fitfully. At six months' distance from the proposed visit, her neutral response to the idea was interpretable, via Heather, as undemonstrative acceptance. But the silence of the last twelve weeks, preceded only by a brief note on a Christmas card, seemed less ambiguous to McHarg.

'But you have to go!' said Heather, upset. 'Perhaps a letter's got lost. You know what the post's like these days. Look, Doug, perhaps if I tried to get in touch with her . . .'

'Inspector McHarg, sorry to interrupt, could I have a word?'

McHarg looked round, grateful to the interruptor till he saw that it was Dr Wainwright, wearing an overcoat and carrying his black bag.

'Hello, Wainwright,' he said. 'Have a drink?'

'Not just now. I'm here on business,' he said, holding up his bag. 'We look after the staff here. I just noticed you in passing.'

McHarg stood up to talk to the doctor. Heather Davison tried to engage her husband in conversation but he made no bones about eavesdropping on what the two men were saying.

'It's about that business last night.'

'Yes?'

'There must have been a mistake. I saw that tongue. It was definitely human.'

'It was dark on the beach,' said McHarg reasonably.

'It was light enough in the police station,' retorted Wainwright.

'But surely without tests . . .'

'Listen. Have you ever looked in a dog's mouth? Even a bloody policeman could tell the difference!'

Wainwright's tone was angry enough to have attracted the attention of other occupants of the bar. Tim Davison stood up, smiling.

'Dr Wainwright,' he said.

'Who the hell are you?'

'Chief Superintendent Davison. I think you're being a bit unfair to the Inspector.'

'What do you know about it?' He scrutinized Davison closely, then added, 'You're the fellow in the car, aren't you?'

'That's right. Look, Doctor, we're just simple laymen caught between experts. I'll tell you what I'll do. I'll have the – er – exhibit sent to the University. Professor Foster there, you may have heard of him, he sometimes acts as a consultant in such matters. Shall we let him have the final word?'

'Send it by all means,' snapped Wainwright. 'Though I don't know why busy people should have to waste time preventing the police from making fools of themselves.'

He strode away, hitting the swing door with his black bag like a battering ram.

'An impressive bedside manner,' said Davison.

'He's not going to let anyone else have the final word,' said McHarg.

'You reckon not?' said Davison thoughtfully. 'Well, let's sit down and finish our drinks or he'll be reporting us for taking extended lunch hours!'

McHarg remained standing and said, 'I'll leave you two to it, I think. You'll want to get into the dining-room.'

'But you haven't touched your whisky,' protested Heather.

'I haven't? So I haven't. Another time, when I really need it. I'll see you.'

He left, a big, broad-shouldered man, rather menacing with his square, grey-thatched head thrust forward and his hands clenched deep in the pockets of his black overcoat. The cold wind tousled his hair and pinched at his leathery cheeks. It had been a childish gesture to leave the whisky. He could have done with its comfortable warmth in his gut. But Davison's cracks about his drinking had got to him, mainly because of their truth. It must be taking its toll of his body. God knows what it was doing to his mind.

He crossed the road on to the promenade. The tide had not been long on the ebb and only a narrow strip of beach was visible, glistening wet and strewn with bits of driftwood, shells, the occasional bottle, a tin or two – all the mingled detritus of man and the ocean.

It was the sight of this rubbish which triggered off the association in McHarg's mind. He recalled a stooping figure; a face almost invisible in a tangle of greying but once gingery hair; those features you could see worn and sculpted like a piece of driftwood to a state beyond nature; a trailing gunny sack; a spiked walking stick.

This was Old Haystacks, no one knew of any other name for him. He was a local derelict, almost invisible because so familiar, keeping out of the way when the beaches were crowded in summer, but as soon as the season was over, he was there, following the receding tide up and down a ten-mile stretch of coast, picking up and making a borderline living out of what the benevolent ocean left behind.

Wainwright had said the tongue was undecayed, had not been long buried, which meant probably the ghastly ceremony had taken place at ebb tide just before dawn that morning. No one would be around at that hour.

No one except perhaps Haystacks whose working life was built around the ebbing of the tides. It was a long shot but McHarg had been shooting long all his life. Turning his collar up, he set out along the promenade, and when that came to an end he climbed down the steps on to the shingle.

Old Haystacks's hut was situated in a tumult of broken sandhills about a mile out of the town. McHarg had stumbled upon it when out walking with his wife shortly after their arrival. He shut his mind against the memory and concentrated on pushing his feet forward. He was finding the walk heavy going but he didn't pause till he reached the sandhills.

His memory told him that wind and weather had

rearranged them since his walks here with Mavis, but he hadn't expected to find Old Haystacks's hut in the same place anyway. 'Hut' was really too dignified a term for what was basically a lean-to of planks and sacking against the steep wall of a sandhill. From time to time the local health authority moved the old man on, but he merely reassembled his fragile shanty in another part of the dunes, treating officialdom as a natural inconvenience like frost or mosquitoes.

The old man had another peculiarity. He didn't beg and he didn't accept gifts of money. On the other hand, whatever he found on the beach was his. McHarg carefully wrapped a few silver coins in his handkerchief and when he finally found the ramshackle hut with Haystacks repairing the piece of sacking which served for a door, McHarg coughed loudly and blew his nose, apparently regardless of the falling coins.

'Nice day, Haystacks,' he said. 'How's business?'

Five minutes later McHarg was beginning to think he'd struck lucky.

Yes, Old Haystacks had been out on the beach early the previous morning. It had been the first calm period after a big storm and he wasn't going to miss first go at the extra goodies likely to have been unloaded by such a stir-up on the ocean bed. In fact, pickings had been disappointingly slim and he had reached the area in front of the promenade with a half-full sack just about the time the tide had been at the ebb.

'Did you see anyone?' demanded McHarg.

The old man scratched his chin through his tangled beard. Dim memories of the unwisdom of becoming a witness might have been flitting through his mind. McHarg placed a foot firmly on a couple of silver coins and ground them into the sand. The old man nodded sadly as though he recalled the unwisdom of not co-operating with the police also.

Yes, there had been two men. Suspecting (because self-interest operates at all levels) rivals in beachcombing, Haystacks had ducked behind a groyne and watched them.

They had been walking away from the sea. No, he couldn't (or wouldn't?) describe them. But they had got into a big silvery blue car on the promenade.

A Jaguar.

This seemed potentially very useful, till further questioning revealed that, just as for soldiers all trees are 'bushy-topped' or 'poplars', so for the old man all cars were Fords or Jaguars.

McHarg took a stick and drew various shapes in the sand and after five minutes or so was hopeful that in this case the old man might have been more specific than he knew.

But it was hardly enough to justify rescuing a case he'd been told in no uncertain terms to jettison.

As he retraced his path across the sandhills he glanced back.

Old Haystacks was standing where he had left him. McHarg felt a pang of mingled pity and approval; pity for the derelict's aimless life, approval that he had dignity enough neither to beg nor to be seen grubbing for the coins he had dropped.

And as he walked on, both emotions were superseded by a vague uneasiness as though something in the old man reminded him, distantly and absurdly, of himself.

8

The morning after the *ceilidh*, Conal Connolly quarrelled briefly with his grandfather, but it was only a token quarrel, a reminder by the old wolf that he still ruled the pack and by the young that he wouldn't do so for ever.

The truth was they needed each other. The old man's frequently expressed wish was to do something great for Ireland before he died. Connolly money and Connolly arms had been available almost on demand for the IRA throughout the 'seventies, but the decisive battle had never been fought. A Connolly in the White House was his last hope of having a significant influence in the future of Ireland, and Conal was the only one qualified. But he in his turn knew that without the Granda's money and influence, he could run for ever and get nowhere.

Rather than use the chopper, he opted to drive into Boston with Dree, who was following Christie's station wagon in her emerald green Porsche (Old Pat's twenty-first present). His ostensible reason was that it would give him a chance to chat, away from fiddle music, jigs and patriotic songs.

But he had relapsed into a moody silence as they left Castlemaine, never once glancing back, and he maintained it almost all the way to the airport.

'Are things really bad between you and Mary?' asked Dree gently.

'Bad enough,' he said. 'And she's a good Catholic girl, which makes them desperate.'

'I'm sorry, Con,' said Dree. 'Politically it won't help, huh?'

'Not much.'

'But you've got plenty of time to sort it out. Or to put it behind you if it won't mend.'

'Plenty of time before what?' he asked.

'Before you start chasing the nomination.'

'Not if I go for it next time,' he answered.

'Next time!' she said, amazed, taking her eyes off the speeding road to glance at his impassive face.

'That's right. I'd be the youngest ever, wouldn't that be something to stick down their throats?'

'Whose throats, Con?'

He shrugged and said lightly, 'Anyone's throats.'

At the airport she said, 'I hope it all works out, Con. Take care.'

'You too, Dree. You take extra special care.'

They kissed and he went out to the waiting plane.

By the time he reached New York the clouds which had been white and fluffy over Boston had thickened into stormpeaks, and as his cab crawled over the Queensboro' Bridge, they spilt a livid light into the canyons of Manhattan and from time to time an italic scrawl of lightning flicked across the sky like a tired neon sign.

The storm broke as he reached his hotel. He checked in and left his bag before returning through the bloated raindrops to the waiting cab. It dropped him on East 62nd between Park and Madison and the storm poured water over him like a shower-bath as he dashed into the apartment block which contained what till recently had been his New York home. But for the past four months his wife and Peggy, their young daughter, had lived here alone. The porter was new and Conal had to show him identification before he summoned the elevator. Even now the humiliation was not finished. He put his key into the lock on the apartment door but found it wouldn't turn. Then it was opened from the other side.

'You've changed the locks,' he said, more accusingly than he meant.

His wife, Mary, was a small blonde woman, with doll-like features and a child's calm untroubled gaze. Her face registered little of the extremes of delight and pain, but she was far from being insensitive to either.

'I had to for the insurance,' she said. 'They like a woman living alone to have stronger locks than the others. You don't grudge us protection, do you?'

Once she had been loving, trusting, yielding, admiring. Now she was a counter-puncher, always ready with a blow.

'Where's Peggy?'

'Out at friends. It's a birthday party.'

'Yeah? Better than the one I've been at, I hope,' he said, sinking wearily into a chair.

'How's the Granda? OK?'

'Same as ever. Annoyed you and Peg weren't there.'

'But you explained why?'

'Yes. I explained,' said Conal. 'Mary, listen, I've come to beg. I haven't got a speech prepared. You can write it for me. Whatever lines will move you, whatever arguments persuade you, you put them in and I'll say them and I'll mean them. For my sake, for our sake, for Peggy's sake; even, if you want, for your country's sake, stick with me now. Please. I beg you.'

She looked at him, blank-faced, a little doll waiting for someone to turn the key so she could speak.

Her voice when it came was most undoll-like.

'After what you told me, Conal? No way!'

'I told you because I trusted you, I needed you, I thought you could help me!' protested the man.

'Did you? Then you were a fool. Poor judgment, that should disqualify you from the White House even if your ethics didn't,' she snapped.

'But why should it make this difference to us?' he asked. 'OK, it's a shock, but it was a weakness, a once-off thing, I'm mortally ashamed, it had nothing to do with us, though . . .'

'Nothing? It had everything. It made disgusting everything we'd ever done; all those things you liked to do, I'd just been puzzled by them before; but what the hell, you were a man, perhaps all men were like that, how should I know, little innocent, straightforward, normal me?'

Her voice had risen and there was a faint, rather becoming flush around her cheekbones as though the dollmaker had lovingly stroked them with a tiny pink-laden brush.

Conal opened his mouth as if to speak again, but instead he threw up his arms in a spontaneous gesture of surrender. Anything more would be rhetoric. Perhaps it had all been rhetoric. One of his political strengths was knowing when he was beaten – sometimes in advance of his opponents knowing they had beaten him.

He stood up. She looked at him in surprise at his suddenness.

'You're not waiting for Peggy?'

'I don't think so. Not today. Goodbye, Mary.'

'That sounds final.'

'Does it? What's final? Remember, any time you decide after all you'd like to be married to the President of the United States, just let me know.'

'I'll always be married to you, Con, whatever you become,' she said steadily. 'Though if you became that, then God help us all.'

'He'd better help me,' said Conal. 'He's all I've got left.'

Mary sat down and remained very still, staring fixedly at the closed door with those shell-blue eyes which looked as if weighted lids would slide smoothly over them if her head fell back. After the silence had stretched for half a minute, she rose and went to the window. After a while she saw Conal come out of the apartment block and stand on the sidewalk. Almost immediately a cab drew up and he got in. He had always been lucky with cabs.

The cab bore him swiftly away. The hotel he had named was not far but during the short journey the driver managed to put the country's domestic problems to rights and Conal's mind and spirit were racked by a storm of thought and emotion which made the turbulent skies above seem placid. But his face showed nothing of this as he paid off the driver and walked swiftly through the hotel lobby.

His bag lay on the bed. He unlocked it but did not begin to unpack. Instead he burrowed his hand in among the clothes till they met the cold hardness of the automatic which he always kept by him at night.

He did not pull it out but sat on the bed, his hand on the gun, his eyes on himself in the dressing-table mirror.

Then he grinned without much humour, said softly, 'Some other time, that's a promise,' released the gun and picked up the phone.

After that he lay on the bed, lit a cigarette and waited.

Half an hour later there was a knock at his door.

He opened it. A broad, motherly-looking woman smiled at him.

'Nice to see you again, sir. Here's Emily, I think you've met before.'

She ushered into the room a girl of about fourteen in pigtails and large round spectacles.

'Yes. Hello, Emily,' said Conal. 'How are you?'

'She's fine, sir. If you'll excuse us just a moment.'

The matronly woman hustled the girl through into the bathroom and shut the door behind her.

Conal didn't move, but stood as if in a trance staring at the closed door till it opened again a few moments later.

The woman came out alone.

'There we are, sir. All ready,' she said cheerfully. 'Would you care to settle now, then there'll be no need to disturb you later?'

Still not speaking, Conal took out his pocket book, peeled off a small bundle of notes and handed them over.

'I'll be back in shall we say an hour, sir?'

He nodded. With a last amiable beam, the woman left.

A moment later the girl appeared at the bathroom door.

She was stripped down to her underclothes, a pair of thick cotton pants and a cheap bra which didn't look at all necessary.

Conal looked at her for a long minute and sighed. At this moment he always got a feeling of nightmare but it quickly passed. The nightmares all lay outside this room, though in a sense they started here.

Turning, he locked the door. The precaution suddenly struck him as absurd and he smiled. Locking doors was an empty gesture in these days of two-way mirrors, micro-bugs, hidden cameras. He should know if anyone should. Hadn't he seen it all on film, heard it all on tape?

And hadn't he been crazy enough to confess it all to his wife in the touchingly naive faith that she would understand and absolve?

But, he reminded himself sardonically, the one positive thing to arise from all these horrors was that he didn't have

to worry about being spied on any more. Once was far and
away plenty.

He made an ironical obeisance to the possible sources of
surveillance around the room.

The girl looked at him warily. She'd probably been
warned about weirdos.

He smiled at her.

'A little private joke, Emily,' he said.

Then he gestured towards the bed and began to undress.

An hour later to the minute, the motherly woman returned
to collect Emily. She left without shutting the door and
before Conal could close it, two men entered. They looked,
dressed and spoke like high-ranking business executives
which in fact was what they were. The first time he had met
them had been in this very room in these very circumstances
only nine months earlier. But his reaction then had been very
different. He had raved, threatened and offered bribes as
they laid photographic prints neatly on the bed and played
tapes. Finally their lack of reaction, their self-contained
silence had driven him silent in his turn.

The older of the two had then begun speaking in
measured, educated tones which had spelt it out to him – *Mr
Connolly, if we publish these photographs and tapes, it will not
only mean the end of your public life and most of your social
life too, it will also mean that you go to gaol.*

They hadn't wanted money, they hadn't wanted anything
except to help him in his political career. *Until I'm President*,
he had said, scornful at their naive prevarication. *Then you'd
own me. Go fuck yourselves.*

We're simple businessmen, he was told. *Ninety-five per cent
of what the President does is of no interest to us. And fifty per
cent of what the President does is due to the influence of
various pressure groups in any case. What's your problem, Mr
Connolly?*

And he had allowed the argument to die. The moment of
decision was still to come, he told himself.

'Just who are you people anyway?' he'd asked.

'Executives,' said the older man mildly.

'Of what?'

They exchanged glances.

'Of legitimate businesses, like this hotel for instance. We specialize in providing unusual services.'

'What businesses? What's your names? I could find out easily enough,' he threatened.

'I'm sure of it, and it wouldn't matter a damn if you did, Mr Connolly. Only if you're going to try, be careful who you involve. We're executives of another less well known business, as you must have worked out. If you pass on even the little you know about us to anyone, you put that person in danger. Just as anyone unauthorized who shares our little bit of secret knowledge about you would be in danger too. Goodnight now. We'll be in touch. In fact we'll never be out of touch. Think about it.'

Yet despite that warning, he'd got drunk that night and confessed everything to his wife. The good Catholic, though long lapsed, still yearns after the cleansing confession. Only this time, instead of absolution, he got an expression of such loathing that it cut through his alcoholic haze like a laser through a morning mist. He had stopped short of telling her about the blackmail. And since that time his desperate efforts to persuade her into some kind of reconciliation had been motivated as much by fear for her life as by self-interest.

But self-interest was never far away. They had him. He either played their way or left the game. And they were very good. They were politically shrewd, excellent strategists, and had access to an amazing range of inside information. In other circumstances, he'd have been delighted to have them on his team.

No; correction; honesty, with himself at least, was his new resolution; he was pleased to have them on his team even in these circumstances. He would be pleased with anything that could give him an edge. And they were pushy too. They it was who were keen for him to go for the nomination in two years' time. They felt sure he could do it. He was beginning to believe them himself.

Now, as always, they came straight to the point and together they spent nearly an hour mapping out directions for the next month. He was no puppet. They were as willing to listen as to talk. It was strange, when they talked political tactics together like this, he could completely forget the sordid circumstances of their compact.

When he thought they'd finished and would soon be going, the elder man took him by surprise by saying, 'Now, do you have anything to tell us, Mr Connolly?'

For a heart-choking moment he thought they must be referring to Mary. They'd worked out that he'd confessed to her and were giving him a last chance to admit it before they killed her!

Then the other man prompted him; 'About your grandfather's will.'

'Granda's will?' he said in surprise. 'Well, yes, but how the hell do you know?'

'Just tell us, Mr Connolly.'

He told them. They examined their notebooks and nodded at each other.

'You really should tell us this kind of thing without prompting,' suggested the elder.

'Hell, you seemed to know it already,' laughed Conal. 'And it doesn't mean anything. It must be an illegal trust. And in any case, Deirdre, my sister's not on the point of running off with this Prince Arthur, is she?'

'The behaviour of young women is impossible to forecast, as are the vagaries of the law, especially when lawyers are being instructed by the Church of Rome,' said the younger of the pair drily.

The two men rose to go.

'But what does it mean?' demanded Conal.

'You're a good investment, Mr Connolly, but part of your attraction is that you're self-financing. Never forget that.

And never forget to pass on to us *all* relevant material. Good day to you now. We'll stay in touch. Close in touch.'

They left as silently as they'd come and Conal lay down on the crumpled bed with his hands behind his neck and stared sightlessly at the high brown ceiling.

9

After his talk with Old Haystacks, McHarg had thought of returning to the Atlanta to have a word with Davison. But the prospect of more probing about Flora from Heather deterred him so he went straight back to Police HQ and set about tying up loose ends in preparation for his absence at the Partington trial.

Just after five o'clock his door burst open and the Chief Superintendent came storming in.

'That bastard Wainwright!' he snarled without preamble. 'I went out of my way for him, rang the University lab, got it from Professor Foster himself that it was definitely a dog's tongue. But when I telephoned Wainwright, he was bloody abusive. There's no dealing with some people. He's a sodding menace.'

'Just because he's rude to you?' said McHarg.

'Oh no. *That* I'm used to from my subordinates. There's more. A few minutes ago I got two phone calls in rapid succession. One from Professor Foster, the other from the editor of the *Post*. That madman's been at them both. Foster he accused of being a charlatan or a dupe. And the editor was all agog at the notion that we were trying to keep the wraps on a South Coast Ripper story. I've just about run out of soothing noises.'

'You'd better call up your reserves,' advised McHarg.

And he described his interview with Old Haystacks. As he

talked, Davison frowned and his ill temper seemed to drain visibly from him to be replaced by something much colder, much more controlled.

'Douglas,' he said. 'I don't want you doing anything to encourage daft rumours. Wainwright made a mistake. There's an end to it.'

'That's hardly the point,' said McHarg, frowning in his turn.

'Isn't it? Well, here's the point, Inspector. Drop it. You hear me? That's an order. And no shit about *your* time, *our* time. *Any* time, you drop it!'

McHarg thought about the conversation the next morning as he prepared for his drive to London. Davison had been as serious as he'd ever seen him. Yet by his own argument, if indeed it had been a dog's tongue, it was an unpleasant but hardly an important matter.

McHarg put it out of his mind and packed his grip, rolling a bottle of Scotch up in his pyjamas. It was still very early, but this way he'd miss the worst of the commuter traffic as he got near to the capital. He did a last check of doors and windows round the cold, empty bungalow. As he did so he wondered why he continued to live here. It was not even as if it spoke to him of Mavis. Their life together here had been all too brief. And the pretence that he was keeping a home for Flora had worn as thin as Thursday's broth.

It was time to go in every sense.

As he drove his old Volvo through the empty streets, he tried to shut out the past and think instead of the day ahead of him. But he knew that the past lay waiting for him there too.

London.

McHarg had once loved it. Now he hated it.

If his cold, comfortless bungalow was bearable because his marriage had sunk no roots there, by the same token London was full of pain for there it was that the good years had burgeoned and blossomed.

There he had met Mavis Finlayson for the first time; he a

soldier on leave with nothing to look forward to but a long journey north and a fortnight of sea and sky with aged relatives, she a Scot also, training as a nurse at Bart's Hospital.

He didn't make the journey north, but at the end of his leave he left her as he had left others before, with a kiss, a gift, a promise to write when he had time, nothing more. This felt different, but McHarg was a canny man. Others took risks, he took precautions.

It took a month back with his unit to convince him. He got a three-day pass, hitched a lift to England on a Dakota carrying mail, and went to see Mavis. One look at her confirmed his feelings. She was the woman for him. It was only after his proposal had been accepted that she told him she was pregnant.

'It's as well I'm marrying you,' said McHarg. 'It's clear you'd never have made a nurse.'

That had been the end of the army for him. Life in married quarters was less than he wanted to offer his wife and child. But life as a civilian proved uncongenial too, until finally he compromised and joined the Metropolitan Police.

He made slow but steady progress, his evident talent for the work usually tipping the balance against his other talent for making enemies by his forthrightness. Above all, he had a strong and evident respect for the job, which Mavis shared as she shared his pleasure at each step forward, particularly his move into the, to her, hugely glamorous world of the Royal Squad.

Flora never understood this. Until about the age of fifteen, she had been her father's greatest admirer. Almost overnight, or so it seemed, she became his greatest critic. Some of the symptoms were conventional. A stage of surly rebellion in her mid-teens manifesting itself in clothes, company and manners, followed in the sixth form and at University by a stage of political radicalism which saw the police as tools of Fascist oppression.

What was not conventional was the effect of the parallel

development of Mavis's illness. McHarg suspected his daughter saw far more of her mother's pain than he was permitted to see. But she didn't seem to see, or wouldn't let herself see, the deep love, and liking, that existed between Mavis and himself; and this bewildered McHarg.

But she was right in some respects. His escort duties with the Prince were taking him away from home for longer and longer periods and what had really got to him was when Flora, recalling stories he had told her in earlier, friendlier days, said bitterly that they'd have had more family life together if he'd stayed in the army.

So, the move to Sanderton. But too late. Too late. Too late . . .

A slight stutter from the Volvo's engine brought him back to the present. The petrol gauge was banging on empty. He discovered that without any conscious effort he had driven through the town and was now on the main London road. He wondered just how much of a man's life was spent in such autonomic behaviour, as if the conscious and subconscious for a period reversed roles. Years perhaps. He found himself wondering if since Mavis's death he had not been in such a state ninety per cent of the time.

He pushed the thought out of his mind and started looking for a garage.

It was still only 6.15 a.m. and the first two he passed were not yet open, but a few miles further on he spotted a twenty-four-hour sign and pulled in. Beside the pumps and the sales kiosk was a small glass-fronted shack full of vending machines.

'Fill it up,' said McHarg to the bright-eyed old man who'd come to serve him, and went to get himself a cup of coffee.

When he tasted it, he wished he hadn't bothered. Not even two years of catering for himself had inured him to stuff like this. He poured it away and chucked the carton into a waste bin.

'You should've asked,' called the old man. 'I'd've warned you. I make my own.'

'Experience is a good teacher,' said McHarg, making a wry face.

'Right,' said the old man. 'And sometimes the sods who warn you are wrong! I went to a Methodist Bible class when I was a lad. Nice folk, but they were wrong about girls and booze!'

McHarg laughed and enjoyed it, like a rare wine, or a good single malt – he wasn't much of a man for the grape. Like something, anyway, which you tasted for itself, not for what it would do for you.

'You were almost dry,' said the man. 'Good job you stopped.'

'It's the gauge,' said McHarg. 'It's old. You lose track of your capacity with age.'

'Speak for yourself,' grinned the old man. 'Oil OK?'

'Take a look,' invited McHarg. 'Tell me, are you the only twenty-four-hour garage along this road then?'

'Unless you head for the motorway,' said the old man. 'Hardly worth it along here any more except in the holiday season. Not that I'm complaining! It suits me down to the ground, this little job. I had forty years on the night shift and I couldn't settle to right ways round when I retired. I've hit it lucky with this. I just wish there was a bit more business, that's all. I don't cost much, but some weeks, it's hardly worthwhile paying me! You'd better have a pint.'

He held up the dipstick for McHarg to examine.

'OK,' said McHarg. 'How good's your memory, Mr . . . er . . . ?'

'Flint,' said the old man. 'Pretty good. Why?'

'Last Monday morning, about five o'clock. Did you have any customers then?'

Now the old man was regarding him with shrewd suspicion.

'Might've done. Who's asking?'

With a sigh, McHarg produced his warrant card.

'This isn't official, not yet,' he said. 'I just stopped for petrol. Then it struck me . . . well, look, what I'm interested in is a large, light blue car, might have been a Jaguar, two men in it . . .'

'Might have been a Jaguar!' interrupted Mr Flint scornfully. 'It was a Jaguar all right, an XJ6, Series Four, four point two litre, automatic, with PAS and speedhold. British *and* best. I had a good look.'

'You mean, it stopped? You're sure?'

'I could count the cars I filled up that night on one hand,' said Mr Flint. 'That was the same night the fire engines were clanging away going to that big fire out Little Pailey way, right?'

'Dead right,' said McHarg. 'Mr Flint, I'd offer you a cup of coffee if you wouldn't be insulted! How's the hot chocolate?'

'Better, they say. But not for me. I'm diabetic,' said the old man. 'I could stand an ox-tail soup, though.'

Over the soup, McHarg discovered that fate had thrown him the ideal witness. Sharp-eyed, intelligent and above all inquisitive, Mr Flint was delighted to have an appreciative audience.

Yes, there'd been two men in the car. The driver had been youngish, early thirties perhaps, very smart, dark-haired, wore a moustache, not one of your modern droopy things but a proper military moustache. He had looked a bit pale. Mr Flint got the impression that it had been his idea to stop, more in order to use the lav and have a cup of coffee than for petrol, though he did ask for his tank to be filled.

And the other man?

Thin-faced, quiet-spoken, hard to pin down anything distinguishing, even his age was doubtful, but definitely the older; wearing a dark suit, expensive – not as fashionable as the other fellow's, but certainly expensive. And despite his quietness, he gave the impression of being in charge.

'What do you mean?' asked McHarg.

'You can always tell,' averred Mr Flint. 'He watched the other fellow, let him drink his coffee (*he* didn't complain!), smoked his fag, picked his moment, then they were off.'

'How did they pay?' asked McHarg.

'Now that was interesting,' said Mr Flint, warming to his task. 'The young fellow started pulling out one of those folders, you know the things, string of credit cards and cheque cards. The other chap, the thin-faced one, he beat him to it, had a wad of notes thick as a Bible in his pocket. He looked the type who'd pay his way.'

'I'm sorry?'

'You know what I mean. Credit cards are OK, but it's money in your pocket that counts in a tight corner, isn't it?'

'You thought he'd be good in a tight corner?' asked McHarg with a smile. He was enjoying Mr Flint.

'Oh yes. What're they supposed to have done anyway?'

'I wish I knew,' said McHarg. 'Were any names used?'

The old man considered. 'They didn't speak much,' he said. 'Hang about, though. When the quiet fellow asked the other chap if he was ready to go, he answered "Yours to command, Taylor," some such thing, making a joke of admitting the other was the boss.'

'Taylor? You're sure?'

'Sixty per cent. Might have been Tyler.'

McHarg believed in following lucky streaks.

'And finally, Mr Flint, what was the number?' he asked as if he had no expectation of anything other than a precise and positive answer.

But he was disappointed.

'There you've got me,' admitted Mr Flint.

'Never mind,' said McHarg. 'You've been a great help. How much do I owe for the petrol?'

Mr Flint took his money and put it in the till.

'I did notice the letters though,' he offered. 'They were something YO. That's London. And it was a Z registration. Any help?'

He offered McHarg his change.

'I'd be honoured if you'd buy yourself a dram on my behalf,' said McHarg, rejecting the notes and silver.

'Get half-a-dozen drams with this!' said Mr Flint.

'Half-a-dozen English measures perhaps,' said McHarg. 'They'll just about make a good Scots dram. It's been a pleasure meeting you, Mr Flint.'

'Likewise. Call again.'

'I will,' said McHarg. 'I surely will.'

Flint had given him much food for thought. Work was an analgesic more potent even than alcohol. Suddenly the day ahead began to seem almost bearable.

10

The semi-euphoric mood lasted McHarg through a transport driver's breakfast and only began to fade when he reported in at the Yard. Security had always been tough but in the old days his had been a familiar face and he could move around with the assurance of an inmate.

Now he knew what it was like to be a stranger. His credentials were carefully checked three times in succession before he was invited to take a seat and await the arrival of Chief Superintendent Highfield, who was in charge of the Partington case. McHarg glanced at his watch. It was still early.

He decided to take a walk.

His look of authoritative certainty carried him through most barriers, but when he finally reached his chosen goal, he found the resistance stiffer.

'Mr Allardyce went two years ago, sir,' said a young sergeant called Williams who had the lilt of the Rhondda in his voice. 'Can I help you?'

McHarg produced the information Mr Flint had given him on the Jaguar and explained that he would like a list of possibilities.

Sergeant Williams pursed his lips and went away and

returned with a uniformed inspector who made McHarg explain himself again.

'You've got authorization?' he said.

'Authorization?'

'That's right.'

'Look,' said McHarg. 'I don't want the key to the Commissioner's private bog, I just want a simple bit of information. You've got the biggest computer in the land at your disposal, or so the hand-outs say. What's it do all day? Work out your pools plan?'

It was not the right tactic. The discussion developed, got warmer and was on the point of exploding when the door opened behind McHarg and the sergeant and inspector stiffened to attention and silence.

'Good morning,' said a quiet voice. 'It's McHarg, isn't it? Doug McHarg. I thought I recognized that voice.'

McHarg turned frowning. But the frown faded immediately and he grasped the outstretched hand.

'Thank God for a friendly face,' he said. 'Freddie Grossmith! I thought they paid you to keep out of the country these days!'

Freddie Grossmith and McHarg had once been very close, not friends so much as members of the same club whose entry requirements were a calm, self-contained competence and a fireproof skin when Sir Robert Mark's purging flames were licking round the building in 1972. In many other respects they were completely opposite. Grossmith was a slight, quiet man who would never draw attention in a crowd. And this anonymity in terms of everything except efficiency had set his career on an upward sweep which had soon sent him soaring high above the plateau where McHarg's uncompromising outspokenness kept him anchored. The difference in rank had begun to separate them just as certainly as the difference in role, McHarg developing his career in the Royal Squad, while Grossmith had become part of the Yard's Interpol link team.

'What are you doing here, Doug?' asked Grossmith.

McHarg explained, both generally then specifically. Grossmith glanced at the bit of paper with the details of the Jaguar.

'Run it,' he said to the inspector. 'Put what you get through to my office. And try to remember, official channels are intended for ease of passage, not for obstruction.'

Outside in the corridor, he said, 'Come along to my office. Let's swap news.'

'What are you now, Freddie?' asked McHarg. 'Chief Super?'

For answer, Grossmith pointed at the legend on the door which they were approaching.

'Jesus,' said McHarg. 'Commander, sir! I'm sorry. What I mean is, congratulations. Commander of what?'

'Same line, basically. Interpol links. International relations are more and more important. We need a constant exchange of information and ideas. No hold-ups, no gaps for the absconder, the smuggler, the terrorist, to fall through. Come on in.'

He ushered McHarg into what turned out to be an outer office. A stocky man of about thirty rose from behind a desk and stood to attention. He was surrounded by banks of filing cabinets plus what McHarg recognized as a computer terminal with visual read-off facility as well as print-out.

'Inspector Elkin, Inspector McHarg. George, ring Mr Highfield's office, tell them Mr McHarg is here with me when they want him.'

'Will do,' said Elkin in a raw East End accent. 'You want some coffee, guv?'

'Doug? Yes, that would be nice. In here.'

He opened the door to an inner office.

As McHarg went through, Grossmith said to Elkin, 'There'll be some information about a car coming through for Mr McHarg. Let me know when you have it.'

The office was comfortably appointed in the unostentatious functional style that Scotland Yard thinks suitable for its top men. Out of the window there was a not very inspiring view of London roofs with a thin glimpse of St James's Park distantly visible between a couple of blocks of glass and concrete.

Grossmith peered out into the grey air and said, 'I was sorry to hear about Mavis.'

'Yes,' said McHarg.

'You had a girl? How's she doing?'

'OK. She's in the States. An academic.'

'Takes after her father?' said Grossmith, trying to lighten the mood as he turned and sat down. 'What's it like down at the seaside, Doug?'

'Sandy. Though even sand has hidden depths.'

Grossmith made a puzzled face and McHarg found himself talking about Wainwright's discovery of the tongue and about Morrison's death. It was shop, but anything was preferable to polite discussion of his personal status, either emotional or professional.

'Interesting,' said Grossmith. 'This man Morrison, I know his stuff. He could write well. You'll be checking on him, I expect?'

'I thought while I was in town,' said McHarg.

'Save yourself some legwork, use the facilities.'

There was a tap on the door. Elkin came in with two cups of coffee on a tray and a short length of print-out paper which he handed to McHarg.

'Yours, I think,' he said.

'George, see what you can get on James Morrison. Freelance journalist. London address not known, but he owned the Mill House at – where was it, Doug?'

'Little Pailey, near Sanderton,' said McHarg, who was busy studying the paper.

There were three names on it.

Samuel Gray, 25, Lea Road, Hounslow.
Edgar Franklin, The Grange, Uppercross Lane, Richmond.

Sayed ibn Aziz, Flat 73, St Bridget's Mansions, Kensington.

'Anything, Doug?' asked Grossmith.

'Not to me. Could we run them?' asked McHarg.

'Of course. George, feed these through too, will you?'

As Elkin turned away he rolled his eyes expressively. McHarg got the impression he didn't care too much to be wasting his precious time on helping out some hayseed from the sticks. McHarg didn't give a sod.

At least Elkin was efficient. By the time they'd finished their coffee and just received news that Superintendent Highfield had finally arrived, he'd collected what information was on record about the four men.

James Morrison was fairly comprehensively covered. As a well-known journalist and therefore a man of potential influence and/or nuisance value, his particulars and background were automatically fed into the computer. McHarg was impressed to see that the record was completely up to date, i.e., it included details of the fire and Morrison's death. His only direct interest with the law (and therefore theoretically the only information necessary for police records) was a conviction for drunk driving and another for causing a disturbance in a London hotel. There was nothing in the background information which obviously suggested a link with Partington.

The Arab too was covered in some detail, mainly because he had some distant link with the Saudi royal family and was therefore regarded as a possible target for terrorist attack.

Edgar Franklin was a company director, aged fifty-nine, and had two convictions for speeding. Samuel Gray was completely unknown.

'Still not much help,' said Grossmith, who had been peering over his shoulder.

'I don't know. If my Mr Flint can be relied on, neither of the men looked Arabic and even the elder of the two was well below fifty-nine. So that leaves Mr Samuel Gray.'

'Unless your Mr Flint got any of his details wrong. About the car, I mean, or about the number.'

'I think I'd back him,' said McHarg.

He stood up.

'I'd better be on my way,' he said. 'Thanks for making me welcome.'

As they passed through the outer office Grossmith said, 'I'll be busy later so I won't be able to see you, but a thought occurs. If you're at a loose end tonight, there's something that might interest you. The BBC are doing a big series on the Crime-Fighters and there's a reception at the TV Centre in Wood Lane tonight to launch it. I can't go, but George here will be there. He did most of the liaison work on the international side, so he deserves the treat anyway. Why don't you go instead of me? Treat yourself at the taxpayer's expense. It could be fun. They go out of their way to please, George tells me.'

'That's right, guv,' said Elkin. 'They dearly love a real life bobby, all these arty-farties. We're like shit to a blow-fly.'

'No thanks,' said McHarg. 'Not my cup of tea.'

'Think about it,' said Grossmith. 'Where are you staying?'

McHarg gave the address of the small private hotel in Victoria where he was booked in.

'George will give you a ring later on in case you change your mind.'

Elkin looked unenthusiastic.

'I think I'll be busy,' said McHarg. 'Goodbye. Thanks a lot.'

Nearly eight hours later, McHarg came out of the Old Bailey into a drizzly evening through which crowds of city workers were scuttling towards home and shelter.

He paused on the steps and glanced up at the figures of Truth and Patience which loom above the entrance. He felt a bit short on the latter quality. The preliminaries had been even longer drawn out than was usual. The defence was clearly determined to fight every inch of the way. His eyes rose higher to the bronze statue of Justice with scales and sword. If Partington was to be nailed, the shining lady would have to hit him with the scales after pinning him down with the sword. It was a good job she didn't wear a blindfold. McHarg as arresting officer would be the first prosecution witness, but he hadn't yet been called. There were many more profitable ways he could have spent the day. Still, it hadn't been altogether wasted.

At lunchtime he had looked up Samuel Gray in the phone directory and rung his home. Mrs Gray had answered. McHarg who had something of a gift for mimicry had put on his best Home Counties voice and spun a line about meeting Gray last – when was it? – Monday night. He had struck oil immediately.

'At the Masonic Dinner?' Mrs Gray had said.

'That's right. I'm sorry he got back so late,' he probed. She didn't mind, she replied chattily. She was used to it on these occasions, had gone to bed with a book and a pill, never even noticed him returning.

McHarg went on: 'Something we were talking about. I said I'd ring him at his office, but I've lost his business number.'

He got it and rang. It was a firm of stockbrokers with an address only a quarter of a mile away from the Bailey. There hadn't been time at lunch but now he turned up his collar against the rain and set off walking. He hoped that Samuel Gray kept respectable office hours and wasn't one of the home-for-tea set.

As he got out of the lift in the building which housed Gray's firm, one of the fattest men he'd ever seen, with a completely bald pate, came dashing out through a door marked 'Enquiries' and jumped into the lift which he completely occupied. He carried a briefcase with the initials S.G. on the side.

McHarg's heart sank. The girl in the *Enquiries* office confirmed the worst. Yes, the portly gent who had just left was Mr Samuel Gray of Hounslow.

It could still have been his car, thought McHarg. But the prospect now seemed gloomy to the point of total obscurity. He had a couple of large Scotches till the crowd of homegoing drinkers began to depress him. Then he went back to his hotel room and had a couple of hefty belts at his own bottle till his own company began to depress him. He needed something to occupy him, someone to talk to.

So when the phone rang and it turned out to be Inspector George Elkin, obediently but unenthusiastically asking how he felt about the BBC reception, to his surprise he found himself hesitating the direct refusal.

'Tell you what, pussycat,' said Elkin. 'I'll leave word at reception you might be coming, OK? That way they can warn the band. Pip pip.'

He rang off.

Cheeky bastard, thought McHarg. Would it bother Elkin more if he came or if he stayed away?

The answer seemed obvious.

McHarg had another couple for the road and set off.

11

Elkin had been as good as his word. McHarg was greeted like a man of distinction at the TV centre and escorted to the reception by a girl with a face like a nun's and a rump like a racehorse's. She'd obviously been told to treat all the guests like top people and at a glance McHarg could see why. The place was full of media-familiar faces. He recognized Justin Greenwood, MP, prominent member of the Tribune Group, talking to his opposite number, Charley Beal, whose membership of the Monday Club went as far back as Sunday (a Westminster joke). There was a whole Punk Rock group present with names like Paul Pee and Tony Turd, standing menacingly around a swinging bishop with an even stupider name. In balance with these was the little throng surrounding Lord Hunsingore, founder of *New Vision*, one of the numerous moral regeneration movements of the 'seventies. McHarg recognized Hymie Small who'd seen the light in Parkhurst where he also discovered you can make more money with a paint brush than a pick handle; Mrs Rose le Queux, one-time leader of the biggest of the new prostitutes' unions, but now one of *New Vision*'s star proselytes; Mrs Ena Dyas, housewife conscience of the nation . . . And so on, as far as the eye could see.

The centaur girl got him a large Scotch and went on her way. He helped himself to half a pound of smoked salmon to keep the thirst coming and another Scotch when it came. A gap opened up ahead of him and he spotted Elkin. The group he was with consisted of an elegant youngish man with rosebud lips puckering beneath a neat military moustache, three or four epicene youths in hemp shirts and tight cords, a woman of about thirty in a wheelchair and a slight grey man with a skull like a death's head whom McHarg recognized as Harry Preston, chief crime reporter for one of the big tabloids.

He went across and joined them. Elkin was doing the PR thing, it seemed, and managed to look pleased to see him, introducing him as *the* key witness in the Partington case. Rosy lips turned out to be Basil Younger, Deputy Controller of News and Documentary. The woman in the chair whose face showed some polite animation on introduction before relapsing into a mask of contemptuous boredom was Betty Woodstock, one of the *Crime-Fighters* research team. The henchmen in hemp were all production assistants with the same name, or so it seemed.

Preston lit a cigarette from the one he had smoked till it scorched his thin lips and said, 'McHarg. Rings a bell.'

Younger said, 'What's poor Partington going to get? I presume it's all cut and dried in advance.'

'Couldn't really say, sir,' said McHarg in his best wooden

constabulary manner. He felt the drink working in him, which was surprising. It had been a long time since booze had got to him.

'Got you,' said Preston. 'You're the one who told Prince Arthur to fuck off.'

'No,' said McHarg.

'No? It would have made a good story,' said Preston, showing his teeth in what might have been a grin.

'Risk hell-fire for a good story, wouldn't you, Harry boy?' laughed Elkin, very jolly.

'One of your colleagues found out about hell-fire the other night,' said McHarg.

There was a silence in the group.

'What do you mean by that?' asked the woman in the wheelchair.

'James Morrison. Did you know him?'

'Did you?'

'Only after the event, so to speak. It happened on my patch.'

'Poor James,' said Younger. 'Yes, I think we all knew him. He was once a pretty big figure.'

'What's that mean?' asked McHarg.

Preston answered through a cloud of smoke. 'He could once ask four figures for a feature. He'd managed to drink himself down to two.'

'Come now. *De mortuis* . . .' said Younger. 'A sad accident. Sad.'

'What's your interest, Inspector?' asked Betty Woodstock.

'No interest. Just my job,' said McHarg.

'Any unusual death, we've got to look into it,' said Elkin almost apologetically.

'But without interest? How's that for blasé,' said the woman.

'I meant disinterested rather than uninterested,' said McHarg.

'You mean, the Partington trial for instance, you don't

care about the result?' asked Younger with a hint of a sneer.

'Can't talk about that,' said McHarg, who was feeling belligerent but not so that he was going to forget the company he was in.

'*Sub judice*, you mean? Well, it's a useful cop-out, if you'll excuse the expression. I sometimes think it goes too far, wouldn't you agree, Mr Preston?' said Younger. 'A little responsible media coverage while the trial's on might do a lot of good.'

'Hard to say without a lot more evidence,' answered McHarg.

Younger's lips pursed like an old woman's, and he said, 'Time to circulate, I think. Lovely to meet you all.' He moved away with the epicenes behind him, fluttering like washing on a line.

Preston's teeth were on show again.

He said: 'McHarg, I could get you a good deal for your memoirs of life with Prince Arthur. You ever want a ghost, you remember me.'

'You'll be the first in my mind,' said McHarg.

'Jesus, McHarg!' said Elkin as Preston moved away. 'They don't teach you no diplomacy down at the seaside, do they?'

'They teach us to keep our noses out of the sun,' said McHarg.

'You know what?' said Elkin. 'You hard bastards only manage your little ego-trips because the rest of us work at keeping the peace. Think about it, pussycat.'

He strode away, leaving McHarg alone with the woman in the wheelchair.

'What are you staring at?' demanded McHarg.

'That's usually my line,' she replied equably. 'Have you had too much of that stuff or not enough?'

'Not enough.'

'What's made you so angry?'

'Who's angry? I'm just – what? irritated. London irritates me. Parties irritate me. Jumped-up shits like that irritate me.'

He made a gesture which comprehended Younger, Elkin and every other semi-famous face present.

'I was once going to marry that particular jumped-up shit,' said Betty Woodstock.

'Younger, you mean? Then you must have had a stroke of luck.'

'That's one way of looking at it,' she said. 'I fell out of a window and landed in this chair.'

'Oh Christ,' said McHarg. 'I'm sorry. I didn't realize.'

'You should have done. You're a detective. Or is that all done via the wallet rather than the brain these days?'

He finished his drink. 'I'll be on my way,' he said.

'Why? Touched a nerve, did I?' she mocked.

He looked at her with distaste. 'I'm not touchy,' he said. 'The thing is, while I don't take bribes, I'm not above a bit of police brutality. Only I haven't brought my special club for beating sitting women.'

'Oh, but I think you have, Inspector,' she replied.

He would have left her then but the *New Vision* group centered on Mrs le Queux and Lord Hunsingore ingested them, amoeba-like, as it drifted past. Hymie Small caught McHarg's eye and smiled, but the smile soon faded in face of the Scot's expression of implacable disgust.

'Betty, how are you?' asked the ex-prostitute, a quietly elegant woman in late middle age.

'Bearing up, Rosie,' she replied. 'And you?'

'Bearing down,' smiled Mrs le Queux. 'But not very often these days. I gather you know Willie?'

Hunsingore, a tall, spindly-limbed man with a narrow aristocratic head rimmed with fluffy grey hair, flapped a hand loosely in a gesture which might have invited a handshake. The invitation was refused.

'I know who Lord Hunsingore is, of course,' said Betty Woodstock. 'But I don't think we've met . . .'

'Am I so forgettable?' he asked in a voice which was high without being shrill. 'You interviewed me once.'

'It depends when it was,' said the woman. 'There's a gap

of about six months in my life when I can't remember anything. I fell on my head.'

'Oh, my dear!' Hunsingore's eyes seemed to take in the wheelchair for the first time. 'I'm sorry, so sorry. Be brave. Never forget, faith really can heal, you know.' He looked at McHarg as though for support.

McHarg laughed harshly. 'Faith makes guid sermons but gey watery broth,' he said.

'Really? You think so, Mr . . . er?'

'McHarg. Detective-Inspector McHarg.'

The hand was fluttered again, rejected again.

'A policeman. Have you been concerned with the programme, perhaps?'

'No,' said McHarg emphatically. 'I've never considered crime to be part of the entertainment business.'

'No?' Hunsingore regarded him with something which might have been amusement. 'I see you are in good company, Miss Woodstock. The Inspector is a serious man. I'm sure he will not allow you to come to harm.'

'He's a little late,' said Betty Woodstock acidly.

'Further harm, then. Nice to have met you both.'

He moved away. The others followed, Rose le Queux last.

'Take care,' she said.

'You too,' said Betty Woodstock.

'Streak of owl-shit,' muttered McHarg when Hunsingore was just about out of earshot.

'What was all that about broth?'

'My mother. What was all that about memory?'

She looked at him sharply. 'When I fell, I didn't just break my body. I cracked some connecting link in my mind and a bit of my life fell off.'

She said it challengingly, but he was losing interest in her and the whole meaningless assembly.

'Can I get you a drink?' he asked abruptly.

'You mean, can you get yourself one, don't you? You've been playing with that empty glass like it was a hand grenade.'

'OK. Can I get myself a bloody drink?' he said rudely.

She was looking at him closely again. He got the feeling she was making up her mind about something.

'How about getting it at my place?' she said finally.

He hadn't been expecting this and his surprise must have shown in his eyes for she laughed again.

'Yes, it's a proposition,' she said. 'Or half a one. I've got to look out for myself these days. You'd be surprised, even Hunsingore would, at how much good old British decency there's still around. Which is all right in its place, but it does tend to stop the decent chaps from trying to touch up a cripple. So I lead the way. But if you're going on to a police ball or something, just say.'

He thought of just saying it, changed his mind, and again, and yet again.

'OK,' he said. 'Why not?'

'I'd hate to sell you a used car!' she said. 'I'll just tidy up. Let's be discreet. I'll meet you in the foyer.'

He bumped into Elkin as he made for the door.

'Off already, McHarg?'

'I think so. So thanks to whoever you say thanks to.'

'I'll do that. Straight home now, pussycat. You country boys need your eight hours, don't you?'

'As much as we can get,' said McHarg equably.

He felt Elkin's eyes on him as he left the room. The little Cockney's advice was probably good, thought McHarg.

He took the lift to the foyer.

12

When Mr Flint came on duty at nine o'clock, the girl he relieved was already sitting in a car with her boy-friend ready to go. He shook his head as they roared off into the night. Then he wandered round the forecourt, tidying up. Jobs, like baths, should be left as you hoped to find them. Next, he did the same in the kiosk, checking the stock of cigarettes, sweets and accessories, totalling the cash in the till and dusting the keys.

Satisfied, he took his electric kettle out to the tap in the washroom and filled it. As he plugged it in, a black Mini heading towards Sanderton turned into the filling station. It halted right in front of the kiosk rather than by the pumps. Probably wanted fags or a pee, guessed Mr Flint as he concentrated on putting a precisely level teaspoonful of instant coffee in his pot mug.

The door opened and the driver came in. Mr Flint recognized him at once. Even without McHarg's visit he would have recognized him, but much more casually. Not that it mattered. The Tyler had not stopped here this evening just to test his response.

He leaned over the counter and gripped the old man's shoulders tightly, pressing his thumbs into the nerve at the base of the neck.

Mr Flint's resistance could hardly be called a struggle. Within seconds he was unconscious.

At his feet the kettle began to boil.

The Tyler went round the counter and regarded the jetting steam with interest. He leaned Mr Flint's body down towards the kettle as if the old man were bending to pick it up. Then he let him go.

His head struck the angle of one of the counter legs as he fell, splitting the skin on his forehead.

The Tyler examined the selection of sweets on the display rack on the wall, helped himself to a packet of large mint humbugs and took one out with his gloved fingers.

Opening Mr Flint's mouth, he dropped the humbug into his throat, forced the tongue back after it and closed the jaws again, holding them shut with pressure on the chin from his left hand while with the right he pressed down on the head and pinched the nostrils.

Mr Flint moved convulsively once, opened his bright, inquisitive eyes, fixed their accusing gaze on the Tyler, then shut them again for ever.

The black Mini drew away from the filling station and continued its journey towards Sanderton. The whole business had not taken more than a minute. The Tyler felt that things were going smoothly. But last time he had been in this area, he had also felt that things had gone smoothly. He frowned. The Præceptor didn't care for loose ends. So far nothing had been said, but it would all be noted.

So this time, it had to be right. Two more calls; at least one more death; that should do it.

That should tie things up very nicely. That would leave nothing but a blank wall for nosey bastards like McHarg to hit up against.

And if he kept on hitting, then something would have to be arranged for him. Something rather more subtle and special than a mint humbug.

Meanwhile he was at a good safe distance. Tonight the Tyler had the freedom of Sanderton.

He saw the town sign ahead and lifted his foot off the accelerator.

There was, after all, no point in attracting the attention of the law.

13

McHarg lay on Betty Woodstock's bed and wished he'd taken Elkin's advice and gone straight home.

'I'm sorry,' he said.

'Think nothing of it,' said the woman. 'All that booze, I knew it wasn't doing you any good.'

McHarg shook his head. 'It wasn't the booze,' he said.

'Don't go honest on me,' she answered sharply, turning her head away. 'Believe me, it's not the best policy. Not now. Not here.'

It had started badly. As they entered the small hallway of her flat, he had noticed a skean-dhu, a Highland dress dagger, mounted on the wall above the door that led to the living-room.

'You have the blood?' he enquired, nodding at it.

'No. Pure sassenach. A gift from a grateful admirer when I was researching a programme on Culloden.'

'What did you do? Tell him Prince Charlie won?'

He must have sounded bitter though there was no reason. He didn't give a damn about the past.

'You're not going to be *that* kind of Scot, I hope,' she said. 'Drunken *and* aggressive all the time?'

There had followed coffee and brandy. They had chatted desultorily, not being able to find a wavelength. Finally bed had come, more at the woman's initiating than his own, as though she might here find a way to say whatever it was he felt she wanted to say to him.

But nothing had happened and he found himself giving way to strong internal urgings to break his usually adamantine rule – never explain, never apologize.

'What I meant was, it's not you. Or at least not the way

you think. You're a fine-looking woman, you must know that.'

'As far as I go, you mean,' she said, running her hands over her firm well-shaped breasts and round stomach down to her upper thighs. There had probably been some muscle wastage, but not yet enough to bother the casual eye.

'No, I mean, it's not you that's put me off.'

McHarg stood up and searched for cigarettes in his jacket pocket.

'My wife, she was ill. Cancer. It went on for years. You want one of these?'

'Thanks,' she said. 'Look, no explanations please. We'll just forget it. I've got troubles enough of my own.'

He passed her a lit cigarette.

'In the last year or so,' he continued as if she'd never spoken, 'sex became a matter of . . . indifference to her. Pain even, sometimes, I suspect. But for my sake she tried . . . she'd offer herself. But in the end, I couldn't. Even though I wanted, I couldn't. Do you follow that? And tonight . . .'

'And that's your explanation?'

She pushed herself up on her elbows and looked angrily at him.

'I didn't know your wife, McHarg. She was probably a very nice woman, but I didn't know her and I can't care about her. Whatever she did or tried to do, it sounds like she was doing it for your sake, so's you wouldn't miss out on your precious rights. But that's not what's happening here tonight, whatever your so sensitive balls may tell you. This was for my sake, McHarg; no charity run for the frustrated fuzz, but *my* choice for *my* sake! So take your sad memories and your heartbreaking apologies and stick them all up your big pointed hat and go home and have a cry over the family album!'

The anger he had felt at the reception, temporarily abated as he'd supped Betty's coffee and brandy, now came flooding back. He dressed quickly and in silence, fearful of what he might say. There were monstrously offensive words and phrases pressing at his lips and he wanted to get out of her sight before they came bursting through.

His anger carried him down the stairs and out into the dark service road in front of the flats, blinding him to the significance of the heavily steamed-up windows in the car parked by the kerbside. As he passed, the driver's window was wound down.

'Excuse me,' said a man's voice.

'Yes?' said McHarg, half stooping, his mind still back in the flat.

Their timing was bad. One of the rear doors began to open a split second before the driver pressed the button on his aerosol can. McHarg heard the internal alarms through his anger and was jerking backwards as the fine spray hit his face. He smelt the ammoniac stench and closed his left eye in agony as some of the liquid hit the naked ball. But the right was hardly affected and he kicked out with great force and accuracy, ramming the driver's door back against the man trying to get out.

At the same time the man from the back seat drove a knuckle-dustered fist deep into his kidneys. His thick top-coat absorbed much but not all of the blow and he doubled up in agony. A third man had got out of the far side of the car. That seemed to be all of them, thank God. But three felt as if it would be quite enough.

The driver was out now. McHarg glimpsed a square face with a slightly twisted nose which he tried to straighten with a flailing left, missed by a mile and felt his arm seized. At the same time the third man had grabbed his right arm and between them he was being stretched out for the attentions of the knuckle-duster. He took one blow hard in the belly.

Then as the fist went back for seconds, McHarg used the two holding his arms as a pivot and swung both feet together against the kneecap of the man in front of him. There was a crack like dead wood in a quiet forest and the man went down, shrieking.

McHarg too was down, pulled out of the supporting holds by his own weight. Keep on your feet was the first law of street fighting but beggars couldn't be choosers. The driver was swinging vicious expertly directed kicks into his belly. Fortunately the third man had let himself be diverted by Knuckle-duster's fate and was stooping over his injured fellow.

McHarg grappled with the driver's legs and unbalanced him, forcing him back against the car.

'For fuck's sake, give us a hand!' the man yelled.

'Sorry, Phil,' said the third man. His voice was shrill, his tone placatory. *Phil*. McHarg stored the name away. It meant something but significance wasn't important here, only survival. The third man was kicking at his spine and swearing obscenely in rhythm with his kicks. He sounded almost hysterical. Better still, he was loud. Best of all, he seemed to be wearing very soft suedes, unlike the man called Phil whose shoes were tipped with fashionable brass caps which made them formidable weapons.

McHarg tried to rise but Phil was having none of that and smashed his fist down against the top of his head.

Hit me there all night, though McHarg with grim and untimely humour. With a bit of luck the man would have broken his hand.

Somewhere above a window opened and a voice cried angrily, 'What's going on down there?'

Wish I knew, thought McHarg. Ring the police, you stupid bastard!

As if his thought had soared upwards, 'I've rung the police!' cried the voice.

'Phil, let's go!' cried the third man urgently.

The thug with the cracked kneecap was already dragging himself into the back of the car. The reluctant man ran round to the passenger side. Only Phil delayed, partly because he was clearly unsatisfied with his performance so far, partly because McHarg was still clutching one of his legs. He brought his knee up hard beneath McHarg's chin, forcing him to let go and rock backwards. Then came a farewell kick.

McHarg didn't, couldn't, avoid it. Instead he gathered the foot to his body like a rugby player fielding a hard-driven grub kick. Cursing wildly, Phil wrenched himself free and fell backwards into the car. It took him several seconds to untangle himself and get the car started but McHarg was in no state to carry the battle after the enemy. He slumped on to the pavement, dragging in huge breaths of air like a man beached by a stormy sea.

He was still there when the police car arrived five minutes later.

14

For the second morning in succession, McHarg was at the Yard bright and early. Everybody – doctor, nurses, policemen – had insisted that he spend the night in hospital which he'd finally agreed to, but only because his internal logic told him he was in no fit state to resist a second onslaught.

However as soon as the dawn chorus of clangs, bangs, buzzers and groans began to fill the ward, he had got up, dressed with difficulty because he'd somehow managed to sprain both thumbs, and discharged himself.

He talked himself into the Criminal Records Office and stated his requirements.

'I want to look at some likelies. Man called Phil. Five ten; twelve, thirteen stone, I didn't see much of his face, comes from south of the river, I think.'

Commander Grossmith found him there.

'Doug, I knew you'd be here. I rang the hospital when I

heard, and they told me you'd discharged yourself. What are you playing at? You look terrible!'

'There were three of them,' said McHarg, wishing it didn't sound like an excuse.

Grossmith just smiled slightly, perhaps pityingly. McHarg couldn't blame him. He must look a sorry sight. And so there'd been three of them. Only a few years before, he'd have broken their backs, one by one. But age, alcohol, the torpor of grief, they'd all taken their toll. It was getting near time to give something up. But what?

Grossmith said, 'Come and have a coffee, Doug. Let someone else sort this one out. You're the victim, remember, not the investigating officer. Have you had any breakfast yet?'

McHarg rose stiffly. 'No,' he admitted. 'I didn't fancy hospital food.'

'You might wish you had,' said Grossmith. 'Let's see what the canteen can rustle up for you.'

McHarg was surprised to discover how voracious his appetite was. As he was half way through his second plate of bacon and egg, Chief Superintendent Highfield who was in charge of the Partington case came in search of him, anxious for reassurance that he'd be fit enough to give evidence.

'I'm fine,' said McHarg. 'They'll need to do more than that to stop me.'

'You think it had something to do with the trial?' asked Highfield. 'What happened exactly?'

McHarg told him. When he got to the bit about the man called Phil, Highfield interrupted him excitedly.

'Phil Wesson!' he said. 'Pound to a penny!'

'Who's he?'

'He's one of the Wessons out of Lambeth. They got big in the property business back in the 'sixties; you know, the kind of property business you carried on with a pair of bruisers and a half-starved Alsatian. Buy a block of flats cheap with sitting tenants, then persuade them all to leave and redevelop.'

'What makes you so sure it's him?' demanded McHarg.

'He's a business associate of Partington's, that's what,' said Highfield. 'He's acted as a front man in half-a-dozen deals. His name turned up when we started our in-depth analysis of Partington's affairs. At the really dirty end of things, where the blood and shit is, that's where we kept on coming across dear Phyllis.'

'Phyllis?'

'Oh yes. Phil Wesson's as queer as a rabbi's Christmas,' said Highfield grimly. 'But don't let that fool you. He's hard and he's nasty.'

'Any way you can get this into the trial?' wondered Commander Grossmith.

'I doubt it, sir,' said Highfield gloomily. 'I'd bet my pension that it was Wesson, but proving it's another thing. He'll have an alibi tighter than a duck's arse. He hasn't even got a record, would you believe it?'

'No wonder I didn't find his picture in Records,' said McHarg.

'He's in my files,' said Highfield. 'We'll get him one day, never you fear. Now we'd better be moving. Couldn't you put your arm in a sling or something, Inspector? The more sympathy we can squeeze for the prosecution case, the better.'

'You don't sound very optimistic,' said Grossmith.

'I'm not,' said Highfield. 'The case is sound enough, on fifty per cent of the counts at least. But he's got good friends, has Partington. Everywhere. It's going to be harder than getting the Royal Family done for speeding.'

McHarg rose. 'Thanks for the breakfast,' he said to Grossmith. 'I'll see you later, perhaps.'

On their way out, they diverted to put the DI in charge of investigating the assault in the picture about Wesson.

'You'll get him at the Queen of Bohemia at lunchtime,' said Highfield. 'It's the bum-boys' employment exchange south of the river. But you'll have to box clever to make anything stick. Come on, Inspector. And try not to look so bloody healthy. The Prosecutor's expecting a wounded hero!'

He was just about right, and McHarg derived a certain cynical amusement from the Prosecutor's solicitous enquiries as to his health which went as close as he dared to suggesting a connection between the attackers and Partington.

Defence counsel was no less sympathetic when his turn came in the afternoon and the time passed slowly if painlessly with gentle repetitious questions about the minutiæ of McHarg's evidence.

Later back at the Yard, McHarg checked with the investigating DI.

'Yes, we've seen Wesson. The Chief Super was right, we found him in the Queen of Bohemia. And he was right about him being a sharp boy too. He was alibi'd up to closing time by all the regulars in the Queen last night, and from then until five this morning by a little gang of the landlord's special buddies who play cards after hours in the landlord's parlour.'

'You mean you take notice of a bunch of bent villains?' said McHarg disbelievingly.

'Bent perhaps, but you'd better watch who you're villaining,' said the DI. 'Two titles and an MP for starters. No, Phyllis is safe, I reckon. Sorry, mate. I could get the local lads to check his tyres and road fund licence.'

'Don't bother,' said McHarg in disgust. 'They'd probably end up giving him a tow.'

On his way out of the building he ran into Elkin.

The man seemed genuinely concerned and McHarg found he was grateful for some real sympathy.

While they were talking, a message came through to McHarg that Superintendent Davison had been trying to ring him from Sanderton.

'Use my phone,' offered Elkin.

Davison sounded anxious. He had heard about the attack.

'I'm all right,' assured McHarg.

'I bet. And the trial? How's it going?'

'Sweetness and light all round today. Tomorrow the defence will put the boot in when I'm no longer the hero of the hour. I hope my part in the charade will be over by mid-afternoon.'

'You sound ready for home, Douglas,' said Davison sympathetically.

'Where's that?' asked McHarg.

'Hang on a mo,' said Davison. There was a pause, then: 'Listen, Heather says if you're driving home tomorrow evening, stop off here and have a meal with us. No, really. She won't be happy till she sees for herself you're all in one piece.'

'I'll see,' said McHarg.

'Don't see. Just come. That's an order,' said Davison. 'Any time after six.'

'Tell her, thanks,' said McHarg. 'Thanks a lot. I'll be there.'

He thanked Elkin and left the Yard. He found himself thinking of last night's party at the BBC. The booze; his anger; Betty Woodstock in her wheelchair, Betty Woodstock naked and frustrated on her narrow bed.

And the thought which had been with him all day suddenly surfaced.

How had Phil Wesson known he was at Betty Woodstock's flat?

He had almost walked back to his hotel. A taxi was depositing a man outside it. On impulse, instead of following the man through the doors he climbed into the vacated cab and gave the driver Betty Woodstock's address.

Outside the block of flats another cab was parked with its flag down. In the cavernous interior McHarg glimpsed a woman as he went past towards the entrance. She looked vaguely familiar, but even more familiar was the high-pitched fluting voice which greeted him as he stepped inside.

'Mr McHarg, isn't it? How are you? I'm so pleased to see

you are up and about after your ordeal. These are terrible times and may grow worse if we take no care of them.'

It was Hunsingore, the evangelical lord, his narrow head fittingly haloed by his fluffy hair and his eyes agleam with missionary enthusiasm. He was standing by the porter's desk and it was to the porter that McHarg, after a grunted response to Hunsingore's greeting, addressed himself.

'I've come to see Miss Woodstock,' he said.

It was Hunsingore who replied.

'I also,' he said. 'But we're out of luck. She's not in, it seems, nor is likely to be.'

'What?'

'I've been thinking about the poor girl ever since I met her again last night. That dreadful accident! Such spirit she shows to be working again so soon, reconstructing her life. I felt I must talk to her, she could be such an example to many we have not yet been able to reach through *New Vision*. But when I rang her at the BBC, I was told she was ill. Now the porter here tells me she's gone away, to convalesce I suppose. Scotland, the Cairngorms, isn't it?'

'That's what Miss Woodstock said, sir,' answered the porter.

'When did she go?' asked McHarg.

'First thing this morning, very early on,' said the porter.

'How did you know her address?' McHarg asked Hunsingore.

'I didn't. Mrs le Queux knows her quite well, though. We've been at a meeting this afternoon and, sharing a taxi back into town, I mentioned my interest and concern . . .'

At that moment the doors opened and the woman from the cab whom McHarg now recognized as Rose le Queux from the BBC party entered.

She said, 'Willie, if you're going to be much longer, I'll have to take the taxi on by myself. I'm late already . . .'

'She's not here,' interrupted Hunsingore. 'Gone off to Scotland.'

'Then there's nothing to keep you, is there?'

'No, of course not. I'm sorry. This is Superintendent McHarg, by the way. We met him last night.'

'Inspector,' said McHarg.

'I remember,' said the woman, though whether she was referring to his rank or his face was not quite clear.

Hunsingore, eager to make up for keeping a lady waiting, now shot ahead through the door.

Rose le Queux hesitated and said to McHarg, 'You're the one who got attacked. I read it in the papers. It was near here, wasn't it?'

'That's right.'

'Had you been visiting Betty, by any chance?'

'What if I had?'

'God, you cops don't give much change, do you?' she snapped. 'It's just that, well, I've seen her a couple of times since her accident. She did some research on a programme on prostitution once and we became quite friendly.'

'Was that before or after you saw the light?' asked McHarg.

'Oh forget it,' said the woman in disgust, turning to go.

McHarg took her arm. 'No,' he said. 'I'm sorry. Carry on.'

She looked at him uncertainly and said, 'It's nothing. Just that I've had the feeling when I've seen her since, which like I say has hardly been more than a couple of times, that she's been in some trouble.'

'Paralysis does trouble some people,' said McHarg.

'No. More than that. Oh, I don't know, I just thought you being a cop and all that, you might have been able to help if you got friendly.'

'We didn't get all that friendly,' said McHarg. 'Besides, if she needs moral support, she'll be OK now that your guru there has got himself interested.'

'Willie?' She laughed lightly. 'He's a dear soul, almost saintly really, but I got the impression that what Betty needed was someone a little more down to earth. I didn't really want him to descend on her like this.'

'Is that why you skulked in the taxi?' he asked.

She looked at him grimly. 'Inspector, or sergeant, or whatever you are, get one thing straight. I believe in Willie Hunsingore and *New Vision* absolutely. Only I don't want my friends to start avoiding me because they think I'm putting the hounds of heaven on the scent of their souls. I dare say that now and then even a policeman likes people to forget he's a policeman.'

'No,' said McHarg. 'Not this policeman. But thanks all the same. This sudden departure of Miss Woodstock's – does that surprise you?'

'Why should it? If she wants to get up and go, she's entitled.'

'But it's in character?'

'Oh yes. From what I know of her, she's a very decisive kind of girl.'

The door opened once more. Hunsingore called plaintively, 'I thought you were in a hurry, my dear?'

'Just coming,' said Mrs le Queux. 'Goodbye, Inspector.'

'Goodbye. And thanks,' said McHarg.

He stood for so long in thought that he found his muscles had begun to stiffen up again when he finally moved. But it was nothing that whisky and rest wouldn't cure.

15

By the time the court rose the following afternoon, McHarg's part in the trial was over. As often happens, the physical and mental after effects of the attack had made themselves felt more strongly after twenty-four hours and he was aware that he had not cut a very good figure in the box. Defence had cleverly niggled away at great length, provoking a couple of irritated outbursts. Grossmith didn't help by expressing doubts about the trial's outcome when McHarg dropped in to say goodbye.

'If he gets off, he gets off,' said McHarg, affecting indifference. 'Our job's catching 'em. The verdict's nothing to do with us.'

'You're probably right,' said Grossmith equably. 'Goodbye, Doug. Till next time. Take care.'

In the outer office Elkin echoed the words.

'Take care, pussycat. Don't park on any yellow lines. And come back soon. Next time I'll try to fix you up with a whole girl.'

The face McHarg turned on him was so frightening in its lack of expression that Elkin raised his hands in not altogether mock defence.

'All right, all right, you like your meals on wheels, that's your business. Hey, McHarg. Something about you that interests me. I just thought it was a bit of the old mythology till I met you. Now I'm not so sure. Did you really get the bust for telling the Prince to fuck off?'

McHarg paused with his hand on the doorknob and remembered. It had been in Italy. The young Prince had charmed everyone as always. Part of his charm was his willingness to fall in with his hosts' plans and when an unscheduled diversion was proposed after his last official function, he raised no objections, particularly as it involved a visit to a graveyard which housed many British dead from World War Two.

The Prince laid a wreath. McHarg, uneasy at the change of plan, was keen to get him back in the car. Looking around, he could not see the usual plethora of Italian security men and he suspected that the cemetery had not received the kind of blanket check made on the rest of the Prince's route. When the Prince was invited to make a short diversion to examine an interesting, possibly Etruscan tomb, McHarg murmured, 'No.'

The Prince glanced at him in surprise, then said to the

man who'd made the suggestion, 'That would be most interesting.'

McHarg gripped his wrist.

'No,' he said. 'Get in the car. Please, sir.'

'Mr McHarg,' said the Prince in a low, angry voice. 'I'm going to take a look at this tomb.'

'You'll do it with a broken wrist then,' said McHarg, increasing the pressure. 'Why don't you fucking well grow up? Just smile, get in the car, and wave goodbye. Sir.'

For a second an expression of sheer fury touched the Prince's face. Then he turned abruptly, pulled his hand free and returned to the long black limousine with McHarg close behind.

As the procession of cars drew away, Prince Arthur said coldly, 'Mr McHarg.'

'Yes, sir?'

Whatever the Prince had intended to say never got said. Behind them there was a loud blast. Bits of interesting, possibly Etruscan, monumental masonry rose high in the air. McHarg eased his gun from its holster.

'Just drive on,' he said to the chauffeur. 'Don't stop for anything, not even little old ladies. Not unless you want to see them shot.'

It was on his return from this trip that Flora had so savagely and directly accused him of accelerating her mother's illness. Three weeks later McHarg was permitted to resign from the Royal Squad at his own request, while at the Yard the popular version of what he had said to the Prince soon reached unprintable proportions.

McHarg did not care. But he remembered now his last exchange with Prince Arthur.

'Mr McHarg, would you really have broken my wrist?' he had asked with genuine curiosity.

'Yes, sir,' McHarg replied. 'But with respect.'

And they had laughed together.

Now he smiled and said to Elkin, 'What do you think, pussycat?'

Outside McHarg stopped and looked back at the Yard. This had been his workplace for many years, in some ways the best years. Now it seemed strange, foreign, frightening almost. He suddenly felt on the outside, spiritually as well as physically, and not just of the Yard but all kinds of things.

He shook his head. Such feelings were all right on the Isle of Barra, but they had no place in a middle-aged policeman.

He went back to his hotel to get packed.

The journey out of London was slow and tedious. McHarg had left it late in the hope of missing the rush hour, but the rush hour seemed to embrace half the evening now.

Once clear of the suburbs he made better time and his mind switched on the autopilot to take care of the driving while his thoughts ranged far and wide. Three thousand miles away, to be precise.

America. What did America hold for him? Nothing, except perhaps a last chance. And perhaps only a fool took his last chance. A wise man should quit with enough in his pocket to show his contempt for the game.

No, that was claiming too much dignity for what he felt. There was nothing dignified about weariness. He felt awash with indifference to his job, his friends, everything. He had a sense of turning his back on things he should be examining closely. The whisky he had drunk before leaving felt sour on his belly and probably smelt sour on his breath. It would be polite to swill the smell away before he saw Heather Davison.

He brought his mind back to the road and saw without surprise how far he'd come. Not far ahead was the garage he'd stopped at on the way up to town. A beaker of their awful machine coffee would be as good a mouthwash as anything. And a chat with that vital old man, Mr Flint, might be a useful mind-wash.

He pulled in.

A long-haired girl in a green overall came out of the kiosk. She looked as if she might be on drugs.

As she topped up the tank, he went to the machine and got himself some coffee. If anything, it had deteriorated since last time.

'What time does Mr Flint come on?' he asked as he paid.

The girl made her blank face look even blanker.

'The old chap who does nights,' explained McHarg, speaking very slowly as though to a backward child.

'Oh, him. He's dead.'

'Dead!'

His reaction was strong enough to penetrate the blankness and the girl continued with more animation. 'Yeah. The other morning. They found him right here.'

She pointed to the floor behind the counter, staring fixedly down as though the corpse might re-manifest itself.

'What did he die of?' asked McHarg harshly.

'Nothing, really. He just fell. Old people do fall, don't they? Banged his head. He was eating a sweet, they said. A humbug. It got stuck in his throat, so I suppose he choked, really. Yes, choked. Awful.'

She nodded. McHarg looked at her with distaste. He had preferred the blankness to this token concern.

He drove away, full of anger. This life which snatched away wives, alienated daughters, put young women in wheelchairs and choked old men with humbugs, how could anyone take it seriously?

The Davisons lived in a pleasant pre-war villa on the edge of a small dormer village a few miles north-east of Sanderton. Heather greeted him with her customary warmth and concern.

Davison had been delayed at work and in his absence McHarg let Heather inveigle him into first admitting the existence and then identifying the cause of his despondent mood.

The Chief Superintendent arrived in the middle of his account of Mr Flint's death and there had to be a re-cap. Davison allowed a look of exasperation to flicker over his face when he heard the reason for McHarg's interest in Flint, but said nothing till Heather had gone into the kitchen.

'You don't let things go, Douglas,' he accused.

'It was a chance,' said McHarg. 'It got me nowhere, but at least Wainwright can't say we didn't try.'

'Wainwright? That fool. We don't work for his pleasure, thank God.'

'Three days ago you were worried enough about the shit he was stirring,' observed McHarg.

'He seems to have got tired of it, I'm glad to say,' said Davison. 'I had a drink with our revered editor this lunchtime, and after trying the provocative bit and failing, he confessed that the daft doctor had changed his tune, says he was probably mistaken, wants to forget the whole thing. I suggest we say a silent prayer of thanks and do the same. Now, tell me about Partington.'

They talked and drank their way steadily through a bottle of single malt till Heather announced the meal was ready. It was the kind of plain, uncluttered food that McHarg liked, washed down with a lot of red wine. He would have preferred beer but found the wine palatable enough and certainly potent, leaving him at the end of the meal with a feeling of drowsy contentment he would not have thought possible a few hours earlier.

It was pleasant to be in front of a fire, drinking large doses of smooth brandy in the company of friends, solicitous about his health and happiness. The Davisons urged him to take some sick leave, perhaps even bring forward his American holiday. McHarg shook his head and refused, but gently, touched by their care.

At ten-thirty the telephone rang and while Davison was out of the room, Heather said to him, 'Have you thought of getting married again, Doug? A man like you needs a woman.'

He looked at her, surprised. The wine and brandy must have got to her as well.

'No,' he said. 'I've not thought of it. Nor will, I doubt.'

'Why not? If you meet the right person.'

'What's right for me?' he asked. 'I've had my time. It was good, I wasted too much of it, it's past.'

Glancing at his watch, he added, more abruptly than he intended, 'I'd better be off.'

'It's early yet,' said Heather. 'Have another brandy.'

'I've got to drive,' he said.

'You needn't,' she said. 'Stay the night. There's plenty of room.'

The door opened and Davison came back in.

'Anything important, dear?' asked Heather.

'No, thank God,' said Davison. 'Some of the things they bother me with, you'd wonder if they had minds of their own. Some more brandy, Douglas?'

'I ought to be going,' McHarg said, but he let Davison refill his glass.

'I've just told Doug he's more than welcome to stay the night,' said Heather brightly.

Davison looked blank for a moment, then said, 'Yes, why not? Why not, Douglas? Come on, we'll finish the bottle, talk about the old days. Excellent idea!'

His enthusiasm seemed to grow visibly, but McHarg suddenly found he had little appetite for the old days.

He downed the brandy in a single gulp and stood up. 'No. I'll be off, thanks all the same.'

'Douglas, are you sure you're OK for driving?' asked Davison anxiously.

McHarg examined himself. The combination of drinks had made things a little hazier than an evening on straight Scotch would have done, but he felt in control. He doubted if there had been many times since Mavis died that a blood test wouldn't have revealed he was over the legal level for driving.

'I'm fine,' he said. 'Thanks, both.'

Outside the cold air cleared his brain, for the time being at least. He started the car, waved at the Davisons framed in the warm yellow glow of their doorway, and set off down the dark driveway on to the equally dark road. He drove slowly, would have driven slowly anyway along these narrow country ways between high-banked hedges, but drove the slower now because inside the car the mists had started swirling around his head once more. But he did not have too far to go once he hit the main road. A fairly steep hill led down to it, straight till it swung sharp left just before the junction. He wound down the window to catch the exhilarating rush of night air as he motored down it. It did its job of clearing his mind once more and he realized he was going a little too fast.

He touched the brake pedal.

Nothing happened.

He slammed it flat, grabbed the handbrake and pulled, his fuddled brain taking a few precious seconds to admit that nothing was going to happen.

The bend was rushing towards him.

He thrust the clutch pedal down, crashed the gears from fourth to first, heard the grinding of metal, saw the lights of a car round the corner, just beginning to climb the hill.

He hit the horn for a moment, then needed both hands to swing the wheel over.

With a clear road he would have made it, but even his diminishing speed was enough to take him wide on the bend.

The other car was a Mini.

There were two people in it, a man and a woman. Or, more properly, a boy and a girl. He saw their youth as clearly as he saw their fear in that moment before the impact.

They hit.

The heavier Volvo drove the Mini into the banking. McHarg was flung forward against the straps of his seat belt. The cars locked together and slewed round athwart the road, creating a centrifugal force that crashed him against the driver's door. His elbow hit the handle. It burst open. Intuitively his left hand hit the harness release button and he fell sideways on to the black road. He rolled to absorb the impact, as he had been taught all those years ago, but his body was older now, his reactions slower. His head crashed against the tarmac and lines of fire fretted his brain. Then he was on the grass verge, lying still, wondering where the pain would start.

But before the pain had time, the fire in his head suddenly burst out into the air before him. There was a sort of fluffy bang, that dull, rather disappointing thump which the experienced ear knows is the real sound of an explosion. Flames leapt from the bonnet of the Volvo, licked backwards to consume the whole of the car, and for a sliver of time as thin and as deadly as a razor's edge their hectic light showed him the couple again, now neither young nor old, nor scarcely anything human. Above the bass of the flame, McHarg could hear a high wavering descant which might have been a scream.

Then another paper bag burst and the Mini too blossomed into fire and soon he could hear nothing but its steady masculine roar.

16

The Præceptor said without reproof, 'It's been very messy.'

The Tyler replied without apology, 'Yes, it has.'

'That beating up: that was . . . amateurish.'

'Yes. I've reprimanded him. It was foolish, but in the circumstances understandable. At least it made up our minds that we had to deal with McHarg.'

'So now everything's tied up at Sanderton? No loose ends?'

'None,' assured the Tyler. 'Two old men, no one to miss them. And the doctor has a young daughter.'

'I see,' murmured the Præceptor. 'McHarg himself is, of course, still alive.'

'He was lucky. But he's finished. Impotent.'

'I hope so. By the way, I too bumped into that girl the other night. She was lucky too, wasn't she?'

Again the tone was neutral, without reproof. But this time there was a faintly defensive note in the Tyler's reply.

'I wanted to finish things, remember?'

'I know you did,' said the Præceptor placatingly. 'But there were other considerations then. Still, I'm beginning to wonder if perhaps you weren't right. I spoke to her briefly . . .'

'You think she knows something?'

'Not about me,' laughed the Præceptor. 'But I don't like coincidences. Better be safe than sorry.'

'I'll test her again,' said the Tyler. 'And if necessary . . .'

'Yes,' approved the Præceptor. 'Now to more immediate matters. Our craft-brothers in America are taking this will seriously. We need to be able to tell them if there's anything to worry about. Is he here?'

'Waiting outside.'

'He did all right the other night, you think?'

'All right. But limited, I'd say.'

'I never doubted that,' said the Præceptor. 'Bring him in.'

When the Entered Apprentice appeared, he was greeted with delighted enthusiasm.

'I've had excellent reports of you. You did well. Congratulations.'

'Thank you,' said the Entered Apprentice with a nervous smile at the unsmiling Tyler.

'Now you have a report for us. What we particularly need is your assessment as to the status of this relationship and whether the Canadian trip will offer a chance to develop it.'

For ten minutes the Præceptor listened attentively, then asked a few questions. Finally the Tyler escorted the Entered Apprentice out.

When he returned he said, 'He's curious. And a bit concerned. If it comes to action there, he'll need good reasons.'

'Better than sixty million pounds and a man in the White House? I'll think of something. I'll be seeing him again before he goes. Now, I'll ring New York tonight and put them in the *picture. They'll make provisional arrangements at their end and I of course am going to be in Boston myself next week, so I'll be able to look at the situation on the ground and decide accordingly.'*

The Præceptor paused and thought deeply for a moment.

'I think on the whole I'd like to have you on hand too. Can you arrange it at short notice?'

'I expect so. You think it will come to action then?'

'I wouldn't be surprised. Like I'm always saying, unbridled passion is a terrible thing.'

The Præceptor gave a high rhythmic laugh. And after a while a rare smile stirred the Tyler's features too, like the shifting of a pike in the depths of some dark, still pool.

Part Two

FACTS OF HISTORY

1

Boston is one of those cities which really persuades you it might be the centre of the universe. A Boston lady, asked by a visitor if she travelled much, is said to have replied, 'Why should I travel when I am already here?'

It was a feeling Dree Connolly could understand.

To the Granda, the house on Beacon Street was merely a symbol; he much preferred Castlemaine. To Christie it was a nuisance, to his wife, Judith, an impressive address. But Dree really loved the old house, and loved Boston too, despite the sad disfigurement of middle-age spread. Particularly she loved it on a brusque March day when each gust of wind brought with it the tang of the sea till, all resistance eroded, she would climb into her emerald green Porsche and head for the marina where the Connolly Dutchman lay restlessly awaiting her arrival.

Her sister-in-law, Judith, had other ideas. Her notion of a good day was to move slickly through two or three expensive stores ending up at an expensive restaurant with as little exposure to the open air as possible. Born in South Carolina, she made a martyr's meal of her sensitivity to Massachusetts winters and she had some evidence to support it.

Now in her early thirties the bloom had gone from her cheeks, the provocatively turned-up nose had become pinched and the seductive drawl was reduced to a plaintive undertone.

Dree was sorry for her, bored by her and entertained by her in equal quantities. Her saving grace was that after a couple of martinis she became amusingly bitchy, parodying the old Southern self which, played for real, was rather pathetic.

Too much drink however turned her merely quarrelsome. At lunch today the proportions remained just about right until Judith summoned the waiter and ordered two large armagnacs with their coffee, despite Dree's protests.

Judith drank hers swiftly.

'Don't you want yours, honey?' she enquired sweetly.

'I said not.'

'Waste not, want not,' said Judith, helping herself to the second glass. She examined Dree quizzically over the rim.

'Dree, honey, how is it you Irish girls keep looking so good, so long?'

Dree smiled but didn't reply.

'Could it be,' continued Judith with a mock-simper, 'that us Southern flowers blossom too early, while in dear old Ireland the girls stay soft and luscious and juicy for ever; like a peat-bog?'

Dree laughed. 'Maybe. I think we should go now.'

She stood up and shook her long hair, which she'd been using as a defensive screen, back on her shoulders.

The gesture seemed to irritate the other woman, who murmured as she rose also, 'Yes, sir. You pluck a petal from a blossom and that's a petal gone forever, but take as many slices as you like from an old peat-bog and you've still got yourself an old peat-bog.'

'This old peat-bog's going to the john,' said Dree, 'I won't be a second.'

There was only one other woman in the rest-room, a girl of about her own age with a handsome, determined kind of face and hair which, while not quite as richly dark, hung just as long over her shoulders as Dree's. She looked up, flashed a brief smile at the newcomer and returned to her makeup.

Dree heard the door opening behind her. Guessing it was Judith and not wishing to be subjected to more of the peat-bog joke, she went quickly into one of the cubicles.

'Well, hello,' she heard Judith say.

'Hello, Mrs Connolly.' The accent was English, the tone politely neutral.

'Enjoy your meal, honey? Must be nice to be able to afford these prices on a research grant, but then, I'm way out of touch.'

'I haven't been eating, Mrs Connolly. Just using the loo.'

'I *see*. Well, feel free, honey. Food's expensive but this is cheap. I thought you might have been using some of your subsidy, that's all.'

'Subsidy, Mrs Connolly?'

'That's what you'd call it, isn't it, honey?' said Judith, her voice thickening in a way which disturbed Dree. 'What else would you call it, what all those poor frustrated lecturers give you for research assistance after midnight? What my stupid fool of a husband gives you! What's the going rate, honey? How's the pound stand against the dollar these days?'

'Mrs Connolly, please, excuse me . . .'

To Dree's horror there was the sound of a violent slap followed by a scream and the noise of scuffling.

She burst out of the cubicle to find the two women locked in each other's arms. Judith had wrestled the other back against the washbasins and was trying to butt her in the face. The younger woman turned her face, which bore the vivid impression of a hand on its left cheek, appealingly towards Dree.

'For God's sake, Judith!' she cried.

The interruption had a momentary effect. Judith slackened her grip and the other woman thankfully broke free. But as she moved away, her assailant cried, 'Whore!' and grasping her long dark hair tugged so violently that she crashed to the ground, her head smashing against the marble basin as she fell.

Dree knelt quickly beside her. She was conscious and the skin wasn't broken.

'You OK?' she asked.

The girl nodded and sat upright.

'Stay there. I'll be back,' commanded Dree.

She stood upright and cast a quick eye over her sister-in-law who was leaning against a basin, panting vigorously.

'You're going home, Jude,' she said, smoothing the woman's elaborate blonde coiffure.

'She's Christie's whore. I'll kill her,' said Judith. But she spoke mechanically, without passion. Her eyes were frightened.

Dree opened the door and stepped out pulling Judith after her. There was no one near enough to have overheard the disturbance. A large man was hanging around by the elevator apparently engrossed in the fire emergency regulations. Dree made a summoning motion with her head and he came across. She had long ago realized the futility of complaining to Old Pat about the presence of a bodyguard wherever she went. There was no way of getting rid of him permanently without recourse to law, though on occasion she had amused herself by setting out to shake him off.

Now at last she was glad of his presence.

'Mrs Connolly's ill,' she said. 'See she gets home.'

The man looked uncertain.

'For Christ's sake, Sam!' snapped Dree. 'We've got trouble. I can sort it, I think, but not with Mrs Connolly around. OK?'

The man nodded.

'Judith, you're going home. I'll see you later,' said Dree. 'Right?'

She didn't wait for an answer but went back into the rest-room.

The girl was on her feet and dipping a handkerchief into cold running water, then applying it to the side of her head where a large purple bruise was developing.

'How're you feeling?' asked Dree.

'As well as can be expected. Who're you?'

'I'm Deirdre Connolly, Judith's sister-in-law.'

The injured woman turned and gave her a clear-eyed stare with a hint of cynical amusement in it.

'OK,' said Dree. 'Obviously I'd like to keep this quiet, but I'm not about to kidnap you, bribe you or bear false witness against you. If you want to make a complaint, I'll tell what I heard and saw. But first let's get you to a doctor.'

'I'm all right,' said the girl. 'Really.'

It was Dree's turn now for the cynical look.

'Maybe. First thing you learn when you're a Connolly is, get the evidence clear. In court six months from now, talk of fractured skulls and brain damage is going to be pretty hard to deny.'

'Forget it,' said the girl. 'You've nothing to worry about. There'll be no court-room drama.'

'OK, I believe you,' said Dree. 'I've nothing to worry about, but you might have. Suppose there is a fracture? For your own sake, please, let me take you to a doctor.'

The girl pressed the sodden handkerchief close against her brow and grimaced.

'For my own sake, then,' she said.

The Connolly name gained them rapid attention at the Massachusetts General and the X-ray plates were processed quicker than holiday film. There was no fracture; there would be a bump and considerable bruising for some days; ointments were supplied for this and pills for any accompanying headache. It took only twenty minutes.

'This beats the National Health Service,' said the girl as they came out of the hospital.

'Only if you're stinking rich,' said Dree. 'You're English, is that right? I don't even know your name.'

The other stopped and turned to face her.

'Perhaps we should get one thing clear, Miss Connolly,' she said. 'What your sister-in-law said was true, in general if not in detail. I have been, occasionally still am, your brother Christie's lover, mistress, whore, I'll leave the term to you.'

Dree thought a moment. 'How about paramour?' she suggested, smiling.

When the girl laughed in reply, Dree said, 'Look, I'd better get back now and check on my sister-in-law. But I'd like the chance to talk a lot more with you.'

'I'd like that,' said the girl.

'OK. They call me Dree, by the way. For short.'

'They call me Flora,' said the girl. 'Neither for short nor long. For precision. Flora McHarg.'

2

McHarg was on the beach again, making heavy weather through the crumbling sand and against a chill sharp wind. But the wind was having an even harder time cutting through the after-haze of a three-day drinking bout.

The boy in the car had been eighteen, his girl-friend seventeen. They were planning to get engaged on her eighteenth birthday. He was training to be an accountant and they had been out celebrating his success in his first public examination.

There was not enough alcohol in the world to wash out their faces behind the flame-lurid windscreen of the ruined car.

There had been a great deal, however, in McHarg's bloodstream, nearly three times the permitted maximum. His claim that his brakes had failed was quite uncheckable in the charred and twisted remains of the Volvo. And his discovery, semi-conscious, in the middle of a field some hundred yards from the accident was being treated as an attempt at flight rather than a search for help.

All this Davison had told him. The papers could not print it all, not so explicitly, but the message was clear, underlined by a quotation of Heather's unconsciously damning, horror-struck reaction, 'Oh God! and we told him he ought to stay!'

Davison himself had come to see him on Saturday afternoon.

'They're going to throw the book at you, Douglas,' he said. 'The CC's terrified of any hint of a cover-up. It'll be manslaughter, almost certainly. The only good thing's that beating-up you took in town. If he's got any sense, your brief'll play that up for all it's worth. Possible black-out. Do you know the name of the doctor who patched you up?'

'Why don't you fuck off?' said McHarg.

'Come on, Douglas! Don't play the hard man still. It's done you no good in the force. It'll do you less out of it.'

'Out of it?'

Davison regarded him with a strange mixture of curiosity and sympathy.

'Hasn't it got home yet? This is the end, Douglas. I'm sorry. Talk it over with your lawyer, but I'm sure the best thing is resign now before the trial, plead guilty, go for a suspended sentence. Judges aren't daft. They know what happens to ex-cops in gaol. You fight it and they'll put you away for sure. And you'll be chucked out of the force anyway. It's over, Douglas. Save what you can from the wreck.'

'Go to hell,' said McHarg harshly. 'In my life, I decide what's over. Go to hell!'

And that was when the drinking bout had started. It had finished not because of any conscious decision but merely because he had run out of booze. He had pulled his overcoat over his shoulders and set out to buy more. But by the time he reached the off-licence, the brain-searing, eye-dazzling greyness of the cold March afternoon had lit his inner consciousness to a point of self-awareness which admitted shame, and he continued past the store, through the blank suburban streets till he reached the beach.

Now as he walked through the sand he forced himself back into contact with the external world, the white-flecked sea, the occasional, quickly repaired rent in the drapery of cloud, the gulls treading air, a group of boys hurling stones into the indifferent water. And, approaching him, a man and a young girl, hand in hand.

It was Wainwright and his daughter.

The two men stopped and silently faced each other. The little girl broke free and made for the water's edge. It didn't seem the time for inconsequential courtesies.

'I read about your trouble,' said the doctor. 'I'm sorry. Will it finish you in the police?'

'Very like. But I'll survive.'

'I hope you do,' said Wainwright, watching his daughter trying to emulate the stone-throwing boys. 'But a man needs something outside himself, something to live for. Don't you think so, McHarg?'

'Perhaps. Within himself too.'

The doctor shrugged. 'We make our own rules,' he said cynically. 'Good luck to you, McHarg.'

He called to his daughter who reluctantly abandoned her unconscious playmates.

'Wainwright,' called McHarg. 'Before you go.'

The doctor paused a few strides away and half turned.

'Yes?' he said.

'That business about the tongue. Why did you drop it?'

The little girl had come up now and her father reached down and clasped her hand.

'The world can look after its own messes,' he said. 'A man has enough to do without minding other people's business. Especially when other people don't want it minded.'

'Other people? Who do you mean?'

Wainwright shook his head sharply.

'I'm speaking figuratively,' he said. 'Stick to your own troubles, McHarg. They're big enough in all conscience. Besides –' and there he grinned lupinely – 'it was only a dog's tongue. Wasn't it?'

And, turning, he walked away.

McHarg too continued his laborious trek, leaving the populous part of the beach behind him till the only signs of life were the wheeling gulls and far out at sea an unidentifiable ship stoically butting its way up the Channel.

There was an idea somewhere in his head but the mists of three days' alcohol swirled around it as the sea-fret swirled about the distant ship, and now it could be seen no more. But the idea was not so easily absorbed.

He stopped and lit a cigarette. It tasted vile but he persevered. Ahead rose a tumult of sandhills. That was where he was heading, he realized. Not directed by reason, but a detective can have his reasons that reason knows not of, especially if his ancestors tilled the soil and tended sheep in the misty wastes of the Hebrides.

He threw away his cigarette and went purposefully forward.

When he came in sight of Old Haystacks's hut, nothing seemed changed. The wormy planks, frosted with salt from long exposure to the insidious sea-mists, leaned against the steep sandhill still. As a man-made structure, it looked ramshackle and impermanent; as a natural arrangement of natural materials, it looked as right as all the rest of that casually spilled landscape.

He called the old man's name, but there was no answer, only a bird-like flapping as the wind caught the sack which stood for a door and whipped it back and forth against the planking.

Through the hole thus revealed, the inside of the hut was so dark that it looked solid. McHarg approached it reluctantly. He had gone through many more uninviting entrances in his time, but this one had some special quality of fear. Was it his island ancestry speaking again?

He knelt down and pushed back the sacking and realized at once his premonition had nothing to do with second sight. His first sight had been good enough. The darkness looked solid because it was solid. The inside of the sandhill had collapsed and filled the interior.

Desperately, because he knew it was vainly, he began to scrabble at the sand.

He didn't have to dig deep.

A couple of feet down his questing fingers touched a

tangle of hair on a frame of stiff cold flesh. His own body blocked the light from the entrance so with fumbling fingers he struck a match and held it in one hand while with the other he brushed the dry grains from the old man's face. After a moment he desisted and let the match go out.

He was a hard man but just now he had no stomach to meet Old Haystacks's questioning stare and to see the old man's cheeks and nostrils puffed out with the sand that had choked him.

But his mind could not be shut off like his sight and in it he was seeing the face of another old man who had been found, bulging-eyed, with the breath stopped in his throat for ever.

When he got home McHarg ran a deep hot bath. While it was filling, he stripped the old crumpled sheets from his bed and replaced them with a newly laundered pair. Next he took his usual cut-throat razor from the bathroom cabinet, held it long enough to observe the slight but persistent tremor in his hand, replaced it and went in search of the almost unused electric shaver which Mavis had bought him for Christmas five years before.

Half an hour later, bathed and shaved, his flesh pink and warm, he sat on the edge of his bed, his mind and body eager for the embrace of the crisp cold sheets. But there was a phone call to make first. He knew enough of human psychology, had listened to enough long rambling explanations in the white hours of the night, to know that reality warps in the heat of self-justification. Equally he knew that in human behaviour, nothing was impossible.

'Hello,' he said. 'Dr Wainwright, please.'

'The doctor's not on duty,' said a high, precise voice. 'If this is a medical call, you should ring – '

'It's not medical. This is the police. Get him,' he commanded harshly.

There was an indignant gasp. A moment later Wainwright's voice said testily, 'Yes?'

'McHarg. I won't keep you. Two questions. First, would

an old man with diabetes be likely to suck mint humbugs?'

'For God's sake, McHarg . . .'

'Come on! I'm serious.'

'*Serious?* All right. No, he wouldn't. Not unless he were a very stupid old man.'

'He wasn't that. Right. Now listen, Wainwright, and listen well. On that hill, my brakes failed. No excuse. Sober, I might still have avoided the crash. But they did fail.'

'What the hell has that . . .'

'*Listen.* Second question. No follow-up. Not now. Not ever. Have you been got at? Don't even answer. Just put the phone down.'

There was a long long pause.

McHarg said, 'Doctor?'

There was a distant click and the line went dead.

Now McHarg slid between the voluptuously cool sheets.

He had time to say a prayer for Old Haystacks. Or more of an apology for leaving him for someone else to find, like a piece of that same flotsam that had been his livelihood. Though perhaps the old man would have liked the idea. Perhaps it was the best hope of us all, to float, to be washed up, to be found . . .

McHarg slept.

3

The jury had taken less than thirty minutes to acquit Stanley 'Sailor' Partington on all counts shortly before lunchtime on the eighth day of his trial.

As he emerged under the portico of the Old Bailey, the press were sucked towards him like iron filings to a magnet and it took a pair of burly constables to clear a small space before him. He turned up the astrakhan collar of his brushed-mohair coat against the chill March wind and regarded the reporters seriously. The open ruddy-complexioned features which had in the past won him many votes looked pale and tired.

'How do you feel, Mr Partington?' yelled one of the pressmen.

'Relieved but weary,' he said.

The reply triggered off a barrage of equally banal questions till someone demanded, 'This verdict seems to bring into doubt the whole basis of the police evidence against you. Do you intend taking the matter any further?'

'You must talk to my solicitor about that,' said Partington, indicating a fat pig-faced man by his side. 'I myself am only too happy to have been reassured that English justice will be done no matter who attempts to bend it.'

This answer brought a renewed spate of questioning but now Partington set off down the steps with the policemen clearing a passage before him and climbed into a waiting car driven by a spectacled brunette recognized by many there as Jane Sykes, his secretary. The car moved away pursued on foot by some of the more enthusiastic photographers, while the unsatisfied journalists took their own routes to Partington's Kensington apartment. Finding it unoccupied, a few of the more energetic headed next to Jane Sykes's more modest flat in Swiss Cottage but were equally disappointed there. Some laid siege to the offices of the porcine solicitor, but the majority retired to El Vino's for lunch taking turns at keeping the telephones in both apartments sounding a vain summons all through the afternoon.

The telephone rang frequently in the bar of the Queen of Bohemia in Lambeth too. Some local historians claimed that the Queen had been the resort of homosexuals since it was built in 1854, while another more macho local tradition asserted that the area hadn't known what a homosexual was till the opening of the National Theatre in 1976.

Phil Wesson in a sense combined both traditions. He was

a local lad and as tough as they came. And he was a homosexual.

The barman was irritated by the frequency with which the phone rang this lunchtime, but he was careful not to let his irritation show when he called, 'Phil, this one's for you.'

Wesson pushed his way to the phone. He was a solidly built man with a sullen, aggressive face that would probably have cleared a way for him even if most of those present hadn't known his reputation.

He took the phone without a thank-you and said, 'Yeah?'

'Wesson?' The line was crackly, the voice indistinct, the accent broad East End.

'Yeah.'

'You heard the news about Mr Partington? Well, he wants a meet. Urgent, like. Like straightaway.'

'What's the panic?' said Wesson surlily.

'Panic is, that bastard McHarg's loose and he's here in the smoke.'

'What's that got to do with me?'

'Listen, pussycat. McHarg gets his hands on you and you'll know what it's got to do with you, right? So get your skates on.'

'Shit,' grumbled Wesson. 'Where's the meet then? Partington's pad?'

'Don't be thicker than you look, you 'orrible bloody fairy,' crackled the voice wearily. 'There's press all over there, isn't there? The other place, right! And don't hang about.'

The line went dead.

Wesson stood at the bar for a moment then shrugged his shoulders and headed for the door, leaving the telephone dangling.

'Thanks a lot,' called the barman after him. But he waited till he was sure that Wesson was out of earshot.

Outside London was grey, cold and windy and Wesson pulled his sheepskin coat close around him as he walked the few hundred yards to Waterloo station. Here he descended to the Underground and headed north on the Bakerloo line to Piccadilly Circus, where he changed to the Piccadilly line and travelled two stops west to Hyde Park Corner. Crossing the bottom of Park Lane, he now headed back up Piccadilly a little way before turning left through gloomy Whitehorse Street into that complex of narrow ways and pavements called Shepherd Market.

Here he slowed down and began to window-shop, examining souvenir trinkets and café menus without much appearance of enthusiasm. Then, suddenly, as a crowd of tourists moved by him, he slipped through a narrow doorway between two shop fronts.

Inside he moved purposefully up a steep, gloomy staircase. There was a half-landing between floors and here he paused to look back and listen, and again on the first floor. Satisfied, he went without pause up to the second floor, where he stopped outside an unmarked door, inserted a Yale key in the lock and turned it.

The man who had been coming stealthily up the stairs behind him abandoned his efforts at quietness and hurled himself forward. His shoulder caught Wesson full in the back sending him crashing against the half-open door with such force that he scarcely had time to cry out against the pain of first contact before the door bounced back off the wall and broke his nose like an old walnut.

Meanwhile the man had let his impetus carry him across the empty room and through a second door straight ahead. Here beneath a powerful light on a narrow bed were a naked man and woman. She was kneeling astride him and he was inside her. An old mahogany wardrobe stood alongside the bed with the door opened so that the full-length mirror inside reflected the scene to the narcissistic couple. The woman had frozen in amazement and terror and the man beneath pushed himself up on his elbows to glare with amazed fury at the intruder. It was 'Sailor' Partington and he'd got his colour back.

'Carry on if you like,' said McHarg with a humourless grin. 'Never start anything you can't complete.'

With a roar of anger, Partington pushed the woman off him and lunged towards the bedside table on which stood a whisky bottle and a couple of glasses. McHarg moved forward smartly and whipped the bottle away from the questing hand.

'Fancy a drink, do you?' he said. And carefully poured the raw liquor over the man's still-rampant member.

There was a noise behind him.

Turning, he fielded Wesson's rush easily with one hand, looked with disgust at the spots of blood which had showered from the man's crushed nose on to his overcoat sleeve, and hit him with the bottle.

The woman began to scream.

He seized her by her fleshy shoulder and bundled her off the bed into the open wardrobe. She stopped screaming and he nodded approval as he looked down at her.

'Miss Sykes, isn't it?' he said. 'One more sound from you and I'll set fire to this wardrobe. Believe it.'

Then he closed the door and turned the key.

Partington was making quite a lot of noise too as he poured water from a large jug over his now considerably shrunken penis.

Wesson on the other hand was making no noise at all as he lay in the corner with blood streaming from a huge gash along the side of his head.

McHarg seized the jug from Partington's hands, saying, 'You could get to enjoy that if you're not careful,' and poured what remained of its contents over Wesson's head.

'I like an attentive audience,' he said.

'Did that stupid bastard bring you here?' groaned Partington.

'Indirectly,' said McHarg. 'I saw your triumphant emergence from the Bailey, but then you shook me off like you shook off all those newshounds. So I went to look for friend Phil instead. And it struck me that I might be able to kill two birds with one stone by sending him after you. It worked. Though I'd have expected something a little more luxurious from a man who's stolen as much as you have.'

'You're mad, McHarg!' gasped Partington. 'You can't get away with this, you know that. I've been acquitted, and this isn't like that time on my boat, this time I've got witnesses.'

'And you're going to call the police?' said McHarg. 'Well, I *am* the police, remember that. But perhaps that doesn't bother you too much. What do you say, Phil?'

Wesson was recovering. He had pushed himself upright and was sitting with his head in his hands, groaning gently. McHarg stooped over him, seized his expensively coiffured hair and forced his head back with such violence that he screamed.

'Right,' said McHarg. 'Quick answers. How'd you know where I was going to be that night?'

'Phone call,' gasped Wesson. 'Like today. At the Queen. Just after closing time.'

'Like today?' echoed McHarg. 'You mean just like today? Like what I'm speaking like now, pussycat?'

Wesson's eyes showed he recognized the parody of a Cockney accent, but McHarg wanted more. He wanted to hear what he had already guessed at.

'Who was it who rang you, Wesson?' he demanded, forcing the bleeding head even further back. 'Come on! Who was it?'

Wesson's eyes, full of loathing and fear, were almost popping out of his head as he screamed, 'Don't you know, you fucking pig? Don't you know? It was your fucking pig mate, Elkin, *that's who*!'

McHarg sighed deeply, released the man's head and straightened up. Sometimes being right left an even more bitter taste than being wrong.

He turned back to Partington who scrabbled away from him in alarm.

'Listen, McHarg, I don't know anything about any of this, believe me, nothing at all, how could I? You know where I've been since the trial began, in custody, you know that, this is nothing to do with me. Nothing!'

The words came out in a series of shrill rising scales.

'You can do better than that,' said McHarg conversationally as he walked slowly towards the naked man. 'Who else could putting me in hospital benefit? That was the intention, wasn't it? To hospitalize me – or worse – so I couldn't give evidence?'

'No. *No!*' screamed Partington as his pursuer's bulk loomed over him like a dark mountain. 'They didn't need to do that, not for me, not for me. I wasn't going to be convicted, there was no way your evidence would get me convicted, so why should I want to fix you? Why?'

His tone had deepened by a couple of octaves in search of a convincing sincerity. McHarg stood very still looking down at him, then slowly he nodded.

'You know, Stanley, I think I believe you.'

Relief rose like an Asian dawn over Partington's face, but as McHarg continued, 'And that being the case, we've got to ask ourselves why?' the relief faded and was replaced by a grey wariness whose colouring derived from fear.

And not just fear of me either, thought McHarg.

'So why was I attacked?' he demanded. 'And where does that wheelchair woman fit in?'

There was a sound of movement behind him.

He turned just in time to receive Wesson's charge. There was little strength in it but the man's weight forced him backwards a couple of paces against Partington and instinctively the naked man began to grapple with his legs. McHarg lost his balance and crashed back against the wardrobe, bringing a peal of terrified screaming from the woman locked inside.

There was no room for subtle manœuvres, decided McHarg. He wrestled Wesson aside and brought his right fist down from a great height on to the base of Partington's neck. The man twitched like an epileptic for a moment, then went still. McHarg swung the edge of his stiff left hand across Wesson's throat. As he fell back choking, McHarg pushed himself upright and drove his foot against the wardrobe door.

'Shut up!' he yelled.

The silence that followed was like a church at midnight.

Then into it crept a distant noise.

The street door opening.

McHarg moved swiftly and silently on to the landing. Below, he could distinguish voices. At least two. Innocent intruders, or friends of Partington, it hardly mattered which. It was time to go.

He ran lightly down to the next floor. The footsteps were ascending the stairs. There were two doors on this landing. The first one he tried opened and he slipped inside.

The windows of this room were shuttered and in the gloom he sensed rather than saw its emptiness. The floor seemed to be tiled with some kind of mosaic pattern and there was an elevated chair between a couple of columns at the far end. A large bathroom? he wondered, but had no time for investigation as the footsteps moved along the landing and began to ascend to the next floor.

He slipped out as quietly as he'd entered and ran down the stairs to the street door.

It was only when he was safely out into the daylight once more and mingling with the afternoon throng in Shepherd Market that it occurred to him.

He had no personal experience to go on, but from what he had read and heard, that room he had glimpsed could well have been some kind of Masonic temple.

4

'Sorry I'm late,' said Deirdre Connolly, a little breathless from hurrying and all the prettier because of it.

Flora McHarg regarded her with cool amusement as she slipped into the chair pulled out for her by the waiter who'd brought her to the table. She had received the same treatment when she mentioned the Connolly name. It was not, she had since noted, universally meted out.

'I had to shake Judith,' explained Dree. 'She suddenly decided she didn't fancy her Catholic Mothers' luncheon club. I thought, Christ! if I bring her along here, we could have the first recorded case of assault with a deadly lobster! Thank God she's taking the kids off on a visit tomorrow, Sunny Carolina. Wants me to go too: *I'd just love that old Southern hospitality!*'

Flora laughed at the unsubtle parody. 'You going?' she asked.

'You're joking! Hey, have you ordered?'

'Now *you're* joking. In places like this I don't order till the bearer of the privy purse turns up. Have you seen the prices? Sorry, of course you've seen the prices! And sorry again. Well-brought-up girls should know how to accept largesse graciously. Which I will now do.'

The two women had met twice since their first encounter. Dree's pleasant open personality was as little spoilt as may be by her wealthy background, but it had allowed her to indulge her spontaneity to the extent of admitting no obstacle or delay to a new friendship. She had taken very strongly to Flora, who for her part, while she was not about to be condescended to, found the Irish girl very easy to like, and when invited to lunch at one of Boston's smarter seafood restaurants had replied gravely that she had no objection to this redistribution of unearned wealth.

Their orders were taken swiftly and efficiently and preprandial drinks brought.

'One thing about you Connollys,' said Flora. 'You're very useful for getting service.'

'I'd have thought you'd have become a little blasé about it by now,' probed Dree.

The other's clear, unblinking grey eyes regarded her mildly.

'You mean with Christie? No, you're wrong. He's an extremely conventional kind of person, your brother. He always insists on going places where he *isn't* known.'

'Oh. That must be, I mean, well, don't you mind being so . . .'

'Furtive?'

'I didn't mean exactly that.'

Flora smiled. 'I've never been particularly furtive, which I suppose is why I get beaten up by angry wives in washrooms. Besides, Christie isn't what you'd call a front-page Connolly. There are quite a lot of pretty respectable places where he's not known.'

The irony was unmaliciously stressed and Dree laughed out loud. 'Sorry. I'm sorry. None of my business anyway.'

'I don't mind,' said Flora. 'Feel free. Then I can take my turn at your love-life with a clear conscience, can't I?'

She smiled again, but this time got no response from the American girl whose expression had become close and wary.

Flora raised her eyebrows.

'No trade, huh? You see, I've almost gone native. And how's that for Connolly timing? Here comes the soup to smooth over your embarrassment.'

After the waiters had retired, Dree bent over her soup as if to inhale the delicate fishy odours and said in a low voice, 'I'm sorry, Flora. I didn't mean to be rude . . .'

'That's all right. I meant to be nosey. I know quite a lot about your family from Christie. About your father and your eldest brother, of course. That must have been hard to take. About the legendary Old Pat who would surely cut you off without a penny if he knew you were wasting his substance buying expensive meals for an English Protestant. About Conal who's already planning to repaint the White House if he can hold his marriage together. But about you, very little have I heard. Hence my noseyness. Sorry.'

Dree laughed. 'Oh Flora,' she said. 'It's good to have met you. You feel like one of the family straightaway.'

'Don't bet your diamond studs on it,' said Flora.

Dree twisted her face in self-reproof. 'There I go again,' she said. 'I'm sorry. Is it bad with you and Christie?'

'Depends how you look at it,' said Flora. 'In every relationship there comes a point of decision. Christie's a good man, he's got a young family, he's a conscientious Catholic. Point of decision! There's a lot of bed mileage in it yet, but both of us know in our hearts that there's no way he's going to leave Judith. That's what made her assault on me so ironic.'

'I'm sorry,' repeated Dree sincerely.

'That's OK. Don't think of it as losing a sister-in-law, think of it as gaining a parasite. This soup's delicious. I may sting you for another bowlful.'

The note of flippancy did not ring altogether true from the mouth of this serious and self-contained girl. Dree observed her sympathetically and suddenly felt a strong temptation to share her own problems, fears and hopes with her new friend. But she resisted it. Flora McHarg created an impression of absolute trustworthiness but their acquaintance had been too brief to risk an indiscretion.

They finished their soup and the waiters removed their dishes.

As she helped herself to another glass of Muscadet, Flora said casually, 'Do you get the feeling we're being watched?'

'What?'

'At the bar. The tall man eating olives like they grow on trees.'

Deirdre glanced and sighed. 'Oh, *him*. That's Sam. The Granda has this neurosis about me being kidnapped or assassinated, so he's hired Sam to keep an eye on me. It's been going on for years. Sometimes it's quite useful, like when Jude beat you up. Mostly it's a pain. From time to time I've complained, but all that happens is he gives me a new one. So in the end I've stopped complaining. At least I can recognize this one. Clever of you to spot him, though. He must be slipping.'

'Not so clever,' said Flora. 'I grew up with that look.'

'What look?'

'Watchful violence. Or violent watchfulness. The cop's look the world over.'

'Yes?' said Deirdre, interested. 'How do you mean, you grew up with 't?'

Flora laughed and sipped her wine.

'You're wondering if I come from a long line of crooks!' she said. '*Au contraire*, or perhaps not all that *contraire*. My father was – is – a policeman, that's all.'

Her tone alerted Dree, who said, 'You don't hit it off?'

'No,' said Flora.

'I'm sorry,' said Dree. 'What kind of policeman is he?'

'Tough.'

'I mean, his job.'

'Now, he's nothing much, I suppose,' said Flora uninterestedly. 'Slapping tickets on topless bathers at a seaside resort. But he used to work at Scotland Yard. He was like your Sam there, in the minding business. But his was royal family while Sam's is . . . royal family too, in a way, wouldn't you say?'

The next course arrived, lobster for Flora, halibut for Dree.

As the waiters served it, Dree sat back looking thoughtful.

'McHarg,' she said. 'McHarg.'

'That's my name,' agreed Flora.

'No. Your father, I mean. Who in special did he look after?'

'In the Royal Family? One of the lesser Princes, for the most part. Arthur, I think. Yes, Arthur.'

Dree choked down another mouthful of wine. It was absurd, schoolgirlish, to let the mere mention of his name affect her like this. How the hell was she going to get through the next week? And how could anything but anti-climax await her at the end of such a nerve-grating, time-destroying eternity of anticipation?

'Are you all right?' enquired Flora, forkful of lobster in suspense.

'Yes, I'm fine.'

'For a second you were showing the classic symptoms of ptomaine poisoning, which would not help your credit with the management.' Flora's tone was light but she regarded the other girl anxiously.

'No, really, it's OK. How's the lobster?'

'Succulent.'

'Great. Your father, did he like his work?'

She was back in control now, recalling a square rock of a face and a probing, unblinking gaze and trying to see points of resemblance in the features opposite her, but failing. Except that perhaps there was a strength, a kind of self-contained watchfulness . . . but no threat of violence, surely?

'Yes, he seemed to like it. More than his family sometimes.'

'And the Prince. What did he think of the Prince?'

This *was* absurd. But the temptation to talk about him was stronger than she could resist.

'Well,' said Flora, sucking at a claw, 'he was no respecter of titles, my father, at least he had that going for him. But he seemed to have a pretty high regard for young Arthur. He felt he'd overcome his deprived background pretty well.'

'That's an odd thing to say.'

'He's an odd man. Why so interested, Dree?' she asked shrewdly.

'Just wondering how the other nine-tenths live,' replied

Deirdre with an attempt at pertness. 'Why did you fall out with him, Flora?'

Flora shook her head slowly. 'My turn to clam up,' she said mildly.

'Sorry.'

She toyed with her halibut for a while. *I have to be adult, restrained, discreet*, she told herself. *As I've been for the past nine months. Longer. But like any good Catholic girl, I've got to believe in signs too, I've got to. I need all the help I can get.*

'Flora,' she said, 'I've decided that maybe we can trade after all.'

5

McHarg was committing burglary.

It was a desperate, foolhardy act, but he had a sense of time slipping away from him. He had covered his tracks in Sanderton to some extent by phoning Davison before he left and telling him, as brokenly as he could manage, that his resignation was in the post and that he was going away somewhere quiet for a couple of days to sort himself out. But his encounter with Wesson and Partington must have blown the gaff where it mattered. He had gone straight round to Betty Woodstock's flat afterwards. Getting no reply, he had phoned the BBC and discovered the woman was still on sick leave. He didn't believe it. The coincidence of her disappearance so soon after the assault was too great. Nor did he give much credit to the story that she was convalescing in Scotland, but there was no quick way to check that.

So McHarg had returned to the St John's Wood flat. There seemed nowhere else to go, unless he made a direct assault on Inspector Elkin. That was certainly on the agenda, but McHarg was a tidy-minded man. He wanted things to be quite clear in his mind before he confronted his ex-colleague. Elkin had sicked Wesson on to him. Elkin had known where he was going to be. And Elkin had introduced him to the girl in the wheelchair.

There the chain of causality snapped.

There was no way to anticipate that the crippled woman would be able to lure him back to her apartment.

All right. It wasn't planned. It had been improvised.

But she still must have told Elkin she was taking his fellow cop home. McHarg had sensed some uncertainty about her, something not quite ringing true. What he wanted to know was why she had passed the information on to Elkin. Where did she fit into this puzzling and terrifying business?

Getting into the block of flats was easy. He simply followed a shopping-laden woman in, politely holding the door open for her after she had used her key.

Betty Woodstock's flat posed a greater problem but one he was equipped to deal with. He worked swiftly and efficiently, pausing only once to scrutinize certain minute scratches he observed on the angle of the lock.

They told him he wasn't the first to get in here without a key.

Once inside, he checked swiftly round to make sure the other uninvited visitor wasn't still in residence.

Satisfied, he then began slowly and meticulously to find out about Betty Woodstock.

She had a sister in California who seemed to write twice a year.

She was meticulous in her accounting, punctual in the payment of bills.

Since her accident she seemed to have bought most of her clothes by mail order. She preferred browns and greys and pastel shades, though the one or two dresses in her wardrobe which stylistically pre-dated the accident were much bolder in hue.

She liked expensive perfume, was worried about dandruff,

had a supply of contraceptive pills which were three years old.

She had an extensive library of reference books. She liked historical romances and P.G. Wodehouse.

There was a desk diary by the telephone.

McHarg thumbed through it. It was liberally sprinkled with appointments, business and social, but nothing particularly revealing. There was no reference to Elkin, nor did any of the names listed with telephone numbers mean anything to McHarg.

All in all he began to feel he was wasting his time.

On top of a heavy Victorian walnut sideboard was a bowl of rather wrinkled apples. He chewed one reflectively as he opened the sideboard doors. A bottle of Scotch caught his eye but he took another bite out of the apple and determinedly ignored the golden liquor. He found nothing else of interest till removal of a stack of table-cloths revealed a fat leatherbound scrapbook.

He sat down and riffled through it quickly. It was full of cuttings that referred to her career, programmes she'd been concerned with, critical reviews, articles from professional journals. Like most scrapbooks, it was meticulously organized to start with but gradually items were merely slipped in loose, to be stuck in later. And after about the halfway point, they stopped altogether.

But this was more than just the triumph of indolence, he realized. The last cutting was dated almost two years earlier. Not long before her accident, he guessed.

The accident. What precisely had happened? he wondered. He tried to imagine what it must have been like for a young woman, bright, lively, carving out a good career for herself, to wake up in hospital and find she was on her behind for ever. No wonder her mind had tried to shut it out! No wonder she had lost interest in her scrapbook.

No wonder she had grown furious with him when he tried to explain his pathetic flaccid response in terms of his own tragedy.

Mavis, or the use of his legs. Given the choice, there could have been no choice. But he shuddered at the thought of it. He turned his attention back to the scrapbook, in particular the final cutting.

After a while: 'Jesus,' he said.

The cutting was from a journal called *Broadcast*.

It was an enthusiastic account of a programme at that time still in the course of preparation.

It spoke highly of the talents of its young producer.

His name was Basil Younger.

It listed the experienced and enthusiastic research team.

They were headed by Betty Woodstock.

Prominent in the list of advisers and consultants was James Morrison.

And the name of the programme was *The Master Builders*.

So rapt was he by the implications of all this that he hardly heard the click of the door opening.

'McHarg!' gasped a voice.

It was Betty Woodstock sitting in her wheelchair in the doorway. She looked terrified and tried to drive her chair into reverse. But McHarg was at her in a flash, seizing the wheels and spinning her round and across the room.

By now she was grey with fear.

McHarg said irritatedly, 'What the hell's wrong with you? Think I'm going to rape you?'

She shook her head, still speechless.

McHarg said, 'I don't know whether that's a compliment or an insult.'

He went to the sideboard and took out the bottle of whisky and two glasses. He poured her a large one, himself a smaller one. His body wanted more but he had a feeling that his body needed to stay in as good a shape as possible, which at the moment wasn't much.

She downed hers in one. Colour returned to her face.

'What the hell do you want, McHarg?' she gasped.

'Nothing much,' he said. 'I just want you to tell me everything you know about Freemasonry.'

For a moment she looked ready to faint.

He refilled her glass, watched her recover.

'McHarg,' she said, 'you're either a sadist or a fool.'

'Just a cop in a hurry,' he said.

She gave him a long, searching glance compounded of uncertainty, fear, distrust and, at last, relief, or perhaps just resignation.

'What the hell?' she said. 'Just keep topping me up and I'll begin.'

6

Betty Woodstock started to cry as she talked. She hardly seemed to notice the tears and at first her voice remained level, controlled, unemotional even. But McHarg quickly realized that the weeping and the words were together part of a single process of great emotional release. He had known long interrogations end like this. All the interrogator could do was sit still and pray to God no one came blundering in.

She said, 'Television research work sounds fascinating, but for a lot of the time you're just following well-worn tracks over old ground. In Freemasonry, this means you start with two groups of people – its defenders and its detractors. There are plenty of both. Generally speaking, they use exactly the same evidence to prove opposing points!

'The apologists say that the ceremonies and rituals are symbolic and no more to be taken literally than what goes on at the official Opening of Parliament. The attackers say that no organization would have evolved such bloodthirsty oaths of secrecy unless it had something to hide. They then go on to suggest the main object of the exercise is to use signs and special handshakes to gain special advantages for Masons, and while the apologists deny this, they also point with pride to many documented instances of Masonry transcending enmity in the American Revolution, the Civil War and World War One. And the list of famous Freemasons (including several American Presidents and some British Royals) is cited by one side as evidence of respectability and the other as evidence of widespread and secret powers.

'Me, I didn't know what to make of it. I didn't care for its male chauvinist side, but women have become Masons and in the US in particular there's a strong line-up of female lodges. At one moment I felt that anything condemned by Hitler and Mussolini as an international Zionist conspiracy must get my vote, then I found that the official propaganda organs of the Roman Catholic Church used exactly the same terms! Certainly there's no denying it *has* exerted political influence, in, for example, the French and American Revolutions, not to mention the question of Irish Partition. But generally speaking, theory apart, I found the actual Freemasons I met were no more, no less, than they seemed to be – ordinary decent citizens with a taste for male fellowship, charitable works and play-acting.'

She paused to take a drink and now her voice was lower and quicker.

'So far it had been mainly history. But if (as seemed proved beyond any shadow of doubt) in the past Freemasonry was often a cover for all kinds of political skulduggery, I found myself wondering why this should just have petered out half way through the twentieth century.'

McHarg took this as a direct question.

'Superseded by superior secret organizations?' he suggested. 'Official, like the CIA, KGB, MI6. Or subversive like the Red Brigade, PLO, IRA.'

'Perhaps. But the whole point of Masonry, especially in Britain and the States, is that it's so bloody respectable! I mean, if you want to attend a secret meeting what better

cover than going openly to attend a secret meeting? If you
follow me.'

'Yes,' said McHarg thoughtfully. 'I'm with you. But had
you come across any real evidence that anything was going
on?'

'None whatsoever,' she said. 'No, to be honest, what
really motivated me at that stage was simple indignation! I
was getting pissed off with all this male exclusiveness. It
struck me that the only way for me to really get an insight
into Masonic rituals and also to assert my equality under the
law, was to attend a lodge meeting. Crazy, you think? That's
what Baz – Basil Younger – said when I put it to him. This
was a serious programme, he said. They'd had a lot of co-
operation from top Masons. He wasn't about to let me snarl
things up by causing offence all round. Well, we were
engaged at that time so I was able to tell him to go and stuff
himself without getting sacked. And I flounced off to pour
my brilliant idea into more appreciative ears. So I hoped.'

'These ears belonging to . . .?'

'The man you were asking about the other night. Jim
Morrison.'

'Ah,' said McHarg.

'You were there when it happened, when he . . . died?'

'Afterwards,' said McHarg.

'What was it like?' she asked almost inaudibly.

'There was just ash. Hot ash,' said McHarg.

'Just ash,' she repeated. 'They said in the paper that he'd
been drinking, it was an accident.'

'Yes,' said McHarg. 'That's what they said.'

She shot him a sharp glance but went on without further
questioning.

'Jim and I had been, were, very fond of each other. Lovers
once. Not any more, not since I got engaged to Baz. But it
left a link, a closeness. He was a Freemason, made no secret
of it, had written articles about it in various magazines. Baz
invited him to act as consultant, just to check the accuracy of
the programme's facts from a Masonic point of view. He was

very useful. Anyway I went straight round to Jim's place and I put my idea to him. I expected him to be amused even if he couldn't help. But instead he got quite angry, told me not to be stupid. Naturally I wasn't taking that.'

'Naturally,' said McHarg with a faint smile.

'At the same time I was really puzzled to find that Jim took it all so seriously. Or rather I'd been quite puzzled all along because Jim didn't seem like the type, but now I became very puzzled. So when I flounced out this time, I didn't flounce very far. I hung around outside his apartment block and waited.'

'To follow him?' said McHarg. 'But how did you know he'd be going anywhere that night?'

'I'd noticed his little box of tricks all ready,' she said. 'I told you we'd been lovers. Well, I moved in for a while, and I knew when he got his little black bag packed, he was off to the Lodge. I just took it as a bit of male daftness then, like playing rugby.'

'So you followed him?' urged McHarg. 'Where'd he go?'

'He headed to Mayfair, to Shepherd Market to be precise. Do you know it?'

'I was there this afternoon,' said McHarg softly. 'Visiting a friend. Go on.'

'Well, you'll know what kind of place it is,' continued Betty. 'Narrow streets, no cars, little shops, pubs, pros. I knew a few of them, I'd done some research for a documentary, that's where I got to know Rosie le Queux who was at the reception the other night. Well, there was a narrow door between a science fiction bookshop and a bespoke tailor. Jim slipped in there. I hung around a bit, not difficult in Shepherd Market if you don't mind the offers, and saw half-a-dozen other men go in. A couple of them I recognized. There was Ray Womack, the TUC man. And Terry Thwaites who started the cut-price airline. I just knew them from their photos, and a couple of the others looked familiar though I couldn't put names to them.

'Well, I waited a bit, but when no one else had gone in for

about ten minutes, I went across the street. There was a plaque on the door, easy enough to miss if you didn't look closely, it was such a scruffy old verdigrised thing. It read *The Templar Thanes of Elba*. There are all kinds of other Masonic orders and side-degrees available for those who really get bitten by the bug, usually with fancy names like *The Royal Ark Mariners* and *The Red Cross of Constantine*. I'd taken a quick look at them and generally found that the names were the most interesting thing about them. I'd not heard of *The Templar Thanes of Elba*, but that fancy title on this scruffy door suddenly struck me as being so sad and pathetic, I almost gave up.

'But then I thought that the men I knew were in there weren't sad or pathetic, so what the hell, I'd try a bit of eavesdropping!

'So I pushed open the door and went in.

'The stairway was narrow and shadowy. I went slowly up it, listening for voices, but I heard nothing except my own breathing and the creaking stairs. After the first few steps I realized I was just going on to prove to myself I wasn't frightened. And at the same time I knew I was terrified. I decided I'd go to the half-landing and that was it. A couple of moments later I reached it and sighed with relief. Then suddenly I wasn't alone.

'He just seemed to appear. I mean, I suppose he was there all the time round the corner, but it was like he just materialized out of the shadows. He didn't say anything, but just stood there a couple of feet away looking down at me. It was funny. He was a quiet, ordinary-looking fellow but something about him put the fear of God into me. A sort of hidden menace. Hey, come to think about it, you've got a bit of the same, McHarg!'

'On with the story,' said McHarg. 'We may be short of time.'

'Jesus! See what I mean?' she said. 'I just looked at him too. Behind him I could see the stairs stretching up into even darker shadows. At the same time because I was at the angle,

I could see the stairs I'd just come up running down to the street door. God, how attractive they looked!

'I spoke first. I said, *Hello ducky. Like to buy a girl a drink?* He said, *Why are you here?* very polite, very soft. I said I'd seen a couple of gents come in and wondered if they might be interested in a bit of company. I don't know how convincing my act was, but he took a step towards me and I got the feeling that sex wasn't uppermost on his mind.

'Then behind him on the next landing, a door opened spilling lovely light all down the stairs. A man appeared in the doorway. He called, *Tyler, would you step inside for a moment? The Præceptor . . .* Then he saw me, stopped abruptly and stepped backwards. And I was off like a flash, I tell you, down those stairs and out of the door into the street. It was as if I'd been hypnotized and the spell had been broken for a second!'

'Tyler,' said McHarg, recalling Mr Flint. 'You're sure that was the name?'

'Oh yes. But it's not a name,' said Betty. 'It's a function. That's what they call the outer guard at a Masonic Lodge meeting. The Tyler. His job is to watch out for and to deal with Cowans. A Cowan is what they call a spy. That's what I was, a Cowan. And even at this stage, this Tyler struck me as being a step or two beyond mere symbolism. I didn't realize how far beyond till later.'

Yes, thought McHarg. Form with substance. Vows with teeth. It was lunatic, but it fitted.

'What about Præceptor?' he asked.

'The kind of high-falutin' title these side-degrees use,' she said. 'Well, I was off out of Shepherd Market like a rabbit. I didn't look back in case anyone was peering out of a window after me. I didn't know how convincing I'd been as a tart, but I didn't want Jim Morrison making a positive identification just yet, not till I'd had time to think.

'You see, I *had* made a positive identification. The man I'd glimpsed through the open door was your dear friend, the Right Hon. Stanley Partington.'

'Partington,' echoed McHarg, nodding his head slowly. 'Well, well. So. So.'

She looked at him curiously.

'You don't seem surprised, McHarg,' she said. 'Why's that?'

'I'll tell you in a moment,' said McHarg. 'What interests me is why were you so surprised. I mean, so our Mr Partington's a what-did-you-call-it? a Templar Thane. So what?'

'So nothing, really. It wasn't that that struck me. No, the thing was, Partington shouldn't have been there at all! Remember it was at that time that the second big wave of public interest was washing around him about his Rhodesian interests. Mugabe had just come to power and lots of odd things were coming to light as his men started going through the books. First there was an explosion of indignation about alleged sanctions-busting via some of Partington's subsidiary companies. Then suddenly that was cut off short and some bright journalist suggested that this was at Mugabe's own direction as he knew that the sanctions-busting had been used as a cover to fool Smith while these same companies were also flogging arms to Zanu!

'Partington was denying everything, of course. I mean, he'd still been in the Government when most of this was going on. The scandal would have been terrific. But it wasn't just the denial that interested me, it was where he was denying it from. He was supposed to be in a sick-bed in a Swiss sanatorium at the time, do you recall? Nervous exhaustion! I'd heard a recorded telephone interview with him earlier that day. Now I went home and listened to the radio news and there it was again. I had the feeling I was into something very scoopish.

'I rang Baz and told him everything. I thought he'd know how best to handle it but he didn't seem much interested and I got very annoyed once more. I told him if he was too dull to see the implications, there were plenty of Fleet Street editors who'd be a damn sight more receptive. After that he got a bit more placatory and asked me to leave it with him. He said he'd get back to me later or perhaps call round.

'So I settled down here and had a drink and waited. Oddly the longer I waited, the less important it all seemed. Researchers should stick to research, I'd decided. Leave the news to the newshounds. Indeed, going over the evening's events I began to see myself as merely ridiculous. When the doorbell rang just before midnight, I was in a mellow mood, ready to be gently mocked before a loving reconciliation landed us in bed which I was now looking forward to very much.

'I didn't check the door, I was sure it was Baz. But it wasn't.

'It was the Tyler.

'He didn't say a word. He looked so calm, so serious, like a solicitor come to draft a will. Yes, that was it, he looked completely, professionally reliable.

'And he was. He closed the door behind him, then hit me in the stomach. Not hard enough to bruise, he just more or less jabbed with his fingers. But it took the breath out of me and I doubled up.

'He caught me over his shoulder, walked across the living-room to that window there. It was open. There's a little balcony outside that overlooks the back area. He stepped out on to it.

'And he tossed me over the side.'

7

McHarg found himself sloshing whisky into his glass. Betty held out hers for a refill too.

'He just tossed me over the side,' she repeated reflectively. 'Sounds simple when you say it fast, doesn't it? Over I went, down I went. I couldn't believe it. It was too absurd to be frightening, even. Suddenly I was flying through the air! It was almost exhilarating!

'And then I stopped flying. There was pain. Just for a moment, a flash. But so intense you could have spread it over a lifetime of visits to the dentist and still had bucketfuls to spare. And after that, nothing. Blackness. A blank. And since that moment, there have been times when I've recalled that pain with the kind of nostalgic longing you usually keep for the Mediterranean sun in a wet February.'

She drank some more whisky, her face deeply troubled. Then with a determined effort at brightness, she said, 'There! I've told somebody. Well, that's a load off my mind. It wasn't so bad after all.'

It was a poor parody of catharsis. McHarg ignored it.

'Why the hell have you been faking amnesia all this time?' he demanded. 'Why not just go straight to the police?'

She sighed deeply and shook her head.

'You're being a great help, McHarg,' she said. 'Listen, will you? For a start when I woke up I was full of dope, cased in plaster, and I genuinely couldn't recall a thing. I mean, really, not a damn thing. Anything I could have remembered, I'd have announced to the world. But everything had gone. My earliest recollection was months earlier, long before I'd started working on the programme. The doctors diagnosed complete amnesia, and prognosed that it might be permanent. If it bothered me, they said psycho-therapy might help. Otherwise, forget it – ha, ha. The police said I must have been sitting on the rail of my balcony when a metal stanchion gave way. A couple of screws had rusted and stripped their threads. The whole thing was dangerous – not just mine, but everybody's. They found my broken glass beside me. They also found enough alcohol in my blood to suggest I might have been a bit unsteady, easily unbalanced.

'I accepted all this. To tell the truth, I wasn't concerned about anything but my health. I'd had a miraculous escape, they told me. I should have been killed in the fall. After a while their stress on my good fortune got through and I realized things must be really bad. So then it came out. Paralysis. Probably permanent. Meals on wheels for life. If I could have got to another window, I'd have made a job of it this time.

'But I couldn't. And I didn't. Instead I got better, or most of me did. I recovered rapidly in some ways. Only a couple of months later I was out of hospital into my chair. Well, I won't bore you with plucky little Betty's struggle with adversity. I did the thing properly, went to a residential training centre; my aim was self-sufficiency, my motives were mixed. In the beginning mainly I wanted to be sure I had the capacity to kill myself if I ever felt like it. Great reason for recovery, eh? Then I began to get the idea that I might be able to walk again. I was sure there was still a bit of feeling there. I wasn't going to let my muscles waste. They had to stop me half killing myself with their therapy exercises!'

'And all the time, no memory?'

'None. Baz was around a lot, most attentive. Everyone was very touched. I came home – I insisted on staying here even though it's so high. I had some insurance money and I got the place fitted out for a cripple. And I wanted to start work again. Baz said he'd fix it. And he could too. His career had taken a rocket turn upwards in the months since my accident. He had got himself into the executive policy-making bracket. He had a lot of experience in news and current affairs when he first started and now he was widely tipped for a top controlling job there. He got me back on to the Crime series which was still in the planning stage. So everything was about as fine as it could be in the circumstances.

'The only thing that really got to me, oddly, was Jim Morrison's attitude. He came to see me in hospital once. He was so upset he could hardly talk. But he didn't come back. And on the odd occasion I came near to meeting him again once I was out and about in my chair, he backed off like a scared rabbit. I heard he was heavily on the bottle. It'd always been his weakness. Now it sounded like it was going to be his death.'

McHarg thought, it probably was, and the woman covered her eyes momentarily as though he'd spoken aloud.

'I'd told Baz that I'd no intention of marrying him by this time, that is a month or so after I'd come out of hospital. It wasn't noble self-sacrifice or anything like that. I just didn't want to, and he was mightily relieved. But he still kept close to me. I thought it was friendship with just a touch of conscience. Perhaps it was. Perhaps it was all a coincidence . . .'

She tailed off. McHarg didn't speak.

'He'd got himself a house on the river down towards Windsor. He was *really* doing well. I stayed there one weekend. Sunday morning it was misty and quiet, not too cold but beautifully still, like we were a million miles away from town. Baz suggested we breakfasted on the water, not the kind of daft romantic idea he usually went in for, but it really appealed. A jug of coffee, half-a-dozen hot croissants, some fresh orange juice and a rug. It was lovely. He lifted me into the tiny skiff he owned, and off we went into the mist. His intention was to moor on a little eyot about fifty yards downstream. Then out of the mist ahead of us appeared another boat. It came slowly towards us almost on a collision course.

'There was only one person in it, a man, and naturally all I could see of him was his back. It was enough.

'*Suddenly* doesn't describe how I remembered. It's not

violent enough. Like a rubber stamp on a blank sheet of paper. Now it's blank. Bang! Now it's not.

'Recognizing him from behind probably saved me. In the two seconds, less, that I had, my mind ran like a Grand Prix engine. This wasn't coincidence. This was at the very best a test. I had to pass it. I stopped my thoughts from running on to what would happen if it wasn't a test but simply an ambush.

'Our oars were going to hit so I gave a shout. That helped too, having a reason for shouting, for being a little afraid.

'Both men glanced round and shipped one of their oars. The boats came close together. The Tyler took hold of our gunwale as though to steady them and looked right into my face.

'I managed to laugh. It was a bit quavery, but I hoped that sounded like relief. He said, *That was close*. I said, *Worse things happen at Henley*. He said, *It's going to be a lovely day*. I said, *Yes, but I think I prefer it like it is now, before the river gets crowded*. He said, *Yes, it's so easy to collide with someone then*. And we laughed again. His eyes never left my face. Then he seemed to make up his mind and he pushed us apart. A few seconds later he was out of sight.

'We went on and had our picnic. Baz chattered away happily, was very attentive. And I responded as best I could. But all the time I was looking at him and wondering how much *he* knew. Had he connived at this meeting? Was his exuberant mood caused by relief that I'd passed the test? Perhaps I should have felt touched to believe so. But I didn't. I was wondering what the bastard would have done if I'd failed. The water flowed past, deep, grey and treacherous. I'd survived my brief moment as a bird, I'd no hope of getting by as a fish.

'I got through the day somehow. I'd no idea what to do. Go to the police? I didn't think much of the police then, McHarg.'

'I'm beginning to agree with you,' said McHarg.

'My story sounded simply hysterical. I'd suddenly

remembered that six months earlier I'd been thrown out of my flat window! And why? Because I'd tried to gate-crash a Masonic Lodge meeting! No, it had to be something to do with Partington.

'Next day I went to the library and got the back numbers of the papers for the week of my accident.'

McHarg interrupted, 'And you found that the day afterwards, the London office of Partington's company was bombed by terrorists claiming to be exacting vengeance for the company's part in repressing their black brothers in Zimbabwe, but also incidentally destroying all relevant records.

'And two days after that, when Partington returned from his Swiss sanatorium, he "discovered" his flat had been burgled and his private papers stolen along with all his valuables. He put it down to the wide publicity given to his absence from the country.'

'So Partington came off clean,' said Betty. 'He's got powerful friends, but everyone knows that. What I knew was just how ruthless they would be to protect their interests. And I was terrified, I tell you. The kind of people I'd glimpsed at that meeting weren't to be taken lightly. And if I couldn't even trust my friends, like Baz Younger and Jim Morrison, who the hell could I trust?

'Only myself, was the answer. An amnesiac cripple would surely get no hassle. I gave up my therapy classes, let it be known I was resigned to a life in this chair. And I've had to learn off by heart what it is I'm supposed to have forgotten. There's a million ways you can give yourself away, you'd be amazed. Like when that silly old fart Hunsingore came prancing up to me at the reception. Of course I remembered I'd interviewed him right at the start of my research for *The Master Builders*. Like half the House of Lords, his family's been into Masonry for years. But it was just at the edge of my alleged blank period. Christ, but it's hard being consistent – and never knowing who's watching. I've lived on a knife-edge, McHarg. I'd got a plan, but it was a long-term one. I've got a sister in California. She's married to a doctor, a gynæcologist. She's been writing to me ever since the accident, asking me to come out there to live with them and try what good old American know-how can do for my legs. I've had to write back that there's no hope. Christ, I don't even trust the mail! But I've been keeping on with the therapy up here as best I can, McHarg. I won't give up hope, not of that, not of that. I won't!'

She began to cry again and instinctively McHarg reached to take her in his arms but she pushed him away.

'That's where I've been. I'd planned to give it a year, make it look natural . . . But after you'd been here . . . I told you I was on a knife-edge. That's why I'd invited you back. You looked honest to me, McHarg. You were asking questions about Jim Morrison, you were giving evidence against Partington, and you sounded like a straight-up guy. So on an impulse I thought I'd take a chance. I wanted a broad shoulder to cry on, some hefty muscle I could trust. Unfortunately things didn't work out right.'

'You mean, I couldn't manage it and you didn't really want it?'

'Oh, don't make me your alibi, McHarg. I wanted it, right enough. It would have been the first time since I got smashed up. I was surprised to find how much I wanted it once we got on the bed! But it was one way traffic and we never got into that nice post-coital confession time. When I heard next day you'd been beaten up after leaving here, I got scared again. I didn't know if there was a connection, but I wasn't going to wait to find out! I headed west as fast as I could move.'

'Leaving word you were in the Cairngorms?'

'You checked that? Well, it gave me a breathing space. My sister was delighted to see me. Brad, that's her husband, arranged for me to have some tests in the paraplegic unit of this huge hospital he works at. I'm still waiting for the results, but I thought, sod it! I can't take London any more, being surrounded by people I don't trust. If Partington had got sent down, I might have risked coming out in the open.

But he didn't. So I came back to do a quick tidy up of my affairs. I'll need money. I own the lease of this place and it's worth a hell of a lot by today's prices. Also I've got some insurance money left, and a handful of stocks and shares. Two days. That was all I needed to be clear and away. Two measly days! And the first thing I find when I arrive is you, McHarg. Christ, why does every time you visit here have to be a disaster?'

McHarg regarded her coldly.

'There are worse visitors than me,' he said. 'I think you've had one of them already.'

As he told her about the scratches on the lock, the speed with which her thin facade of self-containment crumbled into the grey dust of fear made him wish he'd held his tongue. This time she didn't resist when he put his arms about her.

'It's OK,' he reassured her. 'Nothing to worry about. It's OK. They've been, they've looked, they've gone. There's no reason for them to come back. It's OK.'

'You're sure?' she said trembling against him.

'Certain,' he said. 'It's OK.'

The doorbell rang.

8

McHarg said, 'Go through into the bedroom.'

'No!' she cried. 'I can't, I won't, oh Jesus . . .'

McHarg struck her cheek with the flat of his hand, lightly, but enough to be felt.

'It's probably someone selling encyclopædias,' he said.

'Then they'll go away,' she said, rubbing her face.

The bell sounded again.

'Into the bedroom,' McHarg ordered.

This time she obeyed. McHarg waited till she had closed the door before going out of the living-room into the hall, carefully closing that door behind him too.

The bell rang once more, the knuckles rapped imperiously against the door and a familiar voice said, 'Doug, for God's sake, open up if you're in there!'

Surprised but still cautious, McHarg opened the door a fraction, stepping back from it instinctively.

The man outside pushed the door fully open and stepped inside.

It was Freddie Grossmith, his normally inexpressive face crinkled with mingled relief and concern, but it turned to surprise as McHarg, body hunched forward aggressively, said, 'Hold it right there, Freddie. And don't move a muscle till you tell me how you knew I'd be here.'

'I worked it out, Doug,' said Grossmith. 'I used to be a detective too, remember, before I got shoved upstairs. Partington says you tried to murder him and he's got the marks to prove it . . .'

'Hold on,' said McHarg. 'Partington? Why should he complain, I wonder. And especially to the Commander of International Division.'

'Why shouldn't he complain?' said Grossmith in surprise. 'Though to tell the truth, it was more that secretary of his running round Mayfair naked and hysterical! And it wasn't to me directly, but evidently she claimed to have overheard some reference to Inspector Elkin. When CIB come to question my chief assistant, Doug, I make it my business to know what's going on.'

McHarg relaxed slightly. CIB was the police internal investigation unit. It made sense, to a point.

'And you came here because . . .' he prompted.

'I worked it out,' said Grossmith smugly. 'You were following up what happened to you after the reception that night. Partington, Wesson – the next step had to be Miss Woodstock. They told me at the BBC she was off ill. So I came round on the off-chance. Doug, you're in big trouble.

Once CIB get hold of you, they won't let me near. So I thought if I could get your version first, I might be able to help. Is Miss Woodstock at home, by the way?'

'No,' lied McHarg. 'She's still in Scotland, I suppose.'

'So you broke in? Christ, Doug, you really go looking for trouble, don't you?' said Grossmith with feeling, pushing the door shut behind him.

As he did so the door into the living-room opened and Betty came rolling out in her wheelchair.

McHarg looked at her in exasperation. Mavis had been just the same, incapable of obeying even the simplest instruction.

Then he saw her expression change and his exasperation fled. It was fearful to see such terror on a human being's face. It made her shocked reaction when she first arrived seem like a welcoming smile. All colour faded, her mouth sagged open but no sound came, only her eyes spoke and what they said was betrayal.

There was only one explanation of their message and McHarg couldn't believe it.

He turned round to have his disbelief confirmed.

Grossmith had taken a pair of thin black leather gloves out of the pocket of his elegant and expensive camel topcoat and was drawing them on.

'So you have come back, Miss Woodstock,' he said pleasantly. 'Well, that's convenient.'

'Freddie!' said McHarg. 'What the hell is this?'

'No time for explanations, Doug. I doubt if you could take it in anyway. You should have stuck to crofting and let the Kirk look after your thought processes.'

'But Elkin and CIB?' he said stupidly.

'A little embroidery,' said Grossmith. 'I had hoped to persuade you to go somewhere a little more private, but now Miss Woodstock's back, here will have to do for you both. It was Elkin and a friend who found Partington at the Thanes' Lodge. You must have been quite close, Doug. Elkin contacted me straightaway. He's learned his lesson since he panicked last time when he saw you going off with Miss Woodstock. That assault on you was very unprofessional. I apologize, Doug. It wouldn't have happened, but I was busy elsewhere.'

'Mr Flint,' said McHarg dully. 'And Old Haystacks.'

'Don't be sentimental,' reproved Grossmith. 'It's always a mistake and you've got to correct it later. Miss Woodstock, for instance. I knew that some day . . . but there were other voices which insisted . . . and you yourself, Doug. There's no other way. It's been tried, but you keep on coming. You always did, even in training, I recall. You never knew when to stop pushing.'

What was puzzling McHarg as the first shock of disbelief wore off was that Grossmith showed no sign of carrying a weapon. Surely he couldn't expect to do what he clearly planned to do without a weapon? He took a tentative step forward as though just shifting his weight.

'And Morrison?' he said. 'You too?'

'That's right. He'd always been a nuisance, but since Miss Woodstock's accident, he'd become a menace. He blamed Mr Partington mainly, so it seems. But he hid it pretty well except when he was bottled. An anonymous phone call, that's how you got your information, wasn't it, Doug? That was about Morrison's strength. Booze can't give what's not there, can it? But you probably know all about that. We guessed it might have been him. Then he tried to sell an article about Partington's business background – to be published if there was an acquittal. Fortunately he showed it to a friend – a mutual friend. So he had to go.'

'And the tongue?' asked McHarg taking another step.

'Our members have to know that we expect them to mean what they say,' said Grossmith mildly. 'That's reasonable, isn't it? I am the Tyler, after all. I keep my oaths, and I make sure that others keep theirs. It's just another form of law enforcement, Doug.'

McHarg moved.

His left hook had once been famous. Given a bare nine inches of acceleration it would lay out the hardest-headed opponent.

If it landed.

The Tyler barely moved, but the blow whistled wide. The counterpunch didn't, however. A right, buried deep in his gut which age and too much whisky had reduced from steel-plate to foam rubber.

McHarg doubled up. For a second he was entirely vulnerable. But before the Tyler could move in, there was a low rasping scream like an angry cat's. It came from Betty Woodstock who had recovered from the paralysis of terror and with desperate courage was driving the wheelchair into the attack.

Again the Tyler's economy of movement was remarkable. His side-step was not a centimetre further than it needed to be. Using the woman's own momentum, he spun the chair round and with easy strength sent it careering back towards the living-room door. It caught the jamb and overturned, spilling Betty into the doorway where she lay as helpless as a decked fish.

Filled with a great anger, McHarg shook off the effects of the blow to his belly and hunched himself into a defensive crouch. Out of condition he might be, but the old skills were deeply engrained. Wesson and his mates hadn't been able to finish him off and there'd been three of them. Freddie Grossmith, this obscene pantomimic figure of the Tyler, might be OK against old age pensioners, drunk journalists, and decrepit tramps, but this was where he met his come-uppance.

He advanced.

The Tyler watched him and then raised his arms without clenching his fists. A moment later McHarg went reeling back. His nose felt as if it was broken. And this time the Tyler came after him. Those black-skinned hands moved through his defences as though his arms were pipe-cleaners, not solid beams of bone and muscle. What seemed the lightest of taps at the junction of his neck and right shoulder left that side of his body semi-paralysed. Christian-like, he turned the other shoulder and lashed out with his foot, aiming unsubtly at the Tyler's balls. Gratefully the man caught his foot and twisted it. McHarg screamed. He wanted to stay on his feet but he also wanted two feet to stay on.

As he crashed to the ground his foot dragged free from the shoe and the Tyler almost contemptuously tossed it on to his chest. McHarg through his pain thought of Wesson. There was a chain of violence as time brought its revenges. Wesson had beaten him and he had beaten Wesson. Now McHarg, the great fighter, was being taken apart. No wonder Grossmith had been unconcerned about using a weapon. This was a different man from the stylish but essentially light-weight boxer he had known two decades earlier.

This was a finely-tuned killing machine.

He could only hope his turn might soon come round again. But as the Tyler's well-shod feet were finding their way to his body as easily as his gloved hands had done, the possibility seemed remote.

He was ready to give up, ready to embrace rather than evade the unconsciousness which the Tyler was offering him.

Then through his tear-filled eyes and between the Tyler's mohair-trousered legs he glimpsed a movement in the living-room doorway.

A woman stood there.

It took him a painful second to realize it was Betty Woodstock.

The wheelchair lay on its side behind her, its wheel still spinning though it seemed an age since the Tyler's attack. She was hanging on to the jamb of the door with her left hand, but her weight was undeniably, amazingly, on her legs.

And most incredibly of all, in her right hand she held the

skean-dhu which he had noticed hanging on the wall on his first visit.

Two quick steps would have brought her up behind the unsuspecting Tyler, but two steps to her were like a thirty-foot leap to a fit man. Terror had got her to her feet. Now hatred pumped blood through a wasteland of muscle and she took one step forward.

But that was all. She had left the doorway and stood without support in the middle of the hall, her teeth bared like a cornered rat's with the effort of taking the first step and despair of taking another.

The Tyler felt something behind him. Perhaps McHarg's eyes had given the game away. He glanced over his shoulder. To a man of his expertise even an attack from a fully active woman would have presented no problem. But the glance had given McHarg his chance.

Pushing himself off the wall with all that remained of his strength, he hit the Tyler at the knees. The man staggered backwards. A fully active woman would probably have instinctively stepped aside, perhaps making some ineffectual slashing stroke with the knife.

But Betty did not, could not, move. The Tyler crashed against her. She fell backwards and he fell with her, on top of her. He was up almost immediately, with gymnastic grace. McHarg and the woman lay in a grotesque sprawl of limbs, exhausted, defeated. The Tyler put his right hand over his left shoulder with the irritated look of one who feels an unignorable itch on his shoulder-blade.

When he brought the hand back he studied it with interest.

The soft black leather was smeared with russet.

He nodded like a man who confirms the reaching of a long-anticipated conclusion.

'Funny,' he said. 'All those years . . . you always kept coming.'

Smiling slightly, he raised his eyes from his hand to McHarg's face.

'Want a job, Doug?' he said painfully. 'I know . . . a vacancy . . . might suit you . . .'

Then he fell on his face between McHarg and the woman, the skean-dhu protruding from the soft sand-coloured cloth like a cross from a desert grave.

9

They sat opposite each other in the living-room, bathing each other's wounds and drinking whisky.

McHarg talked, filling in all the details of what had happened at Sanderton, in an effort to soothe her nerves, but at the end of it she was pale and trembling still, unable to rid herself of the knowledge that she'd just killed a man.

'Don't worry about it,' McHarg urged. 'Put it out of your mind.'

'I thought you were in it too,' she said. 'When I came out and saw you standing there, talking, like old friends.'

'We were old friends,' said McHarg. 'Something happened. We all change. Something diverts us from what we might have been.'

'They should put up diversion signs, let us choose whether to go on or stay put,' she said. 'Oh Christ. I'm covered with blood. It'll ruin this dress.'

It was a wan attempt at a joke, he realized.

She said, 'I'll have to change it. Help me into my chair.'

It was the first time she had ever admitted the possibility of assistance.

He lifted her from the sofa on which she had been sitting. As he placed her in the wheelchair, she winced slightly.

'Sorry,' he said.

'Don't be. It's my leg. You forget, I'm nostalgic about pain.'

He followed her into the bedroom. She looked at him curiously and said, 'Come for the show?'

'Some other time,' he said, opening the wardrobe. Inside he found a zipped plastic suit-holder.

'OK if I take this?' he asked.

She nodded.

As he went out of the door, she said, 'McHarg. What are we going to do?'

He answered, 'What you planned to do, only even quicker. You're going back to America on the first possible flight. So get together whatever you want to take.'

'And you? What about you?'

'Me? Hell. Perhaps I'll go back to Scotland, grow a beard, run a croft with six hens and a tattie bed.'

She shook her head violently. 'No you won't. It was right what he said about you, McHarg. You'll keep on coming. But you'll need help, you'll have to tell someone.'

'Not till I know who I can trust,' said McHarg. 'It's too risky.'

'I struck lucky,' she said.

They exchanged smiles and he left.

Fifteen minutes later when she joined him in the living-room, he was sitting going through the contents of a wallet.

'His?' she asked.

He nodded.

'Where is he?'

'Gone.'

'What the hell do you mean, *gone*?' she asked in alarm.

'If you must know, he's down the corridor in number 97,' he said. 'It's vacant, I noticed the sign outside when I came in. I've hung him in the closet in that plastic wardrobe. And I've locked the door and dumped the key.'

'But they'll find him sooner or later,' she protested. 'They're not going to sit back and just wait for him to turn up. Neither of his employers.'

'Hopefully later. And better there than here, wouldn't you say? This is interesting, you're not the only one who was going to America. Freddie Grossmith has a ticket too and a wadful of dollars.'

She looked scared again.

'You mean he was coming after me?'

He laughed.

'No. He's bound for the East Coast. Boston. Perhaps there's some international police conference on. I told you that was his speciality. One of his specialities. It must have been useful. Got him all over the world.'

'Why should he have wanted to get all over the world? As Tyler, I mean?'

'I'm not sure,' he said. 'But certainly not to pursue attractive women in wheelchairs.'

But he wasn't sure about that either.

'McHarg, what do you really think this is all about?'

He rubbed his hand over his face. It felt stubbly. He said, 'Do you want what I guess or what I know?'

'How much is what you know?'

'About two sentences' worth.'

'I'll take the guesses.'

'All right,' he said. 'There's a group of men who are working outside the law probably on an international scale. Motivation, probably, though not certainly, or perhaps not solely, money.'

'Why such a large scale?' she interrupted. 'Why not just a little home-grown racket?'

He shook his head. 'The killings. And the rigmarole,' he said. 'It must be really big to be worth protecting in such a way. And all this Freemasonry thing only makes sense if it's really necessary. And it can only be necessary if they need an international umbrella of secrecy to work under. Who needs recognition signals if everybody knows everybody else? It's the big organization, the Mafia-style set-up, that needs structuring.'

'But it's so . . . childish!' she burst out.

'*You* can say that?' he demanded. 'Listen, it stops being childish if you take it seriously. All those blood-curdling oaths – they mean them! The initiate – what do you call him? the Entered Apprentice – has his loyalty tested at some stage by being required to carry out the terms of his oath. That has the double effect of testing the sincerity of a man's vocation, plus it binds him to the group almost irrevocably.'

'All right. I can see that. I still don't know if I believe it, but I know it must be true, if you follow me. Is that as far as your guessing takes you?'

'I'm still working at it. Why they wanted to kill you I can follow.'

'Thanks,' she said.

'But me? Why me?'

'Because of Partington?'

'But I wasn't a risk, not really. They'd obviously got that sewn up. No, Grossmith said that Elkin panicked at the reception and decided to drum up Wesson and his mates to kick my head in.'

'Because he heard you asking questions about Jim Morrison, then saw you going off with me. It must have looked very suspicious.'

'Yes, but more significant perhaps is that the Tyler wasn't there for consultation,' said McHarg slowly. 'Freddie Grossmith heard what I had to say at the Yard that morning and what he saw as the matter of prime urgency was motoring down to Sanderton where he got rid of Haystacks and old Flint as well as shutting up Wainwright.'

'Why not kill the doctor too?'

'Easier to shut him up. Attract less attention. Also perhaps, in a way, he was less important. Which means . . .'

'Means what?'

'The others were more important because . . . oh shit! I'm as thick as a Sassenach! The car. They saw the car. Jesus!'

He jumped up, went to the telephone, dialled.

When the phone was answered, he gave an extension number. Betty looked at him in surprise. His accent had changed, his voice had become flat, controlled, somehow familiar . . .

'Commander Grossmith here,' said McHarg. 'You checked a car number on my authorization last week. That's it, the Jaguar. Could you let me have the possibilities again? No, it's just that the list has got mislaid for the moment. Don't send them up, just dictate them if you would.'

A pause while McHarg scribbled on the telephone notepad.

'Thanks,' he said finally and replaced the phone.

He didn't speak but studied the sheet of paper before him.

'What is it?' demanded Betty. 'Come on, McHarg. No more mysteries, not between us.'

'They checked out the car number, or what they know of it, for me,' he said. 'I saw the computer print-out. There were only three names on it, but it was Elkin who brought it in. There were four names on it when it reached him. He'd torn one off. God, it's so simple, it's absurd.'

'To stop you investigating it, you mean?'

He shook his head. 'More direct than that. To stop me recognizing it.' He read from the piece of paper, 'Captain Edward Jopley.'

'Jopley? Who's he?' asked Betty.

'He is, or at least two years ago he was, equerry to His Royal Highness Prince Arthur,' said McHarg.

He picked up the phone again and dialled.

Betty could only hear McHarg's part of the conversation. He spoke authoritatively, curtly almost, and at the end replaced the receiver abruptly.

'Who were you ringing?' she asked.

'The Palace,' he said, frowning.

She looked at him closely, suspecting a joke, then said, 'Jesus. You know some useful numbers.'

'I don't forget things,' said McHarg harshly.

'I bet you don't,' she said. 'So, what have you found out, for God's sake?'

He looked at her for a long moment, but she didn't feel that he was seeing her. She was right. What he was seeing was a wheelchair.

What he had found out didn't carry him much further forward. Jopley was still Prince Arthur's equerry and currently they were en route to Canada for an official visit. The Tyler had been going to Boston. Coincidence? Probably. It was a long way from Canada and what the hell could be the connection anyway?

He felt himself lost. The great decisive McHarg didn't know where to turn. Jopley. Perhaps if he could get hold of Jopley and give him a dose of what he'd given to Wesson . . .

He shook his head angrily. Had it come to this? The old copper's adage, when in doubt, hit out?

In any case Jopley was on his way to Canada and to get near him while he was on duty would be bloody hard. Dewhurst was no slouch, plus of course all those hard-nosed Canadian security men . . .

But he *would* cross the Atlantic, he suddenly decided. He had his passport, properly visa'd. He had money, his own and the Tyler's. Why not use it? Grossmith owed him something. It would be wise to be out of the UK when they started looking for him in earnest – Grossmith's colleagues, he meant, both in and out of the Yard. There was a trail that led, however faintly, to Boston, Mass. But even without that trail, he had business there which needed to be sorted, one way or another, before he got on with the rest of his life.

Which might not be all that much to get on with, he reminded himself with a grim smile.

The smile encouraged Betty.

'Well?' she said. 'Is the oracle ready to pronounce?'

'I told you before. You're going back to California. Get together whatever you want to take,' he commanded. 'And that doesn't mean the furniture. Five minutes.'

'And what if I don't care to?' she asked.

'You can sit around here and wait for them to sell number 97,' he said indifferently.

'OK. I'm persuaded. And what about you, McHarg? You can't sit around here either!'

'We'll pick up my gear on the way to the airport.'

Her heart jumped, but she kept her face blank. 'You're coming with me?'

'Part of the way,' he said.

She set the chair in motion and started to sort out some papers from her bureau.

'McHarg,' she said, face averted, concentrating hard on her papers. 'You needn't come because of me, you know that.'

'I know it and I'm not,' he said.

'Why then?'

'I don't want to be around when they open 97 either,' he said. 'Besides, I've got family business.'

'Family business?'

'Which means my business. Which means I move at *my* speed. So for God's sake, woman, stop your havering and get a move on!'

10

The Præceptor sat and looked at the phone impatiently. The Tyler had promised to ring more than an hour before and he was usually a man to rely on.

Things had seemed to be going so smoothly the previous night. The Entered Apprentice had been summoned to the Lodge in Shepherd Market for a final briefing and the Præceptor had been in expansive mood and encouraged his questions.

'What I don't understand is why you – we – should be so concerned about this liaison,' he had asked.

The Præceptor smiled. 'Surely, Edward, you don't approve of it?'

Captain Jopley shook his head.

'No, of course not. I believe the Prince's first responsibility

is to his family and his country. And I'm sure he thinks so too.'

'If you could reassure us of that beyond all doubt, then we could forget the whole business,' invited the Præceptor.

Jopley had looked uncomfortable.

'There, you see. No, from what you've told us, Edward, it's quite clear he has not forgotten her. We know they haven't met for some time. We also know that this Canadian visit provides an ideal opportunity for an encounter, and all we want from you is clear warning if any such encounter seems to have been arranged. In which case it will be prevented.'

'Without any risk to His Highness, of course,' the Præceptor added in response to Jopley's frown.

'But I still don't quite see . . .' began Jopley.

'You know what these Connollys are,' interrupted the Præceptor sternly. 'You surely can see what a triumph for the IRA such a marriage would be?'

'Yes, of course. I'm sorry,' said Jopley.

'So, you know how to get in touch. Goodnight then, Edward.'

Jopley accepted his dismissal like a good soldier and left.

'That man bothers me a bit,' said Grossmith. 'I like the people working for me to be motivated by fear and by greed.'

'To each according to his need,' said the Præceptor. 'And I think after seeing you operate on his old school chum, Morrison, he certainly knows all about fear. The old Protestant loyalty should be quite enough if we simply decide to get rid of the girl.'

'That sounds like a good idea,' said Grossmith.

'The Americans think so. I'll decide when I get there. But of course Edward might need some closer attention if there was any threat to the Prince himself.'

'You'd do that?' said Grossmith, showing a rare surprise.

'There's been a great deal of time, money and effort put into the Connolly project,' said the Præceptor sternly. 'It cost a small fortune to arrange for that brother of his to be blown up for a start, but it was necessary to clear the way for Conal. Besides, it got him a lot of sympathy support. And it's never *easy or cheap to protect and promote a man at the same time as you're corrupting and compromising him. If Conal gets disinherited, all this could come to nothing. So of course I'd write young Arthur off if it came down to it. But there's no reason why it should. Everything's under control at both ends.'*

'Don't tempt fate, Præceptor,' grunted Grossmith.

But fate had already been tempted.

The Præceptor heard of Partington's acquittal on the lunch-time news and smiled. It was always nice to have certainties confirmed.

But early in the afternoon the smiling stopped.

The Tyler rang. The Præceptor listened in growing disbelief.

'Partington was screwing his secretary in the Lodge?'

'In the upstairs room,' corrected the Tyler. 'The safe house.'

'It's the same thing. That man can be quite a menace.'

'He's widely regarded as your possible successor, Præceptor,' said the Tyler mildly.

'I am not anticipating a need for a successor,' said the Præceptor. 'In any case our American friends might have something to say. Partington had better take a holiday over there. I'll talk to him in Boston, safer than here. Meanwhile there's an even bigger menace. McHarg. "Impotent" I think you called him?'

'I underestimated him. But not again,' said the Tyler. 'It's my guess he'll make round to the Woodstock woman's flat.'

'Another underestimation, her. But you said she wasn't there?'

'No. But he can get in. I managed easy enough and anything I can open, Doug McHarg can walk through. I'm going round myself.'

'Be careful,' urged the Præceptor.

The Tyler had laughed.

'He's got older,' he said. 'I've just got better. I'll ring you by five at the latest.'

But five had come and passed. Finally at six o'clock, the Præceptor rang Scotland Yard.

'No, he's not back,' said Chief Inspector Elkin. 'Trouble?'

'Go round to Betty Woodstock's flat. See what's happened.'

Half an hour later the phone rang.

'It looks like there may have been a fight,' said Elkin. 'But there's no one there. Not a trace. What shall I do?'

'Do? Nothing. Nothing at all,' said the Præceptor and replaced the phone and sat deep in thought for a long, long time.

Part Three

THE UPLIFTED HAND

1

Prince Arthur had seen a lot of airports and knew how hard it was to make them look festive, but Dorval at Montreal was hitting a new low. A gusty east wind was hurling handfuls of sleet around like wet rice at a punk wedding, lines of bunting flapped soggily like signals of abject surrender, and the guard of honour slouched like a chronic dole queue.

'How long have they had those poor devils standing there?' the Prince murmured to Jopley as he peered through the window of his plane. 'Let's get to it, Edward,' he added, with a sigh.

Moments later, looking merely braced and invigorated by the wind which was the only thing showing any real animation at his arrival, he ran lightly down the steps and another official duty had begun.

How many left? he asked himself mentally with mingled glee and trepidation.

The official welcoming party were (not altogether altruistically) keen to get him under cover as quickly as possible, but Arthur had done his share of military parading and knew what it meant in terms of effort and preparation. Smiling, he ignored the channelling arms which were directing him towards the terminal and strode purposefully towards the double line of men.

'My compliments,' he said in his loudest voice to the officer in charge. 'A splendid turn-out. I would esteem it a favour if you and your men would have a large Scotch on me in the airport bar as soon as you can. Edward, will you see to that?'

'Certainly, sir,' said Jopley, used by now to this kind of

irregular commission. And he had learned the hard way that whatever the Prince commanded, he expected to be carried out to the letter.

Back on the official conveyor-belt, Arthur went through all the inevitable rigmarole, bringing to it that charm and alert interest which removed much of the stiffness and gave meaning to many of the platitudes.

The weather had reduced the public attendance to a relative handful and this made the security presence stand out even more than usual. The Prince counted up those he felt certain were there to keep an eye on him and gave up at thirty.

'They seem to have me well protected,' he murmured to Inspector Dewhurst who was never far away. 'Are the Mohawks restless, do you think?'

Dewhurst smiled dutifully, but the Prince's little jokes fell on stony ground, particularly when they concerned security. He liked and admired the young man, but sometimes felt that he might take his job (i.e., Dewhurst's job) a little more seriously.

In fact, the Prince was taking it all very seriously indeed.

Several hours, introductions, exchanges of compliments and expressions of delight later, the Prince at last found himself alone. Stretching out on his bed, he closed his eyes, but a moment later opened them at a tap on his door.

Jopley stood there.

'Edward, please, I said no interruptions. Not for anything.'

'Except for Mr Emerson, sir,' corrected Jopley.

'Chris? Is he on the phone?' demanded Arthur, leaping up eagerly.

'No, I'm through here wondering where you keep the bourbon.'

Pushing past Jopley, the Prince went into the next room where a craggily handsome man of his own age looked up from the drinks cabinet with a smile on his face. He was dressed in a suede jacket over a tartan mohair shirt and faded denim jeans, held up by a broad leather belt with a huge solid silver buckle.

'Chris! How are you?'

'Just fine, Art. Just fine. And you?'

'Just fine!'

The two men shook hands. They had first met several years earlier when the teenage prince had been sent to do a year's schooling in Canada. They had rapidly become firm friends, a friendship which the Prince had been careful to maintain and nurture after his return to the UK. Long ago a senior member of his family had advised him vehemently, 'When you find a friend, a *real* friend, grapple him to your bosom.' The language had seemed rather florid at the time, but in manhood he had soon come to understand the source of the vehemence. It was very easy for a prince to end up with favourites rather than friends.

'My God, Chris, but you look the part!' said Arthur.

Emerson had inherited his father's huge lumber and mining concern while still in his early twenties and was surprising everybody with his success in running the business.

Now he struck an exaggerated tough-guy pose, sticking his thumbs in his belt, drumming his fingers against the buckle, and drawling; 'Shot the elk and mined the silver with my own hands, yes, sir!'

They laughed together, more at the pleasure of reunion than the joke.

Arthur said: 'Is there really no bourbon there?'

'It doesn't matter. Scotch is fine.'

'No. They really shouldn't cater only for my imagined tastes. Edward, see if you can drum up a bottle without hurting anyone's feelings, there's a good chap. Chris, come and sit down.'

As Jopley left, the two men sank into the huge chintzy armchairs which fronted a large empty fireplace made superfluous by the over-efficient air-conditioning.

'I had a hell of a job getting in here,' said Emerson. 'I had a gang of goons, one at each corner, till they drummed up your groom, or ostler, and he okayed me.'

'Equerry,' smiled Arthur. 'As you well know. Yes, I seem to be very precious in the eyes of your government. Is it going to cause difficulties?'

'Less of the English polite disinterest, you randy bastard!' grinned Emerson. 'Admit it, you're bursting at the seams.'

For a minute Arthur looked offended, an expression which placed him very firmly in his family context. Then he smiled and relaxed again.

'Of course I am,' he said. 'But my intentions are honourable, Chris.'

'I never doubted it. You've made your mind up then?'

Prince Arthur nodded, slowly, hesitantly.

'You don't seem too sure. Have you told anyone?'

'No! I haven't really told myself yet. Not till now anyway.'

It was the truth, more or less. The inward debate which had been raging for these last nine months had frequently seemed to have a quite inevitable conclusion – except that different conclusions seemed inevitable at different times. There were times when he saw quite clearly he was the victim of a self-indulgent infatuation, others when he felt he was an actor in one of the great love tragedies whose climax must be his noble renunciation of personal happiness *pro bono publico*. Then he would swing to the other extreme and feel that in fact his current contribution to the public weal was so little that if you rolled up a whole lifetime of it into a single ball, it wouldn't weigh much against the nine-days' pleasure the public would get out of reading about his romantic defection in the popular dailies.

The truth was, he had been trained to be everything except selfish. Or rather, he had been brought up to think of himself so much in public terms that he was at an even greater loss than young men normally are when trying to worry out what really lies at their core. That was perhaps why friends were so important for him. Family were different – though even there he always had a slight sense of hierarchy. But to unbutton, to be at ease, to be unsuspicious, to be unoffendable – these were the delights he sought in the company of the very few like Chris Emerson. And among that very few there was only one woman. Others he had shared the delights of sex and merriment with, but Deirdre was the only one who relaxed his mind as well as his body.

Perhaps he was being selfish. Or perhaps it was all a form of daydream and when he met her again, the image he had created in his mind would prove to be illusory.

Some of this he tried to explain to Emerson who, when he had finished, or rather stuttered to a stop, said quietly, 'And she may have decided against you too.'

'What?' said Arthur in alarm. 'Has she said anything?'

'No!' laughed Emerson. 'I'm just reminding you, it takes two to make a decision. Listen, I know a lot about Old Pat Connolly and I'll tell you something, Art: I'd rather be in your shoes than hers.'

'Oh God, you're right,' cried the Prince. 'I need people like you, Chris, otherwise it's so easy to start thinking the sun really does shine out of my bum. And I need Deirdre, need her, love her and if she won't have me, I may just kidnap her and imprison her till she changes her mind.'

'You've got the family history for it,' murmured Emerson. 'OK. Here's the plan. Your schedule's still the same, I take it.'

'Yes. If I don't make jokes about Rose Marie, get all my French subjunctives right, and refrain from scalping too many Indians, I get my usual two days' remittance which I am spending with my old friend and thoroughly respectable capitalist, Chris Emerson, in his log-cabin in the Notre Dame mountains. I must say I like "log-cabin", Chris.'

'Yes,' Emerson laughed. 'So do the newsmen. It really is made of logs. But we've got some pretty fancy kinds of moss tucked into the chinks.'

'And is that where we'll meet?' asked Arthur eagerly.

'No way! Shake a pine there and if a mountie doesn't

drop out, a newsman will. Listen, here's what happens. Wednesday morning we go out hunting. Only you don't come back. No, it's OK, I'll have you covered. You're heading south across the border . . .'

'Across the border?' interrupted the Prince. 'Isn't that taking a bit of a chance?'

'It's not the Berlin Wall,' said Emerson. 'Up there, there's any number of tracks that four-wheel drive can just eat up. I had thought of a chopper, but that's more conspicuous, and it's been such a mild winter, the going should be easy enough even for a soft limey to manage. You'll join the highway on the US side and after that it's only a short step to meeting your colleen in another remote primitive log-cabin with a deep-freeze and a charcoal grill!'

'I still don't like it,' said the Prince. 'I would be illegally in America, would I not?'

'Technically, but so what? Listen, Art,' said Emerson seriously. 'You want this meeting to be private, you want to have some time alone together, right? It'd be easy to invite her to my place and put you next door to each other. Only everyone in the Western world would know the next day. Even if the reporters missed it, our security men are there to protect your person, not your reputation. A story like this would be worth a generous pay-off from any paper. But *they* won't be wandering around the US of A. One way or another, this is going to be a big moment in your life, Art. Believe me, this is the best arrangement we could make. Trust your Uncle Pander!'

'All right, all right, I'm in your hands,' said Arthur. 'This other log-cabin. Does that belong to you too?'

Emerson began to laugh.

'Oh no. That girl of yours isn't stupid. Up till now you've always had the advantage, I reckon. She's gone into your world to meet you. This time she's on home ground!'

There was a discreet tap on the door and Captain Jopley came in bearing a fifth of bourbon. The Prince ignored him.

'I'm sorry, Chris,' he said. 'Surely you don't mean . . .'

'That's it, Art,' replied Emerson in a conspiratorial whisper. 'It belongs to Old Pat Connolly. And to cap it all, it'll be St Patrick's Day!'

2

Flora McHarg was in the kitchen of her apartment making coffee when the bell rang. She glanced at the wall clock and frowned. It was only 8 a.m.

Drawing the short travelling robe which was her only garment tightly round her body she went to the door and opened it on the safety chain.

'Yes?' she said to the man who stood outside.

'Flora,' he said.

'Yes?' she repeated; then, 'Oh Christ,' she said.

She closed the door, unhooked the chain, and opened it again.

'You'd better come in,' she said.

McHarg and his daughter regarded each other warily. She saw a grey-haired man with a rock-hard face scratched but not undermined by fatigue, who might have been ten years older than his true forty-five except that in movement or repose some positive quality in his bearing gave him the physical presence, and menace, of a much younger man.

She shivered under her robe.

He saw a girl in her mid-twenties, frowning and unsure, not frightened, but standing with shoulders hunched like a boxer pondering tactics. She had too much of his own solidity of jaw to be truly beautiful, but she was a fine, handsome girl, and in her soft dark eyes and her long dark hair he saw his wife again as she had been when first they met and suddenly the distance between them was too much.

Two paces took him across it.

'Flora,' he said again and folded her in his arms.

She accepted the embrace though she did not return it, letting him bury his face in her hair for a long moment before gently pushing him away. The robe fell open and as his eyes took in her body, for a second he was seeing his lost Mavis again. Almost instantly he turned away but not before the longing and the guilt had shown in his face.

Flora pulled the robe shut, went to the mantelpiece and lit a cigarette.

'This *is* a surprise, Dad,' she said calmly. 'Have a seat. Tell me all about it.'

'What's to tell?' he said, in control again. 'I promised a visit. Here I am.'

'That simple? OK. I was fixing some coffee. Would you like a cup?'

She sounded very American he thought as he nodded. Though doubtless to the Yanks she still sounded awfully British, just as his own Scottishness was only recognized in England now.

He sank into an armchair, leaned back and listened to her clinking cups in the kitchen. The fatigue of the journey was heavy upon him but when he closed his eyes it dragged him down into fantasy not sleep. He tried it again now. The images were still there; fire leaping and a whole queue of dead faces peering through the corroding flames; to them now Mavis, rearing high like a serpent and twisting so that he could see her body, now waxy pale and wasted as it had been at the end, now full and luscious as in her youth.

He forced himself back to reality. Flora was standing over him with a cup in her hand.

'You look awful,' she said.

He took the coffee gratefully. Aware of the shortcomings of her robe, she had found a frilly apron and tied it round her waist to hold it closed. The effect was slightly ludicrous. Like a Bunny girl.

Or a Mason.

He sighed and drank his coffee. To be here alone with his daughter, to have time ahead of them to teach and to learn about each other, to re-shape their relationship – these were luxuries he would be willing to pay much for. Barely a week ago, they might have been his for free, if he had obeyed his own instinct and the urgings of the Davisons.

But now his mind was fragmented among a myriad concerns and ill-equipped to deal with any of them; a crippled woman asleep in a hotel by the airport; an unformulated threat to the Prince, an awareness of his own peril both from within the Law, and outside it.

He had come here first because he had to come, because he owed it to them both, to his daughter and his wife; but also, his irrepressible honesty of self-analysis told him, because there was at the moment nowhere else to go, nothing else to do. The fever of flight, in every sense, was over and arrival had brought with it neither the feeling of refuge nor the power of decision.

'I'm OK,' he said. 'Really I am.'

'Good. So tell me, why have you come?'

'You sound like immigration control,' he tried to joke.

'If you want, we can pretend, Dad,' she said seriously. 'I'm your loving daughter who lives abroad. You're my doting dad, come on a visit. We can put a week in seeing the sights, meeting the citizens. Then a kiss at the airport, a tear in the eye, a wave of the hankie, a long goodbye. Perhaps that's how we should play it. Perhaps there's not time for anything more.'

'Not for that anyway,' said McHarg with a sense of dramatic irony. 'I'm here to find out if I have to settle for being a permanent stranger with my child.'

'Forget the child bit,' she said. 'Dads grow older, children grow up. What's really brought you here? Guilt, is it? You want to be absolved?'

He leaned forward now, making himself uncomfortable so that his tired mind would not be spilling its remaining energies into the seductive upholstery.

'Absolved from what?' he said harshly.

'You say it, Dad. Come on. You really can if you try!'

'I'll say it because there's no time for games!' he cried. 'For your mother's death. You think I'm responsible. Worse, you think I prevented you and her from being together when it happened. Is that what you want me to say?'

'I knew you could do it, Dad,' she applauded with bitter mockery. 'Are you beginning to feel better now.'

'She was incurable,' he said softly. 'You must know that. You're not stupid.'

'Incurable, perhaps. But not inconsolable, not unhelpable, not unlovable!' she flashed back. 'While you were touring the fucking empire protecting your precious fucking prince, who was looking after your proper concerns back home?'

He nodded, not seeing her but regarding the past.

'You,' he said. 'Yes, I begin to see. You.'

'Yes, *me*,' she said fiercely. 'And when you did finally take notice, when you did finally make the big sacrifice which won such universal admiration, what's your first step? That's it. Move away, separate us. King bloody Douglas wants no rival near the throne!'

'*Rival!*' said McHarg. 'Flora, please . . . it was your mother's wish . . . to take pressure off you . . . and for herself, she so loved the sea, the air . . .'

'Did she now? And you? How did you love it, Dad? What did it feel like for you, big hard Duggie McHarg, the royal defender, to find himself out in the sticks? Oh, the time must have stretched away ahead of you dreary and dull as those empty winter beaches. Did you start looking for the signs then, start hoping just a little that it might be next week rather than next month, or next day rather than either . . .'

His hand snaked out, it was pure instinct, the only control left to him being that which unclenched the fisted fingers. The slap cracked against her face like a dry branch snapping.

'Hey you! What the hell's going on here?'

There was a naked man in the doorway, gingery hair bed-tousled, astonishment warring with sleep in his half-closed eyes. He was fortyish, beginning to get paunchy.

McHarg ignored him, concentrating all his ebbing energy on his daughter.

'Understand this, if you understand nothing else. I wanted her to live for ever. And I wanted you to be with us. If I'd had my way you would have been. It was your mother, always your mother, worrying about you, protecting you. Exams! I said to hell with the exams! But your mother, she said . . . she said . . .'

He dried up, like a tyro actor not yet strong enough to carry on in the face of a totally inimical audience.

'*My mother said*,' she echoed. 'Not once did you pay her any heed living. And you expect me to believe you heeded her dying! One thing I know for certain is, I didn't see her before she died because you didn't want me to see her!'

'You must believe I hate you,' marvelled McHarg.

'Hate me? No, that's not true, I never believed that. But resented me, misunderstood me, perhaps feared me.'

'Feared? *What*, for God's sake?'

She considered. She was completely in control. It was indeed fearful to observe her.

'In general terms, it's too complicated to go into. But I often remember something Mum said to me when she was having a bad turn. She said that the pain was bearable because she knew you would not let her bear more than she could. That gave me a laugh at the time. You were in Hong Kong or somewhere. But I've thought about it a lot in the past couple of years. How do you stand on euthanasia, Dad? And who's to care if you jumped the gun a bit?'

McHarg rose. He felt numb but his face must have shown something for the naked man stepped forward to put a protective arm round Flora's shoulders. At the same time the movement made him conscious of his nudity and he dropped the other hand to conceal his privates.

His mouth opened and he said something but McHarg did not hear. He went out of the door leaving it wide behind him.

'Was he your father?' said Christie. 'Jesus.'

But Flora, staring through the open door, did not hear either.

Betty was awake when McHarg returned to the hotel. She took one look at him and without a word put a small tablet into his hand and made him wash it down with a glass of Scotch.

He kicked his shoes off, let his jacket fall to the floor and collapsed on to the bed.

'You'll ruin your trousers,' were the last words he heard.

The sleeping pill was strong enough to hold him in dull blackness for about four hours but as its effect wore off, the flame and the fearful images began to reassert themselves. Once again mingled with them were images of Mavis, now skeletal and now with Flora's ripe heavy body, and McHarg responded in his sleep with the hot feverish lust of an alcoholic orgy. Once he dreamt he awoke but the awaking was so strange that he knew he still slept and he turned feverishly on the disordered bed which seemed to open between his thighs and became soft moist flesh, warm indeed but cool by comparison with the pulsating burning rod he thrust inside in search of relief. It came quickly and violently and for a little while he slept peacefully once more.

Then he awoke and this time knew it a true awakening, though beneath him he found not the tangled sheets he expected but the warm body of a woman.

'God, you're a weight,' said Betty breathlessly.

He rolled off.

'Thanks,' she said.

He looked at his watch. It was mid-afternoon.

'What happened?' he asked.

'There's gallant!' she said. 'You slept, I managed to get your trousers off and put a blanket over you. A wee while ago you threw it off and began tossing around something awful. I thought you were ill till my world-famous powers of observation spotted the root of the trouble. To diagnose was to understand the cure. With true Hippocratic altruism, I offered myself.'

'I'm sorry,' said McHarg, still only half awake.

'Thanks,' said Betty. 'I'll tell you something, McHarg. From my experience you're a damn sight better asleep than awake.'

He rubbed his eyes and sat upright.

'Why'd you do it?' he asked.

'Farewell present,' she said briskly, beginning to dress with that mechanical ease which he found so disturbing. Every movement was precise, economical. Within less than a minute she was easing herself off the bed into the wheelchair alongside.

'Farewell?'

'Yes. In about ninety minutes, I'll be leaving Boston, a city which for ever may remain to me as nothing more than an airport and a quick screw. I'm off to Cal-i-forn-i-a. I fixed it all while you lay sleeping.'

'But why?' he protested. 'Why so soon, anyway?'

His voice faded away. He was being absurd, he realized. He had protested against her insistence that she should travel with him on the Boston flight, told her that she would be a drag on him, commanded her to go directly to California.

Now here he was on the brink of begging her to stay.

'I spoke to my brother-in-law on the phone. They've got the result of my tests,' said Betty, her voice controlled and unemotional. 'There's some hope, they say. Even without some lunatic trying to kill me, there's some hope I'll be able to walk, McHarg.'

'That's grand,' said McHarg dully; then, trying to infuse a proper enthusiasm into his voice, he repeated, 'That's grand. Really grand.'

And finally, ashamed of himself, he said, 'Oh Jesus. I'm sorry. I'm not in a jumping-for-joy mood, but that's the best news I've heard in a long while. I mean a long while. Years. In years.'

She searched his face with unblinking eyes and said, 'I almost believe you mean it.'

'Lassie,' he said attempting a smile, 'when I say *the best*, I mean it. Even if the competition isn't up to much.'

'That's better,' she said. 'That's the real McHarg. Listen. What I'd like very much is for you to come with me. Forget this business, whatever it is. You could be safe out there at my sister's. Sink from view. I've got a bit of money and I'm sure you're a man of vast resource. That's what I'd like to suggest. That's what I'd like to persuade you to do. But I don't think I'll even bother to try, McHarg.'

'Why not?' he asked gently.

'Because I'm finding out about you, McHarg. And I'm certain you wouldn't do it, *couldn't* do it. So why go through the hassle? I don't know what you're going to do. Jesus, if a couple of hours leaves you in the state you were in when you got back here, then God knows what a couple of days may do! But whatever you do, I can only be a hindrance. Fit and upright, there'd be no shaking me off. Like this, well, I may be OK for farewell presents but not much else. Besides, I've killed my one man for this season. So, I'm off in search of a cure. Isn't it nice when altruism and self-interest just for once happen to coincide?'

She was weeping, though her words came out as determinedly merry as ever.

McHarg sat on the edge of the bed and put his arms around her.

'What will you do?' she said.

'I don't know,' he said. 'But you're right. I have to stay.'

'I'm never wrong about a half-wit,' she said. 'Now help me pack.'

As he pushed her through the airport concourse later that evening neither made any attempt at talk. Suddenly, however, he diverted the wheeelchair into the slight shelter of the angle of a magazine kiosk and kissed her long and passionately.

'What did I do to deserve that?' she gasped.

'Nothing,' he said. 'Just a mad impulse.'

Betty laughed disbelievingly. McHarg laughed too, but his eyes were fixed on the retreating back of the man whose emergence through the arrivals channel had been the cause of the sudden detour.

It was Stanley Partington, his open, weathered face concealed by large sun-glasses and disfigured by several bruises.

McHarg watched him out of sight and was just about to push the chair back into the mainstream of pedestrians again when he realized that more familiar faces were in the process of passing.

'Hey,' said Betty. 'Isn't that Hunsingore and his *New Vision* lot?'

'I think it is,' said McHarg, standing very still.

'Come to save Boston probably. Well, at least you should be all right with him in town. He's always on the side of the criminal.'

It was good to hear Betty joke. And he was glad she hadn't seen Partington. She had enough worries of her own already.

Later at the embarkation gate, she said to him, 'I'm not going to let myself fall in love with you, McHarg. Not till I'm back on my own feet and I can see that you're still on yours.'

'That's wise,' he said. 'Take care.'

'You too,' she said.

She didn't look back.

3

After her father had gone, Flora McHarg had retreated to the bathroom. Christie heard the sound of the shower running a few moments later, but when he tried the door it was locked.

His broad amiable face creased with worry, he washed himself in the kitchen sink before returning to the bedroom to get dressed. To some extent he had become anæsthetized to his own family worries, but this was different. Perhaps it was his awareness of how little Flora pressurized him with regard to Judith that made him so sensitive to her own hitherto unsuspected problems.

She was still in the shower when he had finished dressing, so he sat with a cup of coffee and a cigarette and waited.

When she finally emerged she said, 'Hey, it's after nine. I thought you had a seminar?'

'You know me. I always tell them, you think you're so damn clever, if I'm not there you'd better start without me! Flora, are you OK?'

'Why shouldn't I be? I should have thought the Connollys of all people would have recognized a normal healthy family relationship.'

Christie shook his head.

'The Granda's a bit obsessed, true. He thinks you Brits are bent on knocking over all his family one by one. But he doesn't think the family are knocking over the family!'

Flora went into the bedroom and emerged a moment later fastening up a pair of jeans.

'Me neither, not really. Not that he isn't capable of it. My father's capable of anything, Christie. I've always known it. When I was a little girl, I was proud of it. But when I became a big girl, I got afraid of it.'

'And now you're a woman?'

She looked at him, trouble clouding her normally serene, wide-spaced eyes.

'I don't know. Something about him this morning worried me. Even touched me.'

'Christ, you've a queer way of showing it!' he laughed.

'When a McHarg's uncertain, he strikes out,' said Flora. 'But I'm OK, really. Don't neglect your class.'

'All right. Want a lift.'

'No, not this morning.'

'Lunchtime then. Will you be in the refectory?'

She shook her head.

'I've got a date with Dree,' she said. 'So it'll be tonight?'

He looked uncomfortable. 'There's a campus reception I've got to attend,' he said. 'There's this gang of your fellow countrymen, the *New Vision* they call themselves . . .'

'You mean Hunsingore and his lot?' she asked, surprised.

'You know him?'

'Not personally. I was once into that sort of thing a few years back. In and out. It's pretty yucky. Why are they getting the treatment?'

'Boston dearly loves a lord,' said Christie. 'And besides, he's quite a scholar in his own way. Tomorrow I'm hosting the lot of them at lunch. They feel they relate to my department more than to the moral philosophers somehow.'

'I'd watch that,' said Flora. 'Will you be bedding down here again tonight?'

'That's an odd way of putting it,' said Christie.

'All right. Try this. Since your wife's away for another four days, do you propose to spend another night screwing your mistress?' she said with uncharacteristic vehemence.

He tried to conceal his hurt because he did not believe he was really entitled to feel it. She regarded him sombrely as if she could read every thought and emotion as though they were parading across his forehead on a print-out, but she made no gesture of help or affection.

'I'll come if I can then,' he said, a stupid male pride bringing up the rear of the parade.

'I'll be here,' she said wearily. 'I'm a creature of routine, Christie.'

The mailman arrived as Christie left. There was a letter with a Sanderton post mark for her. She studied the envelope for several minutes before opening it. And after reading it, she sat for even longer, quite still, staring sightlessly at the outspread sheets.

At lunch Flora found herself acting out of character by telling everything to Deirdre. They were eating in a crowded diner where the press of customers gave them as much privacy as the discreet distancing of tables in a top restaurant. Sam, Deirdre's minder, was at the counter near the door, chewing on a sandwich and looking more at home with it than with a bowlful of olives.

Deirdre listened unhappily. In an ideal world Flora would have been married to Christie and the two women could have looked forward to a lifetime in which to enjoy and develop their friendship. But the only way that was achievable was via a ruinous domestic bust-up. Dree thought her sister-in-law Judith was on the whole a pain, but she and the four girls didn't deserve the agony of a fractured home, and as for Christie, it would tear him apart. So everything piled up on this young Englishwoman's shoulders.

'Your father, will he try to see you again?' asked Dree.

'I think so,' said Flora. 'The thing is, I'm not sure what he's doing here.'

'Visiting his only daughter, surely?' said Dree in surprise.

'Maybe. He wasn't due for another month and that hadn't been finally settled either. I kept on backing off. No, there's something else. I got a letter this morning after he'd gone. It was from Heather Davison, that's the wife of my dad's police boss in Sanderton. She's a nice woman, a bit of an interferer but she means well. She said he was in a bit of trouble, there'd been a car accident and someone was killed, and Dad was driving. So at the moment he was suspended from duty and feeling very down and a loving letter from me might help. Nothing about him coming to the States.'

'And he didn't mention this?'

Flora said: 'Our conversation didn't develop along those lines. Funny, yesterday I'd have said I was far beyond him, wounds all healed, ready even to establish a simple, guarded, limited relationship. Now I'm bouncing around between love and hate like a pin-ball. And it's opened up my whole relationship with Christie too. I found myself looking at him this morning, comparing him with Dad and not knowing whether I was glad or disappointed at the differences. Oh, screw it all! Let's talk about your interesting neuroses and sexual problems for a change! Have you made up your mind yet?'

'About what?' said Dree automatically, then shook her head. 'Sorry. Defense mechanism. Yes, I've made up my mind. A couple of dozen times a day I make up my mind! Sometimes it's the great altruism bit, with heavy violin music as I retire to a convent. Others, it's all blue lagoon, with the pair of us escaping to some remote island where we do nothing but screw and eat passion fruit. So when I say yes, I mean no. What am I going to do, Flora?'

'You want advice?' asked Flora.

'Yes, please,' said Dree.

'My advice is, don't take advice,' said Flora. 'Follow your heart. Did I really say that? Makes you want to vomit, doesn't it?'

'It sounds like good advice,' said Dree.

'Then don't take it,' said Flora. 'Oh, look, Dree, I'm no person to be giving you advice on how to conduct your love-life. Look at the state I'm in!'

'OK,' said Dree. 'No advice. What about help?'

Flora raised her eyebrows. 'With your love-life? What did you have in mind, dearie?'

Dree giggled.

'No. I'm serious. Just listen and then say yes or no.'

Flora listened.

'Why not?' she said.

4

McHarg had spent a morning drifting.

It was not a feeling he liked. In his book, you met storms by turning into the wind. And if you couldn't ride them out and felt yourself being pushed slowly back towards the rocks, then you should swing about, clap on all canvas and drive boldly across the jagged reefs, preferring to sink proudly rather than drift aimlessly, a useless hulk.

He had started by revisiting Flora's apartment, a little later this time. There had been no reply to his knocking and he had been half relieved. There was only room for one more failure there.

Next he had attempted to pick up the Tyler's proposed trail. The Tourist Information Office told him they knew of no imminent police conference in the city and a call to Police HQ on Berkeley Street got the same response. However, he managed to make himself sound important enough for someone to dig out the information that there was an Interpol conference in New York in ten days' time. That sounded like Freddie Grossmith's cup of tea.

So, why come to Boston first?

Partington was impossible to trace unless he rang every likely hotel. He didn't feel up to it. That was policeman's work. Today he didn't feel anything like a policeman. Thoughts of Flora and Betty floated through his mind. Impatiently he pushed them aside and tried to get a grip on the helm once more.

It was time for action, time to clap on sail and let the forces that were buffeting him generate power and create direction. There was only one thing he knew for certain and that was the owner of the car which had taken the Tyler to Sanderton

that night. Boston was for him a diversion. He didn't
understand its significance.

Except of course as Flora's home.

He paused and took his bearings in time and space. It was
just on midday and he was not surprised to find himself in
the university area. Some internal compass had still been
functioning through all his apparent aimless meanderings. A
few enquiries got him directed to the department of political
and social science. The administration office should be able
to tell him if Flora had any official duties that morning or at
least direct him to the library area where she was most likely
to be pursuing her research. This part of his life had to be
sorted out now. After that there might be little opportunity.
He had other things to do.

As he approached the building a little knot of men and
women came out of it. McHarg's eyes immediately focused
on one of them to the exclusion of all others. It was the big
gingery man he had last seen stark naked in his daughter's
apartment. Simultaneously the man's gaze caught his and
the broad amiable features twitched in a shock of
recognition. But before either of them could make a move,
their encounter was pre-empted by another of the group.

'Hello there! Superintendent McHarg, isn't it? Our paths
seem fated to cross. But how delightful to see a familiar face
so far from home!'

It was Hunsingore, the noble evangelist, his narrow face
alight with the kind of joy he might have been expected to
reserve for an unlikely conversion. His fluttering right hand
grasped McHarg's in a surprisingly firm and rather curious
grip, maintained the pressure for a couple of seconds, then
released him.

'Yes,' said McHarg. 'A real coincidence,' in the dead voice
of one who ceased to believe in coincidence the second time
the midwife slapped his buttocks at birth.

The others had halted a little to one side and were chatting
among themselves. Ena Dyas, the housewife conscience,
was there, and Rose le Queux, the reformed whore, plus

half-a-dozen others, mostly American from the sound of them. Only the ginger man didn't join in the animated talk but silently watched the separated pair.

'Are you having a convalescent holiday, my dear chap? I read about your troubles in the papers. So sorry. Quite dreadful.'

'You could say that,' said McHarg. 'And you?'

'I'm on the lecture circuit. One or two of us from *New Vision* spreading the light, as it were. Most stimulating, these American campuses. Rather naive in many ways, but so intense, so involved. I have a couple of small seminar groups this afternoon and give a lecture this evening. I much prefer the small groups, but you can't have one without the other, it seems. Come along, my dear chap, if you have the time.'

'I'll check,' said McHarg. 'I think your hosts are getting impatient.'

'So organized,' said Hunsingore admiringly. 'We're lunching in the refectory. So democratic.'

The ginger man came across.

'Lord Hunsingore, I think we'd better move if your schedule isn't to get blown.'

'Of course. Professor Connolly, this is an old acquaintance of mine, Mr McHarg. Goodbye now.'

He flapped off and the group got in motion again, but the ginger man made no move to follow them.

'Professor Connolly,' said McHarg.

'Mr McHarg.'

'Do you screw all your students, Professor?'

'Do you beat up all your daughters, Inspector?'

'She's the only one I've got,' said McHarg.

'She's the only one I screw,' said Christie.

The two men examined each other in silence for a moment.

'I've got to see her,' said McHarg finally.

'Why?'

'I'll be moving on. There are things to get straight.'

Unexpectedly Christie Connolly laughed. 'You're not a man who likes uncertainties, I guess.'

'Occupational hazard,' said McHarg.

'Are you going to hit her again?'

'No. That was for my wife. Once was enough.'

'You loved your wife?' asked Christie curiously.

'Yes. I loved her,' said McHarg, adding with the effort of a man instinctively reticent, 'I love my daughter too.'

'Well, I guess that makes two of us,' said Christie, rubbing his hand across his face. 'Come on. She'll be in the refectory, I reckon. I'll take you there.'

They walked side by side, two big men who felt the beginnings of a liking for each other but both doubted for very different reasons if it could ever come to anything.

'Are you married, Professor?' asked McHarg.

'Irretrievably,' said Christie.

'Well, that's honest.'

'Honesty's sometimes the easy way out,' said Christie sadly. 'You're a policeman, you should know that.'

The refectory wasn't packed but there were enough people in it to create a loud buzz of voices and tintinnabulation of implements.

Christie looked around. 'There,' he said pointing. 'She's a creature of habit in some ways.'

McHarg followed the blunt finger's direction. Flora was sitting by a window, eating, with a book propped up against a cruet. The only other people at her table were a young couple, clasping hands and staring soulfully into each other's eyes across plates of congealing french fries.

'Thanks,' said McHarg.

Christie Connolly nodded and moved away to join his party who were already seated together at a table in the centre of the room. Very democratic.

Flora did not look up till McHarg had taken the seat opposite her. She showed no surprise.

'This won't take long,' said McHarg.

'I've still got to eat my pudding,' said Flora. 'So don't rush.'

'I'll put things plainly, because I don't know when I'll see you again. I'm in some trouble.'

She nodded and closed her book.

'I know,' she said. 'I had a letter from Heather after you'd gone yesterday morning. She reckoned you would never tell me.'

'Another minute and she'd have been wrong,' said McHarg. 'It's possible to be wrong about people.'

'You reckon?'

'I've been wrong. A hundred times. A hundred ways. And I've been right too, once or twice. But this isn't a defence, not even a justification.'

'A confession then?' she said, toying with her dessert.

'An assertion,' he said. 'Of the truth. The truth needs to be asserted sometimes. I loved your mother. I love you.'

'Gee whiz,' she said without heat. 'And that buys you a ticket back into my life?'

He suddenly smiled, a little wearily.

'Hell no, Flo,' he said. 'You're missing the point. It buys me a ticket out.'

He hadn't called her Flo since she was nine and had decided that she wanted to be known by her full name.

'Be happy,' he said, standing up. 'I like your fellow. I hope you can work something out.'

Unexpectedly Flora felt herself on the defensive and like her father her instinct was to attack.

'What about you, Dad?' she mocked. 'Are you going to be happy? Get yourself a woman?'

'I doubt it. About being happy, I mean. Or a woman either for that matter.'

She caught at something in his tone and said, 'But there is someone?'

He thought of Betty, safe in her sister's house a thousand miles away, and smiled.

'In a way,' he said. 'But I can't see it coming to anything.'

Suddenly she grasped him by the wrist, a retaining rather than an affectionate grip, but she studied his face so closely it amounted to an intimacy.

'You're going to be OK?' she said. 'This trouble you're in – it's going to pass?'

'Maybe. Maybe not. But most things pass,' he replied.

'Is it being chucked out of the force that bothers you so much?' she asked, her voice a little scornful, but still holding his wrist.

To her surprise he laughed.

'There are worse things to be chucked out of,' he said. 'No, that doesn't bother me. Not seeing you again, that'll bother me, I think. Yes, that'll bother me.'

'And your little bit on the side,' she said, inspired to coarseness in an attempt to resist a wave of compassion that was rising in her. 'Will you not be seeing her again? Or are you off now to walk together into the sunset?'

'Difficult,' he said drily. 'She's in a wheelchair. And no, I don't suppose I'll be seeing her either. Not for a while.'

'In a wheelchair? You mean, crippled?' She whistled. 'Jesus Christ, Dad. You don't have much luck with your womenfolk!'

'On the contrary,' he said.

He slipped his hand from her wrist, then bent forward and quickly kissed her as though frightened she would start back. Curiously that little uncertainty touched her more than anything else.

But there was no time for more talk. He had pushed back his chair and was striding away with that military bearing he had never lost.

When he reached the door, he raised his right hand, the hand that had struck her the previous morning. But he didn't pause and he didn't look round. In a second he was through the door and out of sight.

More than one pair of eyes watched his departure, but only in Flora's breast did it cause such a confusion of feeling. She had rehearsed this second encounter a hundred times in the past twenty-four hours, but it had followed none of the possible scenarios and neither he nor she had spoken any of the hypothesized lines.

They hadn't even said goodbye.

There was something very final about that.

5

The Præceptor was missing the Tyler.

Not that the American craft-brother did not inspire confidence. There was, after all, a long tradition of good old American know-how in these matters.

That was partly the trouble. Because of this they hired outsiders, professionals, to do their removal work. They argued that once you had hit-men on the permanent staff you became a rival Mafia. And you tended to use them because they were there.

The Præceptor accepted this. The last thing they wanted was to get into competition with the Mafia. And removal must always be a last resort.

Reluctantly they agreed that in Deirdre Connolly's case, this stage had been reached. Jopley reported that a rendezvous had been arranged. Whatever its purpose, it was too dangerous to let it take place. As for McHarg, the stage was long overdue. Tracking him through Heathrow had been easy. But it still had come as a shock the previous day to see that looming, menacing figure here in Boston.

And where, wondered the Præceptor, was that other menacing figure? Oh Tyler, Tyler.

'I've sent for Ember,' said the American. 'We've used him before. He's absolutely reliable.'

'He works alone?' said the Præceptor doubtfully.

The American raised his eyebrows. He thought the

Præceptor was being a little hysterical about this McHarg guy. One middle-aged British cop was a mid-morning snack to a man like Ember. OK, so McHarg had dumped the Tyler, but after all he was just another middle-aged British cop.

He said none of this to the Præceptor, however, but went on, 'No. He'll bring an assistant. He picks his own, probably a man named Goldmann. He's very good too. I'm telling Ember we want McHarg removed any which way, but the girl like it was an accident.'

'Why's that?'

'Conal,' said the American. 'He's our investment programme. Put yourself in his shoes. He lives pretty close to the edge. One sniff that we've had anything to do with harming his sister and he could go over.'

'But he'll hold together otherwise?'

'I think so. You see, in the end we're helping him to do what he wants more than anything else in the world to do. But we keep a close eye on him. I'll be checking him out myself tomorrow night.'

'In Washington?'

'New York. He's staying there till after the big parade the day after tomorrow.'

'St Patrick's Day?'

'That's right,' said the American, smiling. 'There's votes there for the collecting, so you can bet that young Conal Connolly will be there to collect them.'

'One more thing. The other girl.'

'Miss Woodstock? That was easy. We've traced her to Los Angeles. She's in hospital there. You'll laugh when I tell you. It's a Masonic foundation!'

The Præceptor didn't laugh.

'Does that mean we have influence?'

'Some,' said the American. 'Just give the word, say what you want done.'

'Nothing, as yet,' said the Præceptor.

'You're not feeling sorry for this girl?' wondered the American.

The *Præceptor* ignored the impertinence and replied in an even tone, '*McHarg is.*'

'*So, she's a weapon? But only while McHarg's still with us, which isn't for long, believe me!*'

'*Yes,*' said the *Præceptor*. '*I'm sure you're right.*'

'*I know I'm right,*' said the American. '*Relax, Præceptor. Come St Patrick's Day and one way or another everyone's troubles are over!*'

Part Four

_____SAINT PATRICK'S DAY_____

1

St Patrick's Day dawned cold and clear all along the Eastern sea-board.

Not everyone saw the dawn.

In a Boston hotel a couple of hours before the sun rose a man left his room and moved slowly along the corridor. For more than four hours he had been meticulously noting the returning guests. There were two distinct possibilities, a middle-aged couple who had returned after midnight, full of booze and giggles, and a man alone who had moved with the dignified over-steadiness of the chronically stoned.

The latter proved to have been too well conditioned. Despite his state, he had bolted the bedroom door behind him. The couple had been more carefree however and the intruder had been able to rifle wallet and purse without disturbing their alcoholic slumber. What he got was small reward for such dangerous work. He had once been big time, but even hotel thieves reach retiring age, the touch goes, the nerve with it, and besides his face was known and he could no longer work the big hotels where the real bread was. Here there was nothing but peanuts and the jewelery wasn't worth the bottles it was made from.

One possibility remained. No one had returned to Number 34, though the room was taken. It was worth a look.

Or perhaps it wasn't, he thought as he searched the almost empty drawers. There was a cheap suitcase on top of the closet. He took it down. It bore the initials D.McH.

He was a man not without culture. *MacHeath?* he thought. Perhaps that's where the guy was, out robbing coaches.

He smiled as his thumbs snapped back the catches.

The blast caught him, lifted him and slapped him back against the wall so hard that it ruptured most of his internal organs and brought a picture off the wall in the neighbouring room. Flames licked across the neatly made bed and for a lot of hotel guests and a good number of firemen, St Patrick's Day dawned earlier than usual that year.

The early editions ran a couple of paragraphs on the story. *Hotel blast. Man killed. Extensive fire damage. Room occupied by English tourist.*

The Præceptor read the report over early morning tea and smiled. The Americans did these things so efficiently. Perhaps the next Tyler should be American?

And how McHarg would have hated that *English*!

Flora McHarg didn't see the report, but her thoughts turned to her father as she ate her frugal breakfast. He had gone so abruptly, she had no way in which she could contact him. Did she wish to contact him? Not particularly, she assured herself. At the same time she knew that for some reason she definitely did not wish to lose contact with him.

After breakfast she showered and got dressed. Usually she was pretty indifferent to what she wore, merely dragging on the jeans and shirt she'd discarded the night before as long as they weren't too disgusting. But this morning she took great care, and with her hair too, and when she'd finished she stood in front of a mirror, her eyes moving between her own image and a sheet of paper she had in her hand.

Satisfied, she now checked her watch and went out. As she felt the fresh morning air on her face, she suddenly felt confident. Everything would work out. Troubles may pile deep as winter snows, but spring comes. In the end spring always comes.

2

Christie Connolly breakfasted late and alone.

Usually he hated St Patrick's Day, but this year, with the old man safely out of the way at Castlemaine, and his wife and daughters even further removed in Carolina, he was looking forward to it. He experienced a strong surge of euphoric optimism. This was going to be one of the *good* days. A good book, a good bottle, and he'd envy no one, least of all poor fools like Conal, stuck in that long dreary crawl up Fifth Avenue in dirty, dangerous, claustrophobic New York.

The door opened and Deirdre came in.

''Morning,' she said.

''Morning. Hey, you look nice and colourful. But where's the green?'

Deirdre was wearing red slacks, a yellow windcheater and had her long hair tied up in a bright yellow scarf with a primrose pattern.

'The Porsche will have to say it all for me,' she said, grinning. 'And I don't see you covered in shamrocks.'

'To be sure, I have them pinned right next to me skin.'

'You enjoy your day,' said Dree, looking at her watch. 'I won't be disturbing you. 'Bye now.'

Sam Nixon, seated in his Mustang Fastback, folded his paper as Deirdre came out of the house. He had just been reading about the hotel explosion, with some small interest. Not that the story meant anything special to him, but as an ex-cop, he'd found himself considering possibilities. Most exotic was the Mob; most likely, a gas-leak. There wasn't a large proportion of the exotic in a cop's life, though perhaps rather more than in an ex-cop's life. Still, the money was good, and the Connollys were pretty nice people.

Miss Deirdre, for instance, she didn't much care to be looked after, he knew that. But she always went out of her way to be nice, like now.

He rolled down the window and said, 'Good morning, ma'am.'

She smiled at him as if she meant it. She was a good-looking girl even with half her face shaded by the big orbed sun-glasses she wore against the bright but unwarming dazzle.

''Morning, Sam. I'll be going down to the marina. I'll probably spend most of the day pootling around on the boat, take her out if the wind doesn't freshen too much. OK?'

'Yes, ma'am, thank you. Will you have company?'

'I'm not expecting any.'

'Right, ma'am.'

It seemed a strange way to him for a good-looking young filly to spend a day. And it would probably seem an even stranger way to Old Pat Connolly for a true-bred Irish lass to spend St Patrick's Day. But that was her business. He was paid to keep her from harm, not report on her private life. She'd made it clear to the old man that this was the only basis on which she would tolerate him.

'Oh, and I'll probably stop for gas on the way,' she warned.

That's what he liked about her, no side and lots of consideration.

The green Porsche drew away and he slid into the traffic after it.

After a few minutes she signalled right and turned into a filling station. He watched as the attendant pumped gas into the Porsche. Miss Deirdre paid and drove forward just a little way clear of the pumps before stopping again outside the ladies' john.

Well, even the very rich had to go when they had to go, thought Sam philosophically.

A moment later she reappeared and ducked into the low-slung car.

Sam followed, yawning. He hadn't been sleeping too well lately. Maybe he could get a couple of hours later in the morning if the girl was going to be bouncing around in that boat of hers. His responsibility ended at the waterline. If Old Pat Connolly wanted her protected beyond that, let him hire a killer whale.

He had registered unconsciously that Deirdre was not driving with her usual panache, but it was not until they reached the harbour area and the steel-grey sweep of the ocean began to fill the gaps between the warehouses that he began to suspect anything might be wrong. For a start this wasn't her normal route, but what the hell, with her money she could drive where she wanted. More worrying was her driving. It might have been uncharacteristic before but now it was plain erratic. The Porsche was pursuing a serpentine path along the highway as though its driver were drunk, or having mechanical trouble with the steering. Anxiously Sam drew close and blew his horn. He knew this stretch of road. Just ahead it dropped down steeply and swung round in a wide curve to join the dockside road – not a good place to have steering trouble.

With relief he saw the Porsche's brake-lights come on and he stamped on his own pedal. He had almost stopped before he acknowledged that the Porsche wasn't slowing down. Brake-lights flickering like a distress signal, it was gathering speed away from him down the slope.

'Holy Mary, Mother of God!' exclaimed Sam whose distant Catholicism, long lapsed, had been an additional recommendation to Old Pat.

The Porsche was now completely out of control. He could see Deirdre struggling to open the door. But there was no time. It shot across the dock road between two horn-blasting container trucks and for a brief second seemed to hang in the air, beautiful as a bird.

Then it was gone, and by the time Sam had tumbled out of the Mustang and rushed to the dockside, there was hardly a trace on the wind-chopped surface to betray the Porsche's passage.

3

The jeep came fast down the hillside, bucking the exposed roots of ancient trees. At the bottom where a great sweep of firs began, Chris Emerson cut the engine and coasted over a thick yielding carpet of fallen needles till they came to a halt in the musty half-darkness between the soaring pillars of wood.

'This is it,' he said.

Prince Arthur leapt lightly from the jeep, removing his red-and-green-checked hunting jacket. A man came out of the trees and took it from him. Also his Robin Hood hat with the little yellow feather.

Inspector Dewhurst, the Prince's personal detective, regarded this transaction with amazement.

'It's all right, Mr Dewhurst,' said the Prince with his most charming smile. 'I'm not being kidnapped. There, I think he should pass muster in the dark with the light behind him.'

He stepped back to examine the newcomer who had now put on the Prince's garments.

'Better than that,' said Emerson. 'He's been practising your funny walk.'

'I don't think I wish to see that,' said Arthur. 'Mr Dewhurst, I owe you an explanation. I'm having a day off, that's all. I've no wish to get you into trouble, so if you wish to come along with me, I'll be glad of your company.'

'I don't understand, sir,' said Dewhurst, his round face expressing puzzlement as his mind raced in search of an explanation for this strange behaviour. 'I'll have to check any change of plan with the RCMP when we get back to the cabin.'

'If you must, you must,' agreed the Prince solemnly. 'Meanwhile, I'll be on my way.'

'Hold it!' commanded Dewhurst as Arthur turned away. 'I'm sorry, sir, what I mean is, I'll have to come with you.'

'Thought you might,' grinned the Prince. 'Right. Jacket off. Hat too.'

Dewhurst was wearing a lumber jacket even more garish than the Prince's had been and on his head was a bright orange tam-o'-shanter.

He removed them, the realization dawning on him that their brightness, against which he had protested when Emerson's foreman had provided them that morning, was very functional.

'Captain Jopley,' he said. 'Do you know what's going on?'

Jopley, seated beside the policeman in the back seat, had no difficulty in looking perplexed. He had been expecting a move, but this had taken him unawares.

He shook his head and said, 'I haven't the foggiest.'

The Prince smiled apologetically.

'Sorry, Edward,' he said. 'Security. Chris will explain all. We'll need your help in the charade.'

A second man had appeared, this one very like Dewhurst in size and shape. He took the policeman's jacket and hat and put them on.

'Come on, Inspector,' said the Prince impatiently.

Slowly Dewhurst climbed out of the back seat and the second man took his place. The first was already seated beside Emerson.

'Mr Emerson, I must protest,' said Dewhurst formally.

'By all means,' said Emerson. 'Everything OK? Enjoy yourself!'

'Captain Jopley, I'll rely on you to inform the authorities . . .' cried Dewhurst, but the rest of his words were drowned in the roar of the engine as Emerson gunned the jeep out of the pine trees.

'Come along, Inspector,' said the Prince in a kindly voice. 'Just a little walk, then I really will explain. I'm afraid we've got rather a long drive ahead of us.'

Together they set off across the carpet of pine needles to where Dewhurst could now dimly discern another vehicle parked deep among the trees.

This is it, he assured himself as he trotted slightly to keep up with the Prince's springy stride. This is definitely it! When this lot was over, it was a transfer to traffic for him. Or down to the seaside like that hard bugger, McHarg. Oh yes. There were no flies on McHarg. None at all. He'd have likely bopped the Prince on the head before he let him take off like this. Whereas he, Charley Dewhurst, was trotting obediently along, like a good little dog, heading God knows where.

Captain Jopley would sort it out. Perhaps. He wasn't as daft as he looked, that one. Perhaps. Well, anyway, there wasn't anyone else. It was all down to Captain Jopley.

Jopley meanwhile was genuinely concerned about the Prince's departure, but not in any way that would have made Dewhurst happy. He had promised to signal the move as soon as possible. The trouble was that Emerson clearly had no intention of going straight back to the cabin and there was no chance of passing on the news while they were stuck out in the middle of this God-forsaken wilderness.

It wasn't his fault, of course. And he had warned the Præceptor that something like this was likely to happen, so he presumed that arrangements had been made.

But as always when any doubts about his role or his performance came into his mind, they were rapidly joined by a picture of the Tyler with scalpel and tongs probing into the chasm of a dead man's mouth which Jopley's shaking hands held open.

He settled back with as much patience as he could muster, eager for the moment when he could get his hands on a telephone.

4

The winch that was hauling the Porsche out of the dock suddenly developed a high keening note as the car broke the surface.

It was entirely appropriate, thought Christie dully as he stood with Sam alongside a little knot of policemen. A small crowd of dockworkers, growing all the time as the news got around, were watching the operation too, but at a greater distance, held back by the crush barriers the police had erected.

Sam was sodden wet, a blanket had been found to drape round his shoulders but he had refused to go and change. In his eyes, he'd fallen down on the job and the least he could do now was stay there and face it out to the finish.

He'd plunged into the water after the car but in the murk could see nothing. After half-a-dozen desperate dives, he had been dragged out exhausted by the dock police who were quickly on the scene.

The news had bereft Christie of speech for several minutes. Then instantly he had rung Old Pat before the prospect entirely drained the courage out of him.

The response had been brusque.

'It's certain, is it? Tell Conal. I'm on my way.'

Then the phone had gone dead.

Conal, dragged to the phone from the preliminaries of the New York parade, had seemed confused. He seemed to think something had happened to Mary at first, but when the truth got through, his anguish was audible over all those miles of wire. And then, sick to his stomach, Christie had headed down to the dockside where a team of frogmen were already diving armed with powerful lights.

The car was on its side, they reported. The passenger door was uppermost. It was either locked or jammed. Not that it mattered at this stage. They could see inside and the open mouth and staring eyes of the drowned girl told them there was no need to hurry.

The best and safest thing was to leave her in there till the whole caboodle could be winched up at once.

Now the car hung motionless in the air, water cascading out of it, molten in the sun glare which struck bright scintillas of light off the vivid green paintwork. Its sleek elegant lines gave it the look of some once fast and powerful marine creature now dragged from its element by a triumphing angler.

Finally the falling water shrank to a trickle and then to a string of glass beads. The winch keened once more and the vehicle was swung round and lowered on to the dock.

The dead woman could be seen quite clearly through the tinted glass. Christie wanted to look away but he couldn't. An ambulance was backed up to the Porsche and two orderlies with a stretcher stood ready.

A police officer opened the driver's door. The orderlies moved forward.

As they manœuvred the body out, they obscured Christie's view. But Sam had a better angle and as the girl was laid on the stretcher he said, 'Hey, hold it!'

He went forward and stooped to the body over which the orderlies had quickly draped a sheet. Pulling this aside, he gazed down at the face.

'Mr Christie, Mr Christie!' he called with excited incredulity. 'It's not her! It's not Miss Deirdre!'

Bewildered, Christie approached.

Sam looked up at him triumphantly.

Christie looked down at the girl.

It was a moment of sheer nightmare.

'It's not Miss Deirdre!' asserted Sam again as though fearful his judgment was being questioned.

But to his amazement and the amazement of all around him, Christie's only reply was a roar of grief and pain and he knelt down and gathered up the corpse of Flora McHarg to his breast, where he held her as though by his own vital warmth he could bring her back to life again.

When Conal reached Boston two hours later he went straight to the Beacon Street house where he found Old Pat in a state of almost manic delight and Christie plunged into near-catatonic grief.

The Granda had no sympathy at all for his elder grandson and was not going to let anything interfere with his euphoric sense of relief.

'But where is Deirdre?' asked Conal after the first wave of joy at the news had rolled over him.

'Off on some madcap jaunt, no doubt,' answered Old Pat almost gleefully. 'Something she didn't want Sam hanging on her coattails at. She really fooled him! She's a real Connolly, slick as they come!'

He shook his head in rueful admiration. He didn't give a damn about anything as long as Dree was alive, thought Conal.

'And the dead girl . . . ?' he asked.

'Some English student she'd got friendly with,' said Old Pat dismissively. 'You know what a nice outgoing girl Dree is, ready to make friends with anything. But it seems she was Christie's whore as well, this girl. He's been blubbering like a baby. Thank Christ that Judith and the girls aren't here to see him!'

'And what caused the accident?' asked Conal.

The Granda poured him a tumblerful of Irish and freshened his own glass.

'The English whore, what would she know about driving a

car like that?' he asked dismissively. 'Your sister now, she has the touch, else I'd never have made a present of it to her.'

Conal shook his head. He felt uneasily that there was a great deal more to it than that and his feeling was confirmed a few minutes later when Captain Gilpin of the Police Department arrived at the house.

'Mr Connolly,' he said, addressing himself to Old Pat, 'we've had some of our people looking over your grand-daughter's car. In their opinion it's been interfered with.'

'What the devil does that mean?'

'It means that someone fixed the steering and the brakes so that eventually if you put any particularly heavy stress on them, they'd give way.'

Conal, despite his suspicions, took longer to digest the information than the old man who in an instant put back the twenty years his relief seemed to have stripped from him – and more.

'They're trying to kill my girl,' he said rising to his feet. 'We have to find her.'

'They?' said Gilpin. 'Who are *they*, Mr Connolly?'

'How in the name of God should I know?' raged Old Pat. 'Do you not think if I knew, I wouldn't be having them shot down like beasts in the forest?'

Gilpin stuck out his pointed chin and said softly, 'There'll be no shooting in Boston unless we do it, Mr Connolly. Remember that. Do you have any idea where your granddaughter is now?'

'None at all,' replied Old Pat surlily, not caring to be reprimanded by a public servant.

'And what was this woman, McHarg, doing in the car, do you know that?'

Old Pat shot Conal a warning glance and said evenly, 'She was a friend of my granddaughter's. She must have loaned the Porsche to her for the day.'

'Generous,' observed the policeman with an ironic inflection. 'We'd better find Miss Connolly as soon as we can, to be on the safe side. I assume if she loaned her car, she's likely to be in town somewhere still? Any ideas?'

The two Connollys exchanged glances and shook their heads.

'OK. She's staying here with your other boy, right? I'd better talk to him. He might have a better notion of her movements. And the bodyguard, I'll want to see him too.'

'Sam? He made a statement to your men, then hung around till I got here. I sent him home to dry off.'

'OK. I'll get to him. Now, Professor Connolly, where's he?'

'Upstairs. The stress of all this has been too much for him. He's pretty shook up, you'll find.'

Gilpin went out, Conal accompanying him to the foot of the stairway to point out Christie's room. As the Captain disappeared, the front door opened and Sam came in.

'Mr Conal,' he said, 'is your grandfather still here?'

'In here,' said Old Pat imperiously from the study door. 'I want to talk with you.'

Sam moved like a recruit responding to a drill-sergeant. The poor bastard must have been terrified for his life when he saw the Porsche go into the water, thought Conal. Now he'd been given a second chance and he was eager to re-establish himself.

'Mr Connolly, sir,' he said, obviously desperate to pre-empt reproof, 'I've been doing a bit of checking. It seemed likely that Miss Deirdre'd need a car, her not having the Porsche and all. So I've been ringing round. I was right. She's rented a convertible, picked it up this morning about fifteen minutes after ditching me.'

He paused triumphantly.

'You've got the licence details and everything?' asked Conal. 'Great. We can get Gilpin to put a trace on it.'

'Hold it,' said Old Pat. 'Not so fast. How long's she rented this car for?'

'Just a couple of days,' said Sam.

'So she wants a couple of days away,' mused Old Pat.

'Let's not be so quick to let the whole of our gabby police department know how she's spending those days, shall we? Sam, have you got enough connections to do a trace yourself?'

Sam shook his head, reluctant to admit inadequacy, but even more frightened to claim more than he could deliver.

'No need,' said Conal suddenly, striking his forehead in a gesture more Latin than Irish. 'I know where she is!'

'What?'

'I remember now. She's booked the Lodge. I overheard her calling old Goffman at the *ceilidh* last week.'

'She never said anything to me,' proclaimed the old man.

'Well, there wouldn't be much point if she didn't want you to know,' mocked Conal, moving towards the telephone. 'I'll ring Goffman.'

There was no phone at the Lodge itself, this being one of its charms for those in search of peaceful isolation.

'No!' snapped the Granda. 'What could that old fool do? I doubt there's any danger for Dree. Whoever fixed that car will still be thinking she's lying on a slab in the morgue, most likely. Besides, we can be there ourselves, just about as quick as he can crawl up the mountainside in that old truck of his.'

'You came down from Castlemaine in the chopper?' asked Conal, quick on the uptake.

'How else would I come, thinking my darling Dree was dead?'

Conal considered the idea. 'But if you're so certain Dree's safe now . . .'

'Now, but not for ever,' said Old Pat. 'I don't know who's done this thing, but I mean to find out before they can try again, which might be sooner than we think.

'Besides,' he added thoughtfully, 'I should like to see for myself what manner of thing it is that turns my lovely open Deirdre into some kind of conspirator.'

Conal too. The shadow of a suspicion had touched his mind. He wiped it away as an absurdity, but he knew there was no way he was going to let the Granda go by himself.

And however you looked at it, it was surely better than prancing up Fifth Avenue in front of an army of potato-brains.

The Granda was heading for the door, pausing only to pick up an old scuffed leather briefcase. It looked to be fairly weighty.

'What the hell have you got there, Granda?' asked Conal.

'My medication,' he replied promptly. 'I'm a sick old man, Con. I daren't be too far from a whole storeful of pills and potions.'

Sick old man, thought Conal. Bullshit!

'What about Gilpin?' he asked, nodding upwards.

'Christie will be spewing his heart out about his English whore,' said Old Pat disgustedly. 'And Gilpin will be lapping up the scandal like mother's milk and wondering whether he dare arrest him on suspicion of murder. That's the way their minds work. Let's be on our way before he decides to take all our fingerprints.'

They left. The cop in the car outside touched his cap. Nice lives these rich Micks lead, he thought settling back comfortably in his seat. No worries, no hassle. And Gilpin would be out soon, full of good whiskey and self-importance. Well, at least it would put him in a good mood.

He closed his eyes and tried to catch a few moments' sleep.

5

The Connollys' mountain lodge was built against a hillside. From the slope below, the trees had been cleared, partly for use in construction, partly to give a clear view away over the darkly forested landscape filleted here and there with a briefly glimpsed strip of silver where a fast-moving river caught the eye of the sun. Behind and above the building the trees remained, mainly tall Douglas firs whose needles and heavy cones formed a rough carpet in the Fall and whose strong trunks provided a necessary barrier against the winter snows which might otherwise have avalanched over the Lodge as spring returned.

The road to the house went no further and its approach was visible for about a quarter of a mile as it snaked down the hillside to where the forest began again. Half a mile further down, it joined the highway which about a mile to the south ran through the small settlement, optimistically called Summit, where the Goffmans lived.

Deirdre stopped to pick up the keys but refused Mrs Goffman's invitation to drink tea and catch up on local gossip.

'That girl's in an awful hurry,' said Mrs Goffman, rather put out.

Mr Goffman, who had long developed a deaf ear to his wife's over-active voice, didn't reply, though Deirdre's haste and agitation had not escaped him. But he also knew the value of a blind eye to the behaviour of those who employed you, and a still tongue when it came to their business.

Deirdre drove straight up to the Lodge at high speed. The private road had been badly pitted by a couple of hard winters and her hired car's suspension groaned protestingly but she made no attempt to slow down. There was no precise time for the rendezvous, and for all she knew, Arthur was already there, waiting for her. Logically the thought should have made her drive slowly, reluctant to begin an encounter the outcome of which was going to cause pain and tribulation whichever way it went.

But the only logic in her heart was the logic of a lover hastening to a tryst.

It was no good! She'd told herself a thousand times. This was no state to start their meeting in. No turbulently emotional reunion could be allowed to pre-empt what had to be a cool, calm and considered decision. But still her foot kept hitting the accelerator and still her pulses raced in time with the high-revving engine. It would be better if he wasn't there, she told herself. Better if she had time to recover her composure, think herself into the role of hostess receiving a weekend guest.

But when she burst out of the trees into the sunlit clearing before the Lodge and saw that no other car stood there, all she felt was a vast cold-drenching disappointment.

Inside she did the usual checks. Mr Goffman had switched the generator on to run the deep-freeze which he had re-stocked. There were fresh gas-cylinders for the oven and for heating too, if required. But the preferred source of heat was the huge fireplace where a wigwam of logs stood ready for lighting. She tossed a match into their centre and soon a plume of smoke was rising above the Lodge, its sharp resiny smell mingling pleasantly with the sweeter natural odours of the forest.

After that Dree went round the building, unlocking the shutters which for security purposes Mr Goffman left to the attention of the new arrivals.

Finally, as there was still no sign of another car, she took a shower and changed her clothes. Water was pumped up from a well beneath the kitchen floor and in addition just a couple of furlongs from the house by the edge of the clearing a fast-moving mountain stream ran. Neither source had been known to dry up.

Refreshed by the shower, she felt herself in control of her emotions once more and set about reinforcing this feeling by busying herself in a conventional domestic role, checking for dust, setting the table, laying out the makings of a meal.

When she heard the sound of a vehicle approaching, she was able to remove her apron and glance in the mirror to check her face and hair with hardly more than a qualm of anticipation, and that too mild to be called either joyous or fearful.

She went to the door and stood there, a welcoming smile on her face.

A jeep came out of the trees, more hesitantly than her own

approach. She saw with surprise, concern, disappointment, that there were two men in it.

But it was Arthur who was driving.

He brought the jeep to a halt some twenty yards from the house and climbed out. He stood there for a moment, fair hair ruffled by the breeze which always blew here as though believing this glade had been cleared for its benefit alone. On his face was a smile, but no more than the smile which he put on to greet the hundreds of reception parties which lay in wait for him year by year as he stepped from plane, train and limousine.

Deirdre felt her own hostess's welcome smile stretching wider and stiffer till it felt obscene and grotesque. She would have liked to step back into the house, escape to her bedroom, turn the key in the lock, but she couldn't move. Perhaps they would remain like this for ever, petrified into effigies of the Noble Lady greeting the Royal Visitor.

The thought released her, but only into its fantasy.

She was wearing jeans, but her hands went out at either side as though gathering a full skirt and she dropped a curtsey.

The Prince's formal arrival smile disappeared as though exorcized. He threw back his head and laughed.

And then they were both running, stumbling over the rough ground between them, till they met thigh to thigh, breast to breast, and mouth to mouth.

After what might have been five minutes or five days, Dree felt her perimeter of perception move slowly outwards again to take in sky and trees and the Lodge and finally the jeep.

'Who's your chaperon?' she whispered.

'Oh God. Dewhurst. I'd forgotten him.'

Turning, he called, 'Do step down, Mr Dewhurst.'

Slowly the policeman climbed out of the jeep. His face was a blank, showing neither disapproval of nor enthusiasm for the situation. As they had driven down from Canada (at speeds which had scared the living daylights out of him till he'd wondered aloud what a traffic cop would make of this pair of speeding limeys), Dewhurst had kept the same lack of expression on his face during the Prince's explanation of what was going on.

'So you see,' he had concluded, 'I'm not really putting you in an awkward situation, Mr Dewhurst. You'll be able to report as fully as you feel necessary because, after this weekend, either the whole world is going to know, or else there won't be anything to know.'

The simplicity of youth, thought Dewhurst glumly. The touching belief that their decisions decided anything! And the naive hope that it would be possible to make a calm, considered judgment on the basis of a two-day reunion in this remote and romantic setting after half a year of separation!

If it wasn't for me being here, he thought cynically as he approached, they'd be inside by now pulling the clothes off each other. Or mebbe even outside.

'How d'you do, Miss,' he said stretching out his hand as the Prince made the introductions. He'd seen the girl before, he realized. But it had never occurred to him that she and the Prince were having a thing, though their families seemed to have got wind of it. Bloody nobs, they always closed ranks, kept it in the family. But if things went wrong it wouldn't be *Sorry, Inspector Dewhurst, we should have told you*, it would be *On your bike, Constable*!

His mood wasn't improved when a quick check round the Lodge revealed the absence of a telephone. And the Prince had the keys to the jeep in his pocket. Still, this couldn't be the only human habitation round here. They had to get their supplies from somewhere. For all he knew these bloody trees screened off a whole building estate in the next glade two hundred yards up the hillside!

He drank some coffee, ate a sandwich and then, partly out of duty because he ought at least to get to know the lie of the land, and partly out of consideration because these two youngsters had been long separated and would clearly prefer to be on their own, he excused himself, to stretch his legs, as he put it, on account of them being stiff after the drive.

Dree and Arthur watched him go with mingled relief and amusement.

'There,' said the Prince. 'Aren't our policemen wonderful?'

'Approaching, no. Departing, yes, they're terrific,' answered Dree.

But now a silence fell between them which made them realize just how useful Dewhurst's presence had been, providing an excuse not to talk as well as an inhibition against going to bed. Had he not been there when they met, Dree guessed – no, she *knew* – they would have made love instantly and talked afterwards. But now that physical burning rage for his body and all its delights which she had felt as they embraced had faded. It was still there in her breasts, her stomach, her thighs, ready to flare up again at a touch, a caress, but now it was talk first. It had to be.

'I want you,' she said.

'And I want you,' he answered.

But they didn't move out of their respective chairs.

'And I shall have you,' she went on casually. 'Even if you've come to tell me your family are marrying you off to some horse-faced half-wit with a pedigree like a Derby winner, I shall still have you before I knock your teeth in. OK?'

'OK. Well, that's something to look forward to,' he said a trifle shakily.

'But first we've got to talk,' she went on. She was surprised to find herself more or less taking control of the proceedings, even more surprised to meet such little resistance from one who she knew to be strong-willed, positive, and accustomed to command. Was that a good sign or a bad? And a good or bad sign of *what*?

'Art,' she said. 'Listen, important things first. Do you still feel the same? I mean, not that you like me, or are very fond of me, or would just adore to jump in the sack with me. No, what I want to know is do you love me, want to stay with me, feel that life would be empty without me.'

Such emotional earnestness was not in his tradition and clearly took him aback. This was more difficult for him, she realized. He was used to dealing in understatement, saving up the intense poetic outburst for moments of high passion. Well, that was OK and she loved to hear it and she accepted its sincerity, but as a precocious schoolfriend of hers had once assured an open-mouthed circle of less-advanced listeners, you could get a grizzly to sing serenades if you got a hold of his balls.

Arthur took such a long time to reply that she began to think he must be seeking the phraseology of evasion, the ambiguities which would make her let-down as gentle as possible.

But in the end all he did was nod and say, 'Yes. I can't add anything to that. And you?'

'Me too,' she said.

They sat and grinned at each other like children. The grins were genuine expressions of joy, but behind them they both felt the start of sadness and pain. For, though not children, they were both very young, younger than their years in that both of them had been brought up in protected environments which prepared them thoroughly for their specific roles but couldn't provide the kind of maturation which comes from struggle and hardship. Dree knew all about the tragic and often sordid history of her forbears, but unlike the Granda in whose mind it was still a living reality, it meant little to her. Arthur had been trained to understand the social and economic problems of his country from an early age, but not all the reading, writing, listening, talking and touring in the world could remove the fact that to him money was mainly an abstract concept and hardship an alternative he sometimes chose in pursuance of military or sporting expertise.

Such upbringings must produce some kind of selfishness,

especially as selfishness is as various as, say, goodness and some of the varieties of the latter are much more harmful than the former.

So even now as they sat and grinned at each other, there was a tiny unacknowledged part of both their minds which wished that the other had offered the easy way out by confessing the death, or at least the dilution, of love.

'Is that end of discussion, or what?' asked the Prince hopefully.

Dree smiled and shook her head. 'Just a clarification of the agenda,' she said. 'Art, you must have thought about this a couple of times in the last nine months, even talked it over with people . . . ?'

He shook his head vigorously. 'No,' he said. 'I mean yes, I've thought about you, about us, day and night. But I haven't talked about it, only with Chris. Frankly I didn't know who I should talk about it with, not back home. The English have a strange sense of duty and I just didn't want any more aggro from the family!'

'What did Chris say?'

'He sees no problem,' said Arthur. 'He says I'm a cypher in an anachronism. Blow me away, and all that happens is nothing happens except everyone moves up a place. He has a quaint turn of phrase.'

'But that's not how you see it?' queried Dree.

'Not quite,' answered the Prince slowly. 'I wish I did. Then everything would be so easy. I don't think I matter much, but I matter. Everything I do every working day tells me I matter, and to a hell of a lot of people.'

'Or to a system.'

'If you like,' he said. 'But it's a system I believe in. It would be easy if I didn't, if I could see my departure from it as a blow for revolution! I don't know, Dree. Am I being too self-important? If it was just a matter of fading quietly away, that would be fine. But I know a lot of people, my people, are going to feel themselves betrayed.'

'All the world loves a lover,' she said lightly. 'Especially when there's objection from up top. Look at Romeo and Juliet.'

'The world didn't start loving them till they were dead,' he said sombrely.

They sat in silence for a moment. Outside, unnoticed, grey clouds were beginning to roll across the sky from behind the mountains to the north and the bright day was snuggling down for an early evening. The logs burnt more brightly in the huge fireplace and the pair of them sat in the flickering light, heedless of the shadows which crowded into the corners of the long room.

'That sounds like a cue for thumbs-down,' said Dree. She felt like a drink, something she rarely did. Not that she didn't *drink*, but it was only rarely that she actively felt in need of it.

'Not at all,' said Arthur. 'But you wanted clarification. That's the way my thoughts have been running. What I am, what I do, may seem daft to healthy democrats like Chris, maybe you too, but as long as my country thinks it worthwhile having special laws about people like me marrying, I've got to take it seriously.'

'Me too, Art,' she said. 'I take it seriously. There's no special laws touching me, but my church has its laws, and I take them pretty seriously. Also there's the family.'

'Yes, I know. At least you've got all your objections concentrated in one package, your grandfather. Once the dear old chap is borne off to the Lake Isle of Innisfree or whatever, your problems are mainly over. Me, I don't have a family, I have The Family.'

'It's worse than that for me, Art,' she said.

Briefly she told him about Old Pat's fury and the new terms of his will. He was aghast.

'But that's monstrous! No court of law would uphold such an outrageous condition!' he exploded.

'Perhaps not. But there's a strong belief over here that a man's money is his to do with what he likes, living or dead,' said Dree.

'But to involve your brothers!'

'Yes. Well, the Granda thinks Con takes far too soft a line on the Irish question anyway, so this is a nice reminder to him of where his duty lies. I don't know what it would do to him politically if he lost the inheritance. He has very little money of his own and the kind of races he will be running really cost. Also, there's a hell of a lot of support might melt away with the Connolly millions and business influence. So it could be fatal. Christie I don't think would give a damn, but his wife would scratch my eyes out!'

She managed a wry smile to lighten the moment and added, 'So, if you were after my money, forget it! We'd have to make do on yours.'

'Which might not be as much as you think,' he answered. 'I'd come off the Civil List, of course, right off it, I mean. However much public support I get, I'm determined I won't take a penny of public money. I'm not setting myself up as a club for the lefties to beat my family with. But at least there's no question of disinheriting anyone else.'

Another silence.

'Oh Art, what are we going to do?' she cried.

He came across to her then, kneeling beside her chair and taking her in his arms. She sobbed a few times, but desire has flames to dry up tears and soon their mutual comforting turned into caresses.

'We said we'd decide first,' she whispered.

'We were wrong,' he said.

'But Mr Dewhurst will come back.'

'He's a good cop. He won't come in without a warrant.'

And picking her up in his arms he carried her through into the bedroom.

Outside the clouds rolled still more thickly out of the north, like whipped cream poured with unstinting hand by the generous aunt with whom Dewhurst had spent his boyhood holidays. But it was only their leading edge which had that rich whiteness against the rapidly diminishing blue sky. Behind, the white quickly modulated through a gamut of greys to the blackness of a horizon where land and air were indistinguishable.

Dewhurst wished he was back in England, back in boyhood, with plump, jolly Aunt Effie in her little terraced cottage in Gloucester. There was nothing out here but trees, trees and more bloody trees, all as tall as a couple of telegraph poles, but with never a wire in sight. He was following the track down to the road with frequent excursions up promising side-tracks in the hope that some form of human habitation lay just out of sight in the forest. Even a gingerbread house would have been welcome, he thought. But there was nothing but bloody trees.

So it would have to be the road. He glanced at his watch. He'd already been away for three-quarters of an hour, what with his diversions and all. Another fifteen minutes maximum to the road, he guessed. Then what? Back north the way they had come there had been nothing for at least ten miles. And south? Damn, he should have brought the map from the jeep. Not that it had done the Prince much good. He'd managed to get lost half-a-dozen times. But wasn't there some kind of town or hamlet marked a little to the south? Dewhurst recollected. But how far? Once he hit the road, he might get a lift, of course. Except that other vehicles had been almost as rare as houses. Shit! He paused uncertainly. He didn't want to be away from the Prince too long. In the circumstances, an hour was diplomatic; anything more might be dereliction of duty. He should have stolen the jeep keys. It would probably have been quite easy once the randy young devil had got his trousers off which hadn't seemed likely to be long delayed.

Should have brought the map. *Should have* stolen the keys. All these *should haves*. He could hear them rolling out at the enquiry. And the *shouldn't haves* too. Especially the one big one – *shouldn't have* let it happen in the first place.

Still, sod 'em all. The problem was here and now. All at once the solution was quite clear. He had to get back. His place was close by the Prince, protecting him. What the hell was he doing, Robin Hooding around among the trees? Also it was getting very gloomy and if his vague memories of school natural history lessons were right, there could be bears in these forests. He loosened his Smith and Wesson uneasily in his shoulder holster and wondered how it rated against bears. They hadn't done much work on bears at the police range.

Then he heard a car.

His first thought was that he was much nearer the road than he'd imagined. But as his directional ear readjusted from the alien natural sounds of the forest, he realized the car was in fact approaching along the track.

His first instinct was to step back into the trees and observe. But he couldn't do that. Once past him, it would be up at the Lodge long before he could get back. He had to know who was in it. He stepped into the middle of the track.

The two men in the car were not in a good temper. Their partnership was purely professional. They did not really care for each other very much and had spoken little on the long drive up from Boston. Each of them was nursing a sense of resentment. The driver who was called Goldmann reckoned his companion, whom he knew as Ember, was to blame. Ember made the deals. This one had been simple. A limey in a hotel room, a rich kid in a Porsche. Then south to sunburnt tit land. Nothing about driving around in this fucking wilderness, for Chrissake.

Ember didn't resent Goldmann. Goldmann was a tool, in every sense. Whenever he made a contract, he checked his list of possible partners and Goldmann had been in the top trio for a long time now. No, what Ember resented was the implication that getting the wrong girl in the car had been his fault. Nothing had been said and they were getting the full rate for this extra action, but the implication was there. And what had been undeniable was the police suspicion of the car. Ember had contracted to do an accident job and that meant it should have been undetectable. He'd never liked accident jobs. Blow away, fly away, that was his motto.

Well, what lay ahead of them wasn't blow away either. In fact, it was much more complicated than he liked, but he hadn't complained. Professional pride made him want to get the details right. Also, while he knew nothing about these people he was working for, he knew enough to know that their kind of money could buy pretty strong disincentives for ineffiency. He regarded the forest streaming past the window. To him as to Goldmann it was a fucking wilderness. But he didn't object to it. Out here they could take their time, get the job right, without any fear of interruption.

The car bucked round a bend and there ahead of them in the middle of the rough track stood a man.

Oh *shit*! thought Ember wearily.

Goldmann brought the car to a halt.

The man came slowly round to the passenger door. His coat was open and his right hand was inside it.

Cop, thought Ember. Most likely a limey cop. The homebred variety would have been coming at them with a handful of metal in the same circumstances. Funny how reluctant the Brits were to believe the worst of people. No wonder these trusting bastards got themselves killed.

He pressed the button and the electric window slid noiselessly down.

'Excuse me, sir,' said Dewhurst.

Ember leaned enquiringly forward and looked up at the policeman.

'What is it, Officer?' he said.

For a moment his head and shoulders had blocked out Goldmann who had been sitting quite still with his hands on the wheel. Now Ember relaxed once more and sank back in his seat to give his companion a clear shot across his body through the open window into Dewhurst's chest.

But the limey bastard wasn't so trusting after-all. It was the word 'officer' that had alerted him. Anyone who recognizes a stranger dressed like a lumberjack in the middle of a forest as a cop is not there to watch birds.

He went sideways and backwards, not fast enough to make Goldmann miss, but far enough to take the bullet in the right shoulder instead of on the button. The pain promised to be excruciating but he postponed it till later and rolled and scrambled his way off the track and into the trees. Now the hit-men made another mistake. Instead of pursuing him instantly, they preferred to let their bullets do it from the comfort of the car, and this was no telescopic sight job, steadied on a tripod, but hand-held, heavy automatics wavering after a moving target in the dusk. A lucky shot burnt its way along his thigh but the others whistled away among the pine needles or crunched fleshily into tree-trunks. By the time he heard the car doors open he was thirty yards away, rolling down into a peatily damp ditch and burrowing his way under a lattice of arboreal debris which wind and storm had lain across it. After a little while, partly to avoid more noise but mainly because he felt what little strength remained to him being pumped out of his riven shoulder with each exertion, he lay still. He could hear his pursuers approaching, but they'd have to move fast to find him still conscious.

His last thought before blackness swept over him thick as the sky-eating clouds above was that the Prince's best hope now was Captain Jopley's sense of duty . . . God help us all . . . Captain bloody Jopley . . .

Below and above, the clouds won.

6

The clouds which were bringing a premature gloom to the mountainous slopes of North Maine had an hour or so earlier done Edward Jopley a favour.

Chris Emerson's intention had been to remain out in the forest all day, not returning till the evening, but the sky had made him change his plans.

'We had an early spring this year,' he explained to Jopley, 'but looks like winter's coming back for a second bite. That's the way it goes out here. And if we don't get home before the snow, they'll be looking for us, which is the last thing we want.'

So they had arrived back at Emerson's 'cabin' in the early afternoon. Flakes of snow were already smudging the air and to any outside observer the quick dash into the house with heads bent was completely natural.

There were telephones here, completely secure, so Emerson had assured the royal party, but Jopley was reluctant to take the risk. His voice talking to a Boston number on some bastard security snooper's tape might rouse interest. Not that there would be any interest to arouse if the Præceptor's word was kept. This was a discreet operation with, preferably, no direct involvement of the Prince. Still, he would have preferred a public phone, but they didn't grow on trees, unfortunately.

His dilemma was solved when he got into the house. There was a message for him from a journalist called Mark Spier, an expatriate Englishman, now working in Canada, and a mutual acquaintance of Jopley and the late James Morrison. Reminders of Morrison were the last thing Jopley wanted, but Spier had booked into the lakeside hotel some fifteen miles to the south, which was the nearest civilized point in this damned wilderness. He was suggesting a meeting, for old times' sake, obviously hoping for some kind of homely inside story on Arthur at leisure. Normally Jopley would have ignored it altogether. Spier was a third-rate chancer. But now he gave Emerson the impression that Spier was a top-liner as well as an old friend, and though Emerson was not too happy to lose Jopley's support in the masquerade even for a couple of hours, he let himself be convinced that the equerry should go.

'Keep it short though, will you?' he said. 'Aside from anything else, this weather's pretty tricky for driving in.'

Jopley said, 'I'll be back in an hour,' and climbed into the borrowed jeep with the aplomb of a man who'd passed every test devised by the Institute of Advanced Motoring.

Things worked out well. As he walked through the snow, much more gentle at this level, from the jeep to the hotel, he saw through a window into the bar lounge where Spier was sitting talking earnestly to a busty middle-aged blonde. Despite the earliness of the hour, they had drinks in their hands and a tableful of empties. Jopley guessed the woman's husband was probably out on the lake or wandering through the forests with a gun in his hand. It was always open season on neglected wives for men like Spier, thought Jopley disapprovingly. But it gave him the chance to get into the hotel unobserved, and perhaps even out again.

He went through the main entrance, stepping immediately into a world of urban luxury and a temperature twenty-five degrees higher. They knew how to do things, these North Americans, he thought admiringly. The best British equivalent in terms of remoteness and height would be a YHA hut.

The reception desk was empty. There was a pay-phone in the corner of the small lobby and he ducked under the soundproofing visor and picked it up. He'd taken the precaution of having a pocketful of change and with commendable efficiency he was rapidly connected with the Hotel Mayflower in Boston. He gave a room number, heard it ringing. Then the receiver was picked up and to his immense relief he heard the Præceptor's voice.

'Hello,' he said. 'I thought I should ring.'

His voice was recognized in its turn.

'I've been expecting you. How's everything at your end?'

He glanced round. No sign of Spier. A couple walking up the stairs. No one within hearing distance even without the soundproofing.

'Fine.'

'Good.' The voice changed, became businesslike. 'So report.'

'He's gone. Late this morning. There was a switch in the forest.'

'Yes. We thought so. The girl went too.'

'I thought perhaps she wouldn't,' said Jopley neutrally, fearful of hinting a criticism.

The Præceptor gave a high-pitched laugh. 'That was the plan, yes. But there was a hitch. There was an accident, but the wrong girl had it. This may amuse you. Her name was McHarg.'

'*McHarg?* Oh Christ! Not . . . I thought that Mr Tyler . . .'

'That's right,' interrupted the Præceptor. '*That* McHarg. And he was here in Boston too. But it's all right. He and his daughter have been united. Permanently.'

'Thank God for that,' said Jopley. 'He was a hard man. Does this mean that Mr Tyler . . .'

'No. I fear the worst there. No word. We have used local talent, recommended by some of our craft-brothers over here. They have been apprised of their error with regard to the girl and dispatched to remedy matters.'

'Won't another accident so soon be hard to believe?' asked Jopley.

'That's very true. Good thinking, Edward,' mocked the Præceptor gently. 'No, no accident this time. An IRA attack, phone calls to the press claiming responsibility, it will all seem very credible.'

'But the old man will never accept that,' objected Jopley. 'Why should the IRA murder *his* granddaughter?'

'Edward, you've done well.' There was a new sharpness in the voice now. 'Just get back with your lumberjack friends and behave naturally. Whatever happens. Remember what you are.'

The line went dead.

Jopley replaced the phone but remained under the visor, his thoughts swirling. The Præceptor had warned him, but against what? But even as the whirlpool in his mind still raged, he knew where it was sucking him down to. There was no sense in mocking up an IRA assassination of the girl. Things had changed now that she'd missed the accident. She was no longer the target.

It had to be the Prince.

Jopley was aghast. There'd never been any suggestion of this. The removal of people who were dangerous, he had accepted the necessity of that. Morrison had been ready to talk; McHarg had been hot on their trail; P. X. Connolly had overshadowed his much more controllable brother; and the girl herself, Deirdre Connolly, she was a menace not only to Conal as a man of potentially vast wealth and power, but also to the Prince. So, remove her. He could stomach that. But not the Prince. Jopley believed in the Prince as part of an ill-defined but noble ideal of global order and authority, based inevitably on wealth and political power and, equally inevitably, needing the support and loyalty of a kind of Prætorian Guard. That was where the Templar Thanes came in. Their work was secret, and ruthless, and at times even squalid. But ultimately it was on the side of order. The Prince and his family were part of that order. It might be necessary to remind him of his duty sometimes, to protect him from the wiles of colonial adventuresses, but to kill him was to reduce the whole affair to a mere money-grubbing, profit-making business. It was not for this he had joined, not for this he had taken and enforced those terrible oaths. The memory of the red ruin of Morrison's gaping mouth rose in his mind and was with difficulty pushed away.

Less than ever he wanted to talk to Spier now. Deep in thought, he walked out of the hotel into the snow-filled air. What was there for him to do? Perhaps face to face the Præceptor could explain, convince? He was a soldier, knew that there were often forces at work far beyond the grasp of the man on the battlefield. Obey orders, that was the soldier's role, that kept him sane.

But why should it have come to this? he asked himself angrily. Someone had been inefficient. If they'd removed the

Connolly girl as planned . . . And what was it the Præceptor
had said? Somehow, crazily, they had managed to kill
McHarg's daughter instead? Jesus!

He shuddered, not at the cold but at the thought of what it
would feel like to have McHarg alive and on the trail still
with that bit of news to put the scent of blood in his nostrils.
Thank God they'd succeeded in killing him at least!

He climbed into the jeep and switched the engine on
straightaway to boost the independent heater. The snow was
thickening. Thank God for four-wheel drive. He was going
to need it. The snow lay against the windows, turning the
inside of the vehicle into a sort of box, shut off from the outer
world and all its troubles, a refuge, almost cosy. He sat for a
moment without turning on the windscreen wipers, enjoying
the feeling of otherness, of respite.

The hand that came to rest on his shoulder felt for a brief
flash of time like the hand of brotherhood, of friendship,
encouraging, reassuring.

But the pressure increased instantly far beyond the power
of his wishful thinking.

He turned his head sharply and shrieked like a woman.
Suddenly his safe cosy box felt like a coffin.

'Hello, Captain Jopley,' said McHarg. 'You and me have
got lots to talk about. But first things first. Where the hell
has the Prince gone?'

7

Arthur looked down at the naked body of the sleeping girl
and marvelled at its smooth perfection. They had made love
with a passionate, almost despairing frenzy twice in very
quick succession and then she had curled up against him like
a child secure at last after much tribulation and, un-

expectedly, suddenly, fallen asleep. He must remember to ask her if it was a compliment to the exhaustive demands of his technique or a comment on his soporific conversation.

He ran his fingers lightly along the curve of her breast and she stirred under the touch and he found himself stirring again also at the sight and feel of her. But there would be plenty of time for that. Or perhaps there wouldn't. Either way he had to think, to work out where it was they had reached in their relationship. Gently he disengaged himself from her light embrace and rolled off the bed.

What is it I want? he asked himself, trying to ease himself into a mood of serious ratiocination. *I want a cigarette* came the frivolous evasive answer. He smoked very little and never in public but now he felt like one. There had been a cigarette-box in the big room, he recalled. Slipping on his underpants as a sop to Dewhurst in case he was sitting out there, he went out of the bedroom.

He had been right. There was a freshly filled box on the old colonial dresser. He lit one with a glowing billet from the log fire and drew in deeply. Dewhurst had not returned, he observed, unless he was elsewhere in the building. Poor fellow, he'd be swanning around outside somewhere, looking for an AA box! This had been a good place to meet, he decided. It gave them as much chance of uninterrupted privacy as anywhere else he could think of. On the other hand its very remoteness and separateness were in a way counter-productive. Instead of getting down to the serious business of working out a future, he found himself inclined to sink into a pleasantly sybaritic state of timelessness and let the world go hang itself.

But a decision had to be made. He hated himself for his uncertainty. To be hesitating now, here, at this stage, with the warmth and scent of Dree's flesh still on him was monstrous, a betrayal. So, be honest, rational. Get the perspective right. OK. His position, his function. That was the obstacle. So what was he?

The answer came pat. He was nothing, unimportant, an

irrelevance, an anachronism; the majority of his fellow countrymen would applaud with delight if he got married to Dree; even his family would not be all *that* disapproving. They would rather he didn't, but there wouldn't be any of that old exile business, nothing like that.

So *why* was he hesitating?

The answer suddenly struck him with the force of divine revelation.

Simply, he was afraid of being married!

He sat down and studied this proposition.

The more he looked, the more obvious it became. He'd seen the syndrome in others, members of his own family even, who had viewed the prospect of approaching matrimony with a mixture of doubt and panic which had seemed almost comic to the outside observer.

It's nothing to do with other people, he realized. Nothing to do with public duty or private loyalty, nothing to do with politics or religion, nothing to do even with his own feelings for Dree, which were as free from ambiguity as such feelings ever could be.

When it came down to it, he was simply terrified at the prospect of being married; public approval or disapproval did not enter into it.

He stood up and tossed his cigarette butt into the fire. It was a gross over-simplification, of course, but it offered hope. This was something different to talk about, something normal, something manageable. Perhaps it would turn out that at bottom Dree had the same fears. Once confronted together, surely they would evaporate?

He headed back for the bedroom, but paused as he heard a noise outside. Dewhurst returning. Not before time. Any longer and he'd have been seriously worried about the poor devil!

The door opened. He smiled in anticipation of the policeman's embarrassment at catching him in his pants.

And the smile remained there, set in that instinctive mask of courtesy which years of conditioning had taught him to wear in the face of no matter what surprises, as Ember and Goldmann came into the room.

'Gentlemen,' he said. 'How can I help you?'

Goldmann glanced enquiringly at his partner. He would have been happy to blast the guy here and now and get on their way. But Ember knew how to take as well as give orders.

'Your Royal Highness,' he said in a light, lilting accent. 'Please to consider yourself under arrest.'

'Arrest?' said the Prince, wondering for one mad moment if these men could be from the US Immigration Office come to get him for illicit entry.

'For grievous crimes you and your family have committed for many centuries against the Irish people,' said Ember. 'You'll get a fair trial.'

It was unnecessary to talk like this without witnesses but Ember believed in working his way into a part.

And now there was a witness.

Deirdre had appeared at the door from the bedroom with a blanket draped over her shoulders. Her eyes were still dewy with sleep and sex, but they cleared rapidly as they took in the newcomers.

Arthur moved towards her.

'Stay still, buddy boy,' ordered Goldmann, who would have needed surgery to give him an Irish accent.

'It's all right, my love,' said the Prince reassuringly, not breaking his step. 'These gentlemen . . .'

Goldmann hit him with the butt of his automatic, catching him just behind the ear and dropping him like a log.

Deirdre shrieked and tried to run to his recumbent body but Ember caught her by the shoulder and spun her round to face him. Enraged, she drove her fingernails at his eyes but he moved his head back and cracked his open hand against her jaw, making her cry out again, in pain this time.

He repeated the blow with the back of his hand on the other side. She staggered back now and the blanket slid from her shoulders, leaving her naked.

'Whore,' said Ember. 'Fornicating with your country's enemies. Filth.'

Goldmann grabbed her hands and forced them behind her body. His eyes ran lasciviously down the slender, sun-tanned body. He dumped her in a hard upright chair and pushed her arms through the wooden bars of the back rest. From his pocket he took a small roll of thin wire with which he bound her wrists together, pulling it so tight that in places it broke the skin.

'What now?' he asked.

'The usual for her kind,' said Ember. 'Cut her hair off.'

'*All* of her hair?' grinned Goldmann.

Ember regarded him coldly. In the little file he kept, Goldmann was marked down as unreliable on jobs involving direct contact with women. Blowing up their cars was one thing, working at close quarters quite another. It was bad enough if the woman had to be taken out. But this one was to be left alive as a witness and what she was supposed to have witnessed was an attack by two IRA fanatics, not a rape by an oversexed hoodlum with a Bronx accent.

'Will you hurry it up?' he said quietly.

Goldmann met his gaze, gave a token sneer of defiance, then took a switch-blade from his pocket and, dragging the girl's hair back so hard that her head cracked against the bulk of the chair, he began to saw away at the long dark tresses.

On the floor the Prince stirred and groaned. Ember watched till he saw that full consciousness had almost returned.

'Stay down there,' he said, levelling his gun. 'Or I'll take your leg off.'

The Prince's eyes flickered to the unwavering barrel and he lay quite still.

'What do you want?' demanded Deirdre, whose pain and terror had receded just enough to make speech possible again. 'What are you going to do to him?'

To *him*. Both Ember and Arthur noticed the altruistic concern. It must be love, thought Ember. Or perhaps she was just bright enough to have worked out that her boyfriend was about to lose more than his hair. It was sometimes a shitty job, thought Ember. He hated close-ups. And he hated play-acting. But it had to be done right. The newsmen were going to be the first to hear of this and what they printed would be the only report his employers were interested in.

'We've some friends outside,' he said. 'Like I said, he'll get a fair trial.'

'Trial for what?' The question ended in a shriek as Goldmann jerked on her hair again. He was taking far too long, cutting a strand at a time, alternately caressing the flowing locks and twisting them painfully. But Ember was ultra-sensitive to people's moods. He usually knew to a millimetre when a victim had tensed himself for a final suicidal dash. Sometimes this sensitivity had saved his own life. And now he knew that he mustn't lean too hard on Goldmann. With any luck the bastard would shoot his load into his pants before much longer and then perhaps they could get this business over and be on their way.

'Trial for what?' repeated the girl.

'For murder, rape, arson, theft and attempted genocide,' said Ember, glancing out of a window.

The snow was easing off, thank God. Being snowed in up here he could do without. But it was definitely getting brighter, and through the softly floating flakes he could see quite clearly the trees which ringed the clearing, their dark ribs picked out now by this lacing of white. There was one a little in advance of the others, tall, slim, elegant, spearing the feathery sky. He'd no idea what kind of tree it was. They were all firs to him. But it would do very nicely, he thought.

As soon as that perverted mother, Goldmann, had finished his barbering, they would take the Prince outside and tie him to that tree and blow his brains out.

8

The chopper pilot had viewed the darkening skies ahead and listened to the weather reports crackling over his radio with increasing perturbation. Conal, in the front passenger seat, had been too rapt in his own thoughts to pay much heed till the pilot dug him in the ribs a couple of times to draw his attention.

'We'll have to go down,' he yelled. 'There's no future in this.'

'What's the trouble?'

The pilot, a fierce dark little man whose immigrant great-grandparents had Americanized their Italian name to Patch, rolled his eyes expressively.

'The trouble is not being able to see. *That's* the trouble!'

'It's that bad, is it?'

'It will be if we keep on going. There's a chance it'll clear up later, but it'll be too dark then, I guess.'

'Don't you have lights?'

'Gee yes, Senator, we have lights. But you do know where we're going, don't you? I've been there before on a bright sunny day, no cloud, visibility clear to Alaska, and *that* was difficult. It's no nice bright helipad down there. It's a tiny hole in a big forest and you get there by following a road and then a track, neither of which I am about to be able to see, let alone the hole. We'll get down in Bangor.'

'Bangor! For Christ's sake, that's miles out of our way.'

During the exchange Old Pat Connolly who was in the seat behind the pilot remained in the posture he had held since they left Boston, narrow tight-skinned head sunk between thin hunched shoulders, dull unblinking eyes fixed on his fragile white hands which clutched, talon-like, at the briefcase he held on his knees. He had given no indication that he was aware of the passage of time or of distance and, looking at him now, it struck Conal that the best place for the Granda at this moment would be a hospital bed.

This was probably a wild-goose chase anyway, prompted by the Granda's senile neuroses and his own unsavoury guilt feelings. Perhaps the McHarg girl's death *had* been accidental, simple mechanical failure compounded by unfamiliarity with the car. The police too had their neuroses.

Anyway, the point was the Granda was not about to contribute to this discussion and the fourth man in the small cabin, Sam, was there to take orders not vote.

'OK,' Conal said to the pilot. 'Put her down. We'll hire ourselves a jeep.'

Patch nodded his relieved agreement.

Then Old Pat spoke.

'No,' he said.

Patch glanced at him, raised his eyebrows, and shook his head sadly.

Conal said, 'Are you OK, Granda?'

Old Pat ignored him. His skinny thumbs were pressing on the catches of his briefcase.

It snapped open. He reached inside.

When his hands came out they were holding the old Webley ·45 revolver which for so long rested in the cabinet on his study wall.

He found it so heavy that he had to hold it in both hands, but when he rested it against the back of the pilot's seat with the muzzle about three inches from Patch's neck, it was steady enough.

'Keep going, Patch,' he said.

'Granda, don't be so stupid!' yelled Conal.

'Keep going,' repeated Old Pat.

Conal twisted round and looked at Sam who was directly behind him. He signalled him with his eyes. It would be easy for the security man to reach over and grab the Granda's gun.

But Sam shook his head.

Oh shit! thought Conal. He's expiating guilt feelings too. Only Patch had no axe to grind and he was taking a long look over his shoulder at the Granda's face.

'OK,' he said finally. 'I'll try. Though I think that either way we all die.'

'No tricks,' said Old Pat. 'Keep that road in sight even if you've got to run along it.'

'Yes, sir,' said Patch, dropping the chopper a couple of hundred feet. 'There it is now. Not much traffic now. Think how lucky we are. It must be a hell of a day for driving!'

The jeep was aquaplaning so smoothly across the snow-covered road surface that it might have been a sleigh. Jopley had glanced once at the speedometer, then he glanced no more but sank a little deeper into the passenger seat and from time to time studied the map on his knee by the light of a flashlamp.

There had been no resistance on his part, little overt pressure on McHarg's. Somehow, despite the security net, the man had got close enough to the cabin to see their return from the hunting trip through his binoculars. Bright shirts and fancy hats had meant nothing to him. Their three-second dash from the vehicle to the building had told him the Prince was not in the party. And when Jopley had re-emerged only a few minutes later, he had followed him.

Now Jopley had leisure to analyse the ease of his agreement to co-operate. McHarg he'd always feared. There was in the man a centre of stillness and strength which he had always felt as a rebuke to his own secret uncertainties. He had been pleased when McHarg left the Prince's service, horrified when he learned he was somehow on the track of his car after the dreadful night at Sanderton, doubtfully relieved when he heard of the frame-up accident, and incredulously delighted when the Præceptor assured him of the man's demise.

Well, the incredulity had been right, the delight premature. The man was indestructible. His very essence was menace, with no need of gesture. And oh, sweet Jesus! what would he be like when he learned that his daughter was dead? The anticipated horror of that moment had created enough terror in Jopley to make him readily co-operate.

But he could salvage something of self-respect by the genuine identification of something more than just fear of McHarg in his motivation.

His shock at working out that the Prince's death was now purposed had been real and deep. He had neither the means nor the courage to attempt to thwart this purpose himself. But if anyone could, it was McHarg.

So it had been easy to let himself be carried unresistingly along, with all his own thoughts and emotions retired into a kind of limbo. Time enough to let them loose again when he saw how things were turning out.

But curiosity is not so easily switched off. The headlights penetrated only a few yards into the swirl of snow and even less was visible out of the side windows. Even though the speedometer told him that they were moving along at a suicidal rate, it was easy to relax and let the sense of speed be substituted by that sense of cosiness he had momentarily experienced just after leaving the hotel. Outside the dark, the cold, the unfriendly; inside the warm, the comfortable, the secure.

He said: 'McHarg, why are you doing this?'

'Doing what?'

'This US Cavalry act which is likely to get you killed if you don't slow down.'

McHarg thought. 'Answers,' he said. 'I want answers.'

'No, you don't,' said Jopley. 'If you just wanted answers, you'd have spent more time toasting me over a low fire to find out exactly what I know.'

'There'll be time for that,' said McHarg grimly.

Jopley shuddered. He believed it.

McHarg continued: 'But the job comes first. Always must. Do the job. Let the answers come if they will.'

Yes, that was it, thought Jopley enviously. That was McHarg's strength. He took the nearest way. Doubts, uncertainties, pains, profits, all were diversions. Drive straight on. Go for the throat.

Whereas he, Edward Granville Jopley, impeccably pedigree'd in birth, education and military service, was, always had been, a parcel of evasions and deceits.

McHarg spoke as if reading Jopley's thoughts. The Captain was ready to believe he had.

'And you, why've you done this?' he asked.

Jopley did not need to hesitate. He had thought all this through a thousand times. And this box they were in, so remote from time and realilty, had something of the qualities of the confessional.

'Because in openness I could see no way to potency,' he replied.

McHarg shot him a curious glance, but asked no more. He knew when an interrogated man needed no further prompting.

'I believe . . . certain things,' resumed Jopley. 'Details don't matter. I have always wanted to be influential in my beliefs. But there have been no opportunities. What I am . . . openly, what those who make decisions found to admire in me, was in fact limitation. I have no skill for money-making which is one way to power; no talent to rise to more than a moderate military elevation. I thought when I was invited to be the Prince's equerry that here, at last . . . but I'm a social secretary, an upper-class valet, that's all. So I let myself be recruited.'

He broke off abruptly. Even his powers of confession were limited. In openness there is no potency. And sexually too. He could find nothing to take, nothing to give . . . there had been dreadful moments of shame and fiasco till he had discovered that it was through shame, through debasement, through subjugation, that he became potent . . . and after that, ah, the sweet agonies, the soaring depths . . . till they had found him out, or more likely sought him out . . . the

Tyler with his rolls of film, another man of quiet terror, not unlike McHarg . . .

'McHarg, have you killed the Tyler?' he asked abruptly.

The silence was affirmative. Oh Jesus. His own reminiscences were preferable to that thought.

It had seemed like simple blackmail at first, but they had asked nothing. There had been questions, probings, over a long period, till it must finally have occurred to them that here they had something better than a pressed man, they had a volunteer.

Even then they were not content till they had grappled his soul to them with bands stronger than their threats – his own promises. And strangely, after the horror of that night in Morrison's cottage had passed, the realization that for the first time in a life full of form and symbol he was involved with symbols and forms that actually meant something, had filled him with a greater sense of strength and security than he had ever known.

He was ready to obey unquestioningly and indeed even now would have obeyed with only private questionings had not McHarg appeared, *deus ex machina* – no not a god, and needing no machine – a force of nature . . . avalanche . . . blizzard . . .

He fell asleep.

When he awoke the snow had almost stopped and McHarg was studying the map as he drove.

'I'm sorry,' said Jopley. 'I felt so . . . tired.'

Relaxed, he had been going to say.

Into the headlamps' beam loomed a sign. It read SUMMIT pop. 522.

McHarg slammed on the brakes and used the slushy road surface to spin the jeep round in a dozen yards.

'We've overshot,' he said. 'Let's have the map.'

It was hot in the jeep and Jopley wound down the window to get a few draughts of reviving coldness. Somewhere close he heard the familiar pulse of a helicopter's vanes, then it was gone.

'Back a couple of miles. A track off right,' said McHarg. 'Watch for it.'

They moved at a more sedate pace now but only till Jopley spotted the narrow track. There was a sign saying *Private* and a simple gate that someone had passed through and not bothered to shut. McHarg slewed the wheel over and next minute they were thundering through the trees.

The thin patina of snow gave the surface of the track a deceptively even look but underneath it was hard and deeply rutted. The trees flew past at arm's length. All the previous illusion of calm and immobility was completely replaced by an impression of headlong, dangerous flight which was not at all illusory. Terror of seeing made Jopley close his eyes, then greater terror of not seeing made him open them again. It was as well he did, for he spotted the slight movement first. A dark shape at the edge of the track ahead, a rotting branch perhaps, a drift of needles; but it moved!

'McHarg!' screamed Jopley.

The jeep lurched to a halt just short of the moving shape. McHarg killed the lights, kicked open his door and leapt out, with Jopley close behind. They had both realized simultaneously it was a man who lay before them, and now McHarg crouched low by the side of the jeep and tried to pierce the grey shades which folded all around. But Jopley went straight to the man and shone the flashlight in his face.

'It's Dewhurst,' he cried.

McHarg joined him. The moist pain-filled eyes strained up at this new face which loomed over him in the penumbra of the torch, then something like a smile of recognition flickered there.

'McHarg . . .' If he could have asked for any man in the world . . . he strained upwards and groaned more with the effort than the pain which loss of blood and the cold had almost anæsthetized.

McHarg put his arm round his back, saw him wince and looked more closely at the right shoulder.

'Nasty,' he said. 'What happened?'

'Two men,' whispered Dewhurst. 'Shot me . . . looked for me . . . hidden . . . gave up . . .'

'How long ago?'

The eyes managed another flicker of amazement at the absurdity of expecting measures of times.

'. . . seconds . . . minutes . . . hours . . . days . . .' he murmured.

McHarg ran his hand inside Dewhurst's coat and grunted with satisfaction. He came up with the policeman's revolver firmly grasped in his broad fist.

'Hold him,' he ordered Jopley.

He went back to the jeep and reappeared with a rug and half a bottle of Scotch, standard equipment almost in these climes.

'Here,' he said. 'Feed him this. Keep him warm as you can.'

He climbed back into the jeep.

'McHarg!' cried Jopley. 'Surely we ought to take him up to the house . . .'

'He'll be safer here for the time being. You too. I want you safe, Captain Jopley, so don't be taking any walks through the woods.'

Jopley saw the lips stretch in a humourless smile. Then the headlights leapt forward once more and the jeep bucketed away up the track.

Soon it was out of sight and the shadows came running back with the echoes of the fading engine.

When everything was quite quiet again, he thought he caught the throb of the helicopter's vanes once more, but he might have been mistaken.

He unscrewed the whisky cap and dribbled a trickle of the warming liquor into the wounded man's white, stretched mouth.

The chopper pilot's mouth was also white and stretched with the tension of the past hour. The heavy pistol barrel resting on the back of his seat had never wavered, but enough was enough and fifteen minutes earlier he had been ready to call the old bastard's bluff when suddenly the weather had started to ease. It still wasn't good, but at least there was a chance of seeing something. His eyes moved to the fuel gauge. Low but still leaving a bit of a margin. Not that that worried him too much. Once he put this thing down, he was setting off out of range of that pocket cannon strictly under his own power.

He had been flying blind on several occasions and was no longer certain of his position. Coming low to get a visual fix was a dangerous business in this high country but it had to be done. He swung from east to west in a short arc and almost at once picked up the road, then equally quickly lost it again. Another swing and there it was once more, its narrow line running through a small settlement, whose lights twinkled against the early evening gloom.

'Hold it,' said Conal. 'Is that Summit?'

The old man glanced down.

'That's it,' he said.

Patch wished he could feel so positive. One road looked much like another, and one huddle of buildings too, from up here. But obediently he flew on, seeking for the track which ran up to the Lodge. This was even more difficult in the murk, for the trees closed in across the forest tracks and even the clearing in which the Lodge stood was easy to miss if you didn't get right above it.

'There! Is that it?' demanded Conal. 'Look, where the lights are.'

Momentarily Patch glimpsed what looked like the headlights of a car swimming fast beneath the ocean of green. Then they stopped moving and suddenly disappeared.

He swung the chopper round in a tight circle, eyes straining. For a while, nothing.

'Look! There again!' cried Conal.

He saw them, away back and to the right.

Christ, he thought as he watched the light cascading

through the pines, surely no one would be travelling that fast down there?

But unless it was a will-o'-the-wisp, someone was.

He laid in an interception course and dropped down to follow.

Ember heard the helicopter as he stood shivering in the clearing. Goldmann heard it too but he neither paused nor accelerated in his meticulous binding of the Prince to the chosen tree. It wasn't like cutting the girl's hair, he got no perverse pleasure out of it, except in the simple sense of the word in that it pleased him to make Ember impatient. All this fucking rigmarole was none of Goldmann's choosing. But if Ember wanted a performance, OK, that's what he would get.

'Move it, will you?' demanded Ember. The noise of the chopper had made him uneasy. He knew that they were common enough up here – forest rangers, fire-watchers, they all had them. But this one sounded close. Would they be able to make out what was happening if they flew right overhead? He doubted it. The branches of the pine spread out wide and thick a few feet above the Prince's head. A little further in a minute when he shortened it, he thought with an uncharacteristic flash of macabre humour.

Christ, he'd been on this job too long. If he wasn't careful, he'd end up like Goldmann getting kicks from it.

'Why are you doing this?' Arthur asked in a clear, calm voice.

Ember looked at him in surprise. He'd thought the poor bastard was half conscious and in a state of shock, but the head was upright now, the eyes clear and steady.

'You're no more Irish than I am,' Arthur continued. 'So why? If you're being paid, I think I can top their best offer. A prince's ransom is still pretty handsome.'

This was the English royals just like in the movies, thought Ember. All guts and a bit of comedy. He met the man's gaze. He saw there intelligence and genuine curiosity.

The poor bastard really wanted to know what it was all about! He almost wished he could have told him.

What Arthur saw in return was a brief flash of something that might have been pity, then confirmation of his death.

He nodded.

'Dree – the girl – is she to be killed too?' he asked.

'No,' said Ember, after some thought.

'Thank you,' said the Prince warmly.

This guy was something else! thought Ember.

Goldmann said: 'Finished. Let me do the honours.'

He raised his gun to the bound man's head.

'No!' said Ember with sudden ferocity. 'I'll do it.'

Goldmann looked at him in surprise, shrugged and began to walk away. Time for one more look at the naked girl perhaps.

The noise of the helicopter was louder now. He paused and looked up, trying to spot it against the low dark sky.

Ember raised his gun. Arthur didn't close his eyes.

The clearing was full of noise. And it wasn't just the chopper.

'Ember!' yelled Goldmann. 'We got company!'

The headlights of the jeep came slicing through the trees. Ember turned his head. The muzzle of his gun was pressed against the Prince's temple, his finger was white upon the trigger.

And now Arthur did close his eyes, thought a little prayer which was surprisingly ecumenical for one whose family led the Established Church, and kneed Ember in the balls. As the man doubled up, the gun at his temple exploded.

Goldmann had his automatic out and with a two-handed hold was pumping slugs through the windscreen of the fast approaching jeep. No driver was visible but the vehicle held its unremitting course. The killer did the right thing, kept his finger on the trigger till the magazine was empty and held his ground till it was too late for the jeep to follow his evasionary leap. But the snow-covered grass and his thin city shoes betrayed him. Instead of leaping he slipped. And the front right wheel of the heavy jeep ran a groove across his pelvis which provided just enough resistance to turn the steering so that the rear right wheel crushed his chest and neck.

For the jeep was travelling unattended.

As the first bullets crazed the windscreen McHarg had hit the accelerator and left. It was many years since he'd done a parachute drop, but he hit the ground with his body curved and rolling and would have been amused if he'd ever realized that his left hand still swung hard against his chest to hit a non-existent release catch.

In his right hand, he held Dewhurst's gun. He had taken in the scene instinctively as the jeep emerged from the trees but now he was momentarily disorientated, and besides the light had gone. The jeep had continued its mad career across the clearing and there was a tremendous crash as it struck one of the cars parked outside the Lodge. The headlights shattered. Black night poured in from the forest. Only the snow seemed to offer any source of illumination.

Then suddenly, as the fuel line broken by Goldmann's final bullets spilt petrol on to the ruptured battery leads, they shorted and the tangled vehicles blossomed into flame. At almost the same instant, the helicopter's floodlights hit the centre of the clearing as Patch, estimating that the gun at his head was closer to going off than ever before, obeyed Old Pat's injunction to land.

Ember and McHarg faced each other, only a few yards apart. The pain in Ember's crutch was still excruciating but he raised his gun unwaveringly and took aim. He got his shot off first and it might have finished McHarg had not the violent down-draught of the chopper's vanes rocked him with its force. His bullet flew wide and McHarg, who had once spent his days falling out of gun-ships and assuming the firing position as if on an indoor range, showed the uncertainties of age by putting a second shot into Ember's chest when his first had already exploded the man's heart like a fairground balloon.

Now he rose and sprinted to the man bound to the tree,

ignoring the helicopter whose passengers were spilling out of it almost before it touched the ground.

The Prince hung slack in his bonds. The bark above his head was splintered by Ember's bullet and the air was full of the acrid smell of burnt hair.

For a second McHarg thought it had all been too late. Then the Prince stirred and groaned.

It took McHarg a long minute to untie Goldmann's cunningly contrived knots. Arthur slid down the tree and stretched himself out on the ground like a fatigued man ready for a long sleep. McHarg examined the groove in the thick fair hair. The bullet had scorched the scalp but not actually broken it as far as he could see. He plastered it with handfuls of snow and the Prince's eyes opened.

'Mr McHarg,' he said faintly but without surprise. 'I've missed you.'

'Yes, sir,' said McHarg, checking him for other wounds. Apart from a nasty bruise at the base of the neck, there seemed to be nothing.

'That fellow, the one I kicked in the goolies, what happened to him?' croaked Arthur.

'You're lying on him,' said McHarg flatly.

The Prince pushed himself upright and looked down at the crumpled body he had pillowed himself upon.

'Oh God. I didn't kick him *that* hard.'

Then his eyes took in the helicopter with its still slowly rotating blades, the burning jeep, the Lodge beyond, and he cried out, 'Dree!'

He rose to his feet, staggered, but pushed McHarg away when he tried to help and set off at a drunken run towards the building.

McHarg followed in close formation.

Here I am again, he thought ironically. Back in the same old nursemaid job. Only this time no one can say I'm neglecting my family to do it.

Ahead of him Arthur burst through the doorway of the

Lodge and halted instantly, so that McHarg almost ran into him.

Over the Prince's shoulder he saw a strange tableau. A naked girl, with her hair chopped so short that in places the scalp had been torn, was sobbing convulsively in the arms of a very old white-haired man. Kneeling beside them among the tangles of the girl's shorn locks was a younger man, dark and saturnine of expression, with his arms encircling but not touching the other two. Behind them with a gun in his hand which was trained on the door was a third man who had 'cop' written all over him.

The Connollys, identified McHarg. And one of their minders. A strange way for Prince Arthur to meet the family at last.

'Dree!' said Arthur, taking a step forward.

The girl looked up.

'Oh Art!' she cried. 'Thank God.'

She struggled to free herself from the old man's arms. His bright birdlike eyes flickered from her face to Arthur's. There was a wildness in them which McHarg did not like the look of.

Then the girl was free and in Arthur's arms. They looked as if they might be occupied together for some time. McHarg stepped by them into the room and instantly the cop-like man was by his side, gun ready.

'Who are you?' he demanded harshly.

'Who are *you*?' replied McHarg indifferently.

'I look after things for Mr Connolly,' said the other. 'Sam Nixon. And you?'

'McHarg. I used to look after things for His Highness here. We haven't done so well, either of us, have we?'

Sam lowered his gun. 'McHarg,' he said hesitantly as though trying out the name.

'That's right.'

Something about the man's reaction puzzled him.

He said, 'Does it mean something?'

'There was a girl. In Boston,' said Sam slowly.

'My daughter,' said McHarg. Then with a violent intensity which penetrated even to the embracing lovers he said, 'What do you mean – *was*?'

Only Old Pat Connolly was unaffected. All his ears heard and his eyes saw was the English voice and the English face of this English Prince who had brought his beloved granddaughter to this pain and humiliation. Under his hand was the gun which his great namesake had put into his hand all those years ago, not long before he, Young Pat Connolly then, had fled from the ruins of the Dublin Post Office waving his American passport before him like a talisman.

For sixty years he had never told a soul of those moments of terror and total surrender, but the shame of that memory had been with him night and day ever since.

Now here, now at last, there was a chance of expiation.

The face before him became the single mocking face of all those evil Protestant bastards who had riven apart his beloved country, driven his grandfather and his family into exile, and foully murdered his own darling grandson in a Belfast bar. Destroy this face and he would be destroying everything he had hated for all these years.

Trembling, he raised the gun.

Sam was speaking, slowly, reluctantly.

'She's dead, Mr McHarg. There was an accident in the car. No, not an accident. It was meant for Miss Deirdre . . .'

McHarg's head reeled.

'Dead?' he cried. '*Dead!*'

And again he had been miles away, protecting others, looking after this Prince and his Irish whore, while his own beloved Flora . . .

Old Pat Connolly cried, 'Death to the persecutors of Ireland!'

'No!' cried Conal, stepping forward.

'No! No!' cried Deirdre as Arthur pushed her aside.

And '*No!*' screamed McHarg in a long wavering cry of pain as the gun exploded.

Part Five

THE LONG DESCENT

1

The Præceptor looked down on Boston from a great height, like Jesus on the exceeding high mountain, and did not need to be tempted.

It went without saying that all this was desirable. And there was no doubt in the Præceptor's mind that sooner or later it would all be obtained, along with the rest of the wealth and power of this great country.

But now it seemed likely to be later rather than sooner.

There should have been a signal from Ember the previous night and none had come.

What had come was word from a contact in the coroner's office that the man blown to pieces in McHarg's room had not been McHarg. So, no signal; and McHarg alive.

In the Præceptor's mind there was no doubt that the two things were connected.

And the fact that twenty-four hours later not all the careful probings of the New England craft-brothers had been able to pierce the security blanket thrown over events up in Maine confirmed beyond doubt that the Prince was safe. Protection was for the living, not the dead.

The Præceptor took it all phlegmatically. It had been a fiasco. But business ventures had to be able to take losses as well as gains, and there was as yet no indication just how great or small this loss had been.

The longer there failed to be an indication, the smaller the loss was likely to be, thought the Præceptor not without amusement.

Killing the McHarg girl instead of Deirdre Connolly had clearly been the plan's ruination. On the other hand, paradoxically, the girl's death could now mean salvation if, as seemed likely, McHarg had got his hands on Captain Jopley. For, if the Præceptor read McHarg aright, he would want to keep it purely personal now.

The phone rang. Leaving the balcony on to which the huge penthouse window opened, the Præceptor moved back into the hotel room and picked up the receiver.

'They're here, both of them. They're on their way up. Is that OK?'

'I said so, didn't I?'

Replacing the receiver, the Præceptor went to a chair in front of a large television set and sat down. By the chair on a low table was a VTR machine with a cassette in position. The Præceptor lit a cigarette, and studied for a moment the thin elegant fingers that held the burning match. Did they tremble slightly? No, not a jot, though it would have been no surprise if they had done, considering the dangerous moments ahead. Were there safer ways of dealing with the situation? Probably, but every way they had attempted since this chain of disasters began had proved ineffective. In the end, no matter what your elevation, there were some things you had to do yourself.

Besides, the Præceptor was not above curiosity, and had always enjoyed the thrill of personal danger inherent in a long career of manipulating potentially violent and ruthless men.

There was a tap on the door. It was a good start. A blinding, door-smashing fury might have proved impossible to deal with, but where reason controlled, reason was controllable.

'Enter,' called the Præceptor.

The door opened.

Edward Jopley stood there. Not the dapper Captain Jopley familiar to the denizens of that privileged triangle bounded by the Palace, Whitehall and St James's, but an unshaven, haggard man dressed in boots, cords, a tartan shirt and a fleece-lined hunting jacket.

But the voice was the same that might have ushered a visiting dignitary into a royal drawing-room.

'Someone to see you, Præceptor.'

He stepped into the room and to the side.

Behind him, McHarg.

A big man, not tall but broad.

A face which looked as if weariness had tried its worst and finally itself grown weary.

Eyes blank, unblinking, like peepholes in a dungeon door behind which some unimaginable captive sits, calmly waiting to crash out.

Grizzled hair; a brow corrugated like the tundra by endless winds driving across immortal ice; a strong, square jaw.

And black-gloved hands which held a dull black revolver.

It hardly seemed necessary. The man brought with him into the room an aura of menace like a force field. Indeed, thought the Præceptor, seeking reassurance in fantasy, he felt alien enough to have just arrived from beyond the stars, coldly defying the earth's powers to resist.

The fancy brought no comfort but a sudden touch of real fear.

Then an emotion touched McHarg's face. It was surprise, the Præceptor realized. Surprise that there was no one else in the room. It made McHarg mortal once more. And therefore malleable.

The Præceptor let out a high, trilling laugh.

'Mr McHarg. You look surprised. Really, Edward should have warned you.'

'I kept my oath, Præceptor,' said Jopley, adding honestly, 'But he didn't really make serious enquiry.'

McHarg spoke.

'I thought Partington. Or Hunsingore maybe. But no matter.'

The Præceptor made a moue of disapproval.

'Partington? Useful but limited. And *Hunsingore*? That poor old fool has suffered the worst of fates. He is what he seems to be, though he provides a nice ironic kind of cover for my travels. But I'm disappointed that it doesn't matter to the great McHarg that I'm a woman!'

And Rose le Queux laughed again, but this time the deep throaty laugh which put men at their ease and invited their complicity.

McHarg said, 'It didn't matter to my daughter.' And raised the gun.

'Now hang about!' protested the woman. 'Not so hasty. Surely your male arrogance is curious to know how it arises that a mere woman controls this organization?'

He laughed now, a single bark like a gun-shot, making her start slightly despite all her efforts at calmness.

'*Controls!*' he mocked. 'It's a shambles. That's why I'm here.'

Rose le Queux relaxed slightly. Once get them into intercourse, of whatever kind, and the reins (metaphorically or physically) were in your hands.

'No,' she said seriously. 'You're here because I knew you'd come and I cleared the way for you. I wanted to see you, to talk to you. But first there's something I'd like you to see.'

Her finger pressed the start-button on the VTR. At the faint click, McHarg's finger tightened on the trigger, but relaxed again as a picture formed on the television screen.

It showed the interior of a large hall, not unlike a gymnasium. At one end a narrow strip of matting about twenty yards long was laid between two hand-rails.

A woman in a white towelling robe was setting off to walk along it. Her progress was painfully slow and for long periods she was clearly dragging her whole weight along by the strength of her arms alone.

The camera zoomed in to close-up.

It was Betty Woodstock, her face contorted with effort and pain.

Then, a few feet from the end of the walk, she suddenly drew herself upright, her face a blank of concentration, released her hand-holds, and took three unfaltering, unsupported steps forward, before collapsing over the rails once more. But this time her face was alight with the joy of achievement. It radiated almost tangibly from the screen.

A young white-coated man moved towards her smiling too and obviously congratulating her, though the sound was turned down.

Rose le Queux touched a button and the girl's face was held in big close-up.

'The man's Dr Kitchingman,' she said approvingly. 'He's very good, I believe. That's really remarkable progress in a couple of days, isn't it? That was yesterday. I had the tape flown in overnight as soon as I realized I might be going to need it.'

'Need it for what?' grated McHarg.

'For you, Mr McHarg,' said le Queux. 'As soon as we knew you were in Boston we had Betty traced. It wasn't difficult. And it's odd, this may amuse you, but the hospital she's being treated at is a Masonic foundation! I mean, a genuine charitable institution, nothing to do with us directly, except of course that we have influence. Oh, believe that, Mr McHarg. It's a complex course of treatment that Betty's undergoing. Manipulation, psychology, exercise, drugs, and a bit of surgery too. The prognosis is good, but there are dangers. One slip and she could be back not just to what she was, but even further. Total paralysis. Messages by flickering the eyelids. Food through tubes. It doesn't bear thinking of.'

Her finger moved. For a moment Betty's happy face loomed even larger. Then the picture faded.

Rose le Queux studied McHarg's face closely. She was long an expert in reading men's expressions but this one gave nothing away or at least nothing that she wanted to see. There was another button on the table at the base of the VTR. Press this and help would move in fast. But not fast enough, she felt. And besides, her vanity was at stake. The basis of her power was that men were vulnerable. She could only hope that behind that iron mask her threats were working. She was relying on his superhuman powers of control. The second important discovery she had made about men was that their strengths were as useful to her as their weaknesses. In some you channelled passion, in others control. It was just a matter of getting it right. She felt an impulse to stand up, move around, remind him (and perhaps herself too) that she was a woman. But until she was sure she'd got it right, she wasn't getting out of reach of that alarm button.

'Edward,' she said seeking momentary diversion, 'tell me, what's happening up there?'

'Chaos,' he said promptly. 'Prince Arthur's alive and well. The Connolly girl too. Once the local police realized just who was involved they had the wit to go right to the top. I expect the whole thing's being controlled through the White House and the British Embassy by now.'

'And who is not alive and well?' enquired le Queux.

'Your two men,' said Jopley. 'Mr McHarg saw to that. The Prince's bodyguard is seriously wounded. Old Pat Connolly is in hospital with a stroke. And his son . . .'

'Conal, you mean?'

'That's right. Conal,' said Jopley. 'A bit of a disappointment there, Præceptor. Conal Connolly is dead. He took a bullet meant for the Prince. Fired by his own grandfather.'

For a second the calm brown eyes screwed up in thought and the woman's true age appeared. Then all went smooth and calm again. She's worked it out, thought Jopley, admiring. Her men dead, no evidence. Conal Connolly dead, no profit. So forget it all. Only McHarg remains.

'And Mr McHarg, I take it, when he heard about his daughter, decided to keep his mouth shut and with your help to deal with things personally?' she said.

She felt quite pleased with herself. It was exactly as she had worked out. Except perhaps McHarg. He was way out, beyond anything she would have guessed at. She focused all her attention back on him.

'Mr McHarg,' she said, 'I'm deeply sorry, believe me. We have unwittingly caused each other a great deal of trouble but I admit that in the end you have been the greater sufferer.'

Jopley regarded her admiringly. Years of work wasted, the glittering prize of control of the White House snatched from her grasp, and here she was, earnestly, sincerely, assuring McHarg that his loss was the greater!

'Your daughter's involvement with the Connollys was a desperately unhappy and unforecastable coincidence. But do remember, it was the Connollys themselves who got her mixed up in this, not us.'

McHarg's expression did not change but after a few moments he moved, walking in a small arc to a table stocked with decanters and glasses. The muzzle of his gun held as fast to Rose le Queux's breast as a compass needle to magnetic north, but the woman felt her tension ease by another notch.

'Us? Who's *us*?' said McHarg, unstopping a decanter with his left hand and pouring himself a finger of Scotch.

'Our organization,' she said. 'Or rather, federation. It's grown pretty large, you see. A loose union of near-independent entities, bonded by common interests and old loyalties. Rather like the Commonwealth used to be.'

'With you as the Great White Mother?' gibed McHarg.

She smiled, relaxed another notch. This was going well.

'I was a whore, Mr McHarg,' she said calmly. 'A good one too. But intelligent enough to recognize it as a limited career. I worked in England and America. In fact I was a bit of a pioneer in being one of the first to work the transatlantic jets. Better than the motorways where I started, I can tell you!'

'So, a jet-bag,' said McHarg. 'So?'

'I started making a bit on the side by doing jobs for interested parties. Sometimes it was straightforward blackmail, setting up a naughty tableau, then in bursts the photographer. Sometimes it was Mata Hari stuff, wheedling a bit of information out of a man, or going through his pockets. In the end this became more profitable than the screwing and when I began to establish my own little houses here and there on both sides of the Atlantic, I set them up as much as information agencies as knocking-shops. It wasn't easy at first, there was a lot of bother, a lot of mistakes. In the end I began to get tired of just being a middle-man, so to speak, and I looked for ways of using this intelligence-collection service for myself. I found plenty of businessmen, captains of industry and politicians who were interested. I knew them because they'd sought to buy information from me. Or some I knew because they were my other clients and I could recognize, and of course encourage, their readiness to join us.'

'You mean, you blackmailed the poor sods,' corrected McHarg.

'Some, of course,' agreed le Queux. 'But before you jump too quickly to their defence, Mr McHarg, you should be one of the first to recognize that most men given a choice of being blackmailed or bribed will usually opt for making a profit. Well, to cut a long story short, once things got moving, they really moved. Secrecy was of the essence, of course. The secret world of women is a sexual one, that's where their power lies. I had wide control of that. To find an equivalent male secret world didn't seem possible until one of our executives who was a thirty-two-degree Mason said, why not Freemasonry? Once suggested, it was obvious. An internationally recognized secret society ready made for us. Even the suspicions and opposition it aroused worked to our advantage. They had gone on so long that no one really took much notice of them any more. The best place to hide a poisoned needle, Mr McHarg, is not in a haystack but in a sewing-box. You'd have to prick yourself with each in turn to find out the deadly one.'

'So you hid your secret society in a secret society,' said McHarg half admiringly. 'Clever.'

He'd finished his drink. Now he poured himself another.

'And what are you after? Political power or just profit?'

'The two often go hand in hand,' she said. 'Me, I just

provide the information, or the muscle, and vet the schemes. I've no desire to get us involved in anything that would bring us into disrepute.'

'Like arming an inefficient terrorist group,' mocked McHarg.

'Oh no, Mr McHarg, you misunderstand,' she said with a smile. 'It's failing to make a good return that brings you into disrepute in the world of business. We would supply a gang of paraplegics with blowpipes to attempt a coup against the Kremlin so long as we had our money upfront. But that end of the business has become too involved. You can get your fingers burned, especially if you overestimate your own cleverness like our Mr Partington. No, generally we stick to recruiting men of influence, actual or potential, willing or unwilling. We thought we were on to a winner with Senator Connolly. Alas, it turned out otherwise. We'll have to find ourselves another boy. It shouldn't be difficult. Your fellow men are often a sad, disgusting lot, Mr McHarg. Men like you are pretty rare.'

McHarg laughed. It was more like a real laugh this time.

'You mean, men who are going to kill you, Mrs le Queux?'

'Oh no,' she said, laughing too. 'Every man who comes into a whore's bedroom is potentially one of those. I mean men who are reliable, inexorable. Men like Commander Grossmith, our late lamented Tyler. I take it he is late lamented?'

'Late,' said McHarg shortly. So they hadn't found him yet? Property must be moving more slowly than of yore on the London market.

'He'll be hard to replace,' mused le Queux. 'Very hard.'

She fluttered her eyelashes significantly towards McHarg, whose face registered disbelief.

'You must be crazy!' he exploded.

'Why? You've just heard me expound our technique,' she said, growing in confidence every minute. 'First, get a hold on them to make them listen. Then show them where their advantage lies. OK, in most cases it's spurious, self-deceiving. But not with you, McHarg. What's the point of seeking revenge? Revenge for what? An accident, you know it was an accident. I genuinely regret it, what more can I say? But the harm we *have* done you, deliberately and with malice aforethought, what does that amount to? You've survived! You're probably better mentally and physically than you've been for years.'

'Thanks,' said McHarg sarcastically. 'Except that I'm out of work and on the run.'

'That's nothing. Listen, McHarg. We can make you a hero, get you back in at the Yard. We need a top man there again. There's a lot of small-timers like Elkin, but he'd stick out like a sore thumb if he got much higher. We wouldn't try to hide what's happened to you recently, no, we'd use it! Like me; too many people knew I'd been on the game for me to dare to risk simply changing my identity when I wanted to go respectable, so instead I flaunted it and became a publicly reformed harlot under the auspices of *New Vision*! We'll devise a scenario for you which would fit everything that's happened and is on the record into an acceptable pattern. You'd have influence, authority, status in a world you could help shape to your liking.'

'All that?' said McHarg softly. 'And how many people would you want me to kill a week?'

Rose le Queux made an exasperated gesture.

'We don't like killing people. It's a last resort. We try everything else first. Besides, I know you, McHarg. There's no way I could make you kill anyone you didn't want to. Though once you make up your mind, by Christ, you've shown a pretty talent in that direction!'

Now there was another silence, longer this time, interrupted only by the chink of crystal on crystal as McHarg filled his glass again.

Jopley, a silent auditor still, viewed the protagonists in this enthralling bout with mingled admiration and sadness.

His admiration was for the Præceptor who was slowly, inexorably, gaining the ascendancy. His sadness was for McHarg, this powerful, desperate, violent man who at the end by being false to his own principles of instant, straightforward action was minute by minute being staked out with threads and needles like Gulliver in Lilliput. He saw in process now what he had guessed at intuitively before, the Præceptor's technique of holding before each new recruit a glass in which the terror, crime and raw capitalism of the organization was distorted into shapes to fit the individual's fractured vision of life. But there was in his mind no thought or will to resist. When champions meet, mere mortals hold their breath and tremble at the thunder.

'And Betty Woodstock?' said McHarg nodding at the TV screen.

'No harm. Hopefully a full cure,' said le Queux expansively. 'Back to her career. She's a very bright kid. Just the kind of woman a top cop needs at his side.'

Suddenly Jopley could read her thoughts like subtitles on a screen. She was thinking that given another year, if Betty Woodstock showed any signs of still wanting to tell all, le Queux reckoned she could get McHarg himself to put her out of the way! She was high on her own power, he could see that. And, more horrifyingly, he could not be altogether sure she wasn't right.

'I'd need to think,' said McHarg.

For the first time the gun was lowered, the muzzle pointing at the carpet.

Rose le Queux felt such an upwelling of delighted self-congratulation that she could have wrapped her long shapely arms about herself and hugged her own body in glee. She realized with surprise that for the first time in many years she felt like having a man. She regarded McHarg speculatively. That would be the finishing touch, their physical orgasms matching her orgasm of ego-power. But first, be sure. She was not going to take any more risks.

'McHarg,' she said, the huskiness of her voice no longer

assumed, 'think as long as you like. But we're down to details now, aren't we? No need for guns between us.'

It was McHarg's last chance, thought Jopley.

He was looking straight at Rose le Queux, their unblinking gazes twisting round each other like strands of a single rope.

'No,' he said at last, tossing the revolver on to a chair. 'No need for guns.'

And now she rose and took a step towards him, exerting the full force of her sexuality. It had been a long time since she had been called upon to do this professionally, but all the old power was still there. And this time it was for herself.

'You look tired,' she said. 'There's a bed next door. A long lie-down might help your thoughts along.'

'Yes,' said McHarg putting his glass down and running his fingers through his hair. 'It might.'

He moved towards her. Eagerly she went to meet him.

Well, so much for the Great White Hope, thought Jopley. It was game, set, and match to the Great White Mother.

They met and embraced. Rose le Queux yielded willingly and eagerly to the passionate strength of his arms around her, pulling their bodies close together as though he purposed to take her here, now, his force ripping through their very clothes.

And then the pressure of his arms increased and pain struggled through to the surface of her passion, and she opened her eyes and saw his face.

She opened her mouth to shriek but he brought one hand from behind her back and pressed it over her mouth. She reached out a desperate arm towards the alarm button by the VTR machine but she was yards short.

He said softly in her ear, 'I thought you'd never move, Rosie. And no motorway tart's worth dying for.'

Her eyes bulged like a great Boston cod's as she took his meaning.

To Jopley all this looked like the mere physical abandon of an obscenely erotic embrace. And even when McHarg lifted the woman off her feet, he thought it was just a simple continuation of the same.

Then McHarg took one, two, three, four steps to the open window and as a man might carelessly toss away an empty cigarette packet, he threw the woman over the rail of the penthouse balcony.

He didn't stay to watch her descent twenty-four storeys to the car park below but turned instantly and went back to the table with the VTR machine. He pressed the rewind button and removed the cassette which he slipped into the capacious pocket of his donkey jacket. Recovering the revolver, he dropped it in the other pocket. Finally he finished his drink.

'McHarg!' choked Jopley in terror.

Slowly the man turned to him, then jabbed out a finger, more menacing than a pistol.

'Tell them what happened,' he said. 'Tell them you saw it happen. Tell them the charade's over. Tell them that's what the future holds for anyone who troubles me or mine. Tell them that just a scent, a trace, a mere suspicion, and the air will be so full of falling bodies, the birds will complain. Just tell them!'

The words seemed to hang between them as though carved on the very air.

McHarg turned and made for the door.

'McHarg!' cried Jopley once more. 'What shall I do?'

McHarg turned and smiled grimly. He held up his black-gloved hands.

'I'd wipe anything you touched,' he said. 'Then I'd get out of here before someone comes. Goodbye, Captain Jopley.'

He stepped out of the room and the door closed quietly behind him.

Part Six

LEAVES FROM A SCRAPBOOK

1

Washington Post   March 19
News of the tragic death of Senator Conal Connolly in a
hunting accident in Maine has stunned his colleagues on
Capitol Hill. Widely regarded as a presidential hope for the
not too distant future, Senator Connolly stood for much
that is best in the vital young political life of the country. One
of the great Boston-Irish families, the Connollys have been
dogged by tragedy and this latest sorrow has hit the
immediate survivors hard. Old Pat, the nonagenarian
patriarch, had a stroke when told of the news and is
currently dangerously ill in the Massachusetts General.
Professor Christie Connolly of Boston University was not
available for comment but was reported to be under medical
observation himself, while the Senator's sister, Deirdre
Connolly, is said to have suffered a nervous collapse and to
be recuperating in a private clinic . . .

Boston Globe   March 22
A verdict of accident was reached in the coroner's enquiry
into the circumstances surrounding the death of Mrs Rose le
Queux, an English visitor who fell from the 24th floor of the
Mayflower Hotel. Mrs le Queux was alone in her room when
the incident occurred. Lord William Hunsingore, leader of
the *New Vision* evangelical movement under whose auspices
Mrs le Queux was visiting the United States, assured the
coroner that there was no possibility of suicide. 'Mrs le
Queux was a very strong-minded, mature and balanced
person,' he said. 'Her life had a deep-rooted religious base.
To her, human life was sacrosanct, whether others' or her

own. She will be deeply missed both personally and as a force for good. God moves in mysterious ways . . .'

Montreal Star   March 24
Despite still being visibly affected by the severe cold caught while staying at Chris Emerson's mountain retreat last weekend, the Prince managed a smile as he climbed aboard his plane at the end of his highly successful tour . . .

Miami Herald   April 1
The alarm was raised by a business associate when Mr Partington, one-time member of the British Government's inner cabinet and more recently acquitted of alleged crimes involving bribery of officials and illicit trading, failed to keep an appointment. A pile of clothes found on the remote stretch of beach where Mr Partington had said he was going bathing was identified as his and it is presumed that he was swept out to sea . . .

Pet-Pro Monthly Bulletin   May 4
Interesting news from head office at Sudbury is the appointment of ex-Chief Inspector Elkin as head of company security. Till recently engaged in the international division at Scotland Yard, it is expected that ex-Chief Inspector Elkin will bring many new insights into the growing problems of security within the firm . . .

The London Gazette   May 13
Captain Edward Jopley has resigned from his post of equerry to Prince Arthur and returned to active duty with his former regiment currently serving in Belfast.

Sanderton Evening Post   June 2
At the postponed inquest into the deaths of John Parker (21) and Moira Griffiths (18) in a car accident in March, the coroner heard new forensic evidence that the car that struck Mr Parker's Mini, a Volvo owned by Detective-Inspector

D. McHarg of Sanderton CID, had been tampered with. Inspector McHarg, the court was told, had recently been the victim of a vicious attack with a suspected revenge motive . . .

Daily Express   December 11
Buckingham Palace yesterday refused to comment on rumours of an engagement between Prince Arthur and Miss Deirdre Connolly. An angry reaction is expected from Ulster religious and political leaders who have in the past demanded reassurances about the constitutional issues involved in marriage with a Roman Catholic. Miss Connolly's grandfather, whose wholehearted support of the Republican movement would have been a major obstacle to such a marriage, died last month. He had been bedridden since March this year when . . .

The Times   April 30
The news of the marriage took even the most informed of observers by surprise but if anything this was surpassed by the impact of the simultaneous revelation of the completeness with which Prince Arthur intends retiring into private life. All Civil List income has been completely renounced and with it all titles and their privileges, even though this may require an Act of Parliament. It is believed that the young couple intend to settle in America . . .

The Scotsman   May 2
To Elizabeth and Douglas McHarg of Gulvain Lodge, Inverness, a son, Angus, 7 lbs 3 ozs.

Betty pasted the back of the last cutting and pressed it firmly on to the page of her scrapbook. McHarg had not been pleased when she had insisted on putting the announcement in the paper but she was adamant that things had to be done properly. Like marrying a girl you'd got pregnant. Dr

Kitchingman had been furious when he found out and had made it quite clear to McHarg who he blamed. Betty had sat with her best demure look on, remembering her assiduous and inventive campaign to get McHarg inside her as frequently as possible till the desired result was achieved. And McHarg's thoughts had gone back a quarter of a century to his lost Mavis who had also assured him that all precautions were taken. But nothing of this showed in his expression or speech. All he said was: 'It won't be born in America.'

Surprisingly, far from impeding Betty's progress in regaining the use of her legs, the pregnancy seemed to aid it. At least it surprised the doctors to start with, but as usual with their kind, they rapidly developed explanations which eventually devolved into foreknowledge.

Privately Kitchingman had expressed his doubts to McHarg whether Betty would ever achieve anything beyond a sixty per cent recovery. Casually McHarg passed the opinion on. The reaction was what he had anticipated.

'By the time I'm done, I'll be able to walk that cocky sod off his feet!' she averred angrily.

Well, that time was still a long way off, but now, freed from the weight of young Angus, she was looking forward to bringing it a bit nearer every day.

She closed the scrapbook and put it away. Then she went to the open window and peered out. It was a fine soft morning and Angus was lying in his pram on the stone flags behind the house, enjoying the good Scots air.

McHarg was out on the estate somewhere, but she expected him back for his mid-morning break. He nearly always returned two or three times a day, no matter how distant his work. It had won him a reputation for uxoriousness among the estate workers, though none dared make even the gentlest of jokes to his face. And even Betty did not know the number of times in a day he would clamber to some vantage point of tree or scaur and scan through his binoculars the long narrow road winding between the loch and the heather-deep braes which was the only approach to the house. If he saw a strange car on it, then no matter what he was doing he would abandon it and head straight home.

There was one this morning, a Ford Granada.

He caught it in his glasses, followed it along the road for a while, then turned abruptly and plunged down the hillside towards his Range-Rover. The two foresters with whom he had been discussing a new plantation moments earlier watched his departure with knowing grins.

Drive as fast as he could, he was unable to get down to the house before the Granada.

He parked the Range-Rover some distance away, deliberately slewing it across the estate road, and stepped out, his shotgun in the crook of his arm. He moved lightly towards the house. He could hear voices, not from the interior, but somewhere round the side. Carefully he approached the angle and peered round.

There were two of them with Betty, a man and a woman. The woman was bending over the pram, lifting Angus out of it.

McHarg stepped forward. They all looked round.

'Here he is now!' said Betty.

'McHarg! How are you? And many congratulations!'

It was the Prince; beside him, with Angus cradled lovingly in her arms, Deirdre Connolly. Her hair beneath a headscarf was still cut short, her face would probably never recover that fresh girlish clarity which had been the envy of her sister-in-law. But the pain had gone from her eyes, and from the way she held Angus, she was eager to create a family of her own to replace the one which the previous year had taken away from her.

'I'm fine, sir,' said McHarg. 'We weren't expecting you.'

'Good,' said Arthur with a grin. 'If you weren't, then the press won't be. With a bit of luck, they'll still be staking out the estate we were staying on in the Bahamas. One thing I learned in my old job was how to get out of places unobserved!' He grinned engagingly.

'Is Mrs MacTavish expecting you?' worried Betty, who had a healthy respect for the fierce old housekeeper who looked after the Castle which wasn't really a castle at all but a comfortable small mansion, more French château in style than Scottish baronial.

'She's expecting a small party to come up for the fishing,' said the Prince. 'I've often loaned it out in the past. McHarg, tell me, how are you liking it here?'

'It's fine,' said McHarg.

It had been the Prince's idea. Gratitude had made Arthur more than willing to restrict his curiosity, and that of others, about McHarg's part in the series of events which culminated in the violence in Maine. That was all that McHarg asked, a smoothing of his path to a resumption of something like normal life. But the Prince wanted him to have more, a reward, employment, *something*.

Finally, learning of McHarg's marriage and intent to return to Britain not as a policeman (he had formally submitted his resignation) but as a private citizen in search of peace and quiet, he had offered him the job of estate manager at Gulvain, the small Inverness-shire estate which had been left to him as a child by one of his great-uncles and which he felt he could morally hang on to when he slipped out of public life.

McHarg had protested his ignorance of the work involved.

'We're all going to have to learn new tricks,' Arthur had replied.

'You're set on marrying the girl then?' McHarg had probed shrewdly.

'If she'll have me. And I'd feel comfortable with you somewhere around me, McHarg.'

To which McHarg had answered, 'I'll have a wife. And soon a child. They'll come first to me, no matter what. You should understand that, sir.'

Arthur had laughed and said, 'I'll settle for third. And

don't be deceived, McHarg. I'll be over the estate books with a magnifying glass. I'll maybe need the money!'

And so he had come here, alien at first, but not so alien as he expected. And ignorant at first, but quickly learning, and quickly teaching too that he did not take his job or himself lightly.

It was the kind of existence they both wanted, perhaps not for ever, but certainly for now. Here they could grow together, take stock of their lives and experience, study the future of their child.

He had reassured Betty they were safe. It was all over. But he knew that he lied. There'd be a chain of succession, another Præceptor in another Lodge. Partington's disappearance, Jopley's and Elkin's resignations, these were evidence of reorganization not dissolution, sops to confirm him in his silence.

They would know that he had only spoken as much as was necessary to preserve his own position. What point in saying more? Who would believe? More importantly, who was there to be sure of? All he asked was to be left alone.

There'd been only one voice from the past, a letter from Heather Davison full of affection and concern. He hadn't replied. A man's tongue that had become a dog's tongue, and an old Volvo that had been tampered with while he ate dinner and drank brandy, lay between him and Tim Davison. There were some things he didn't want to be sure of.

From now on he would take care of his own. Surely they had learned that he was capable of that?

Evidently they hadn't.

There had been a visitor to the glen one dark January night. A mere boy. McHarg had not realized how young he was till he shone his torch on to the still features, cast in a pale mask of surprise as the head lolled at its strange angle from the broken neck. An apprentice, sent to prove his vows, he guessed.

He buried the body deep in the forest where the frost had not yet got the earth in its iron grip. The motor-bike the boy had travelled on McHarg dismantled and dropped piece by piece from his rowing-boat into the deepest trough of the loch.

There was nothing more he could do. Silence was perhaps the best message. Indeed it was the only message. He prayed there would not be a next time, but if there were, he would talk a little with his visitor, and listen too, before he killed him.

Rose le Queux, he told himself without much relish for the irony, had turned him into a Tyler after all.

One irony he did relish came to him a little later that day.

The Prince and Deirdre shared the McHargs' lunch, indeed seemed well contented to sit out the rest of the afternoon with them.

Finally Betty had announced that it was time for her daily exercises and invited Deirdre to keep an eye on Angus while she did them, an invitation accepted with alacrity.

'McHarg will want you to try his single malt,' she said as the women went out of the room. 'He's got his own still up the mountain.'

'True?' asked the Prince, ready to believe anything.

'Not so. But I do have a friend. Here, try a dram of this.'

It was tried, pronounced excellent.

'Your wife calls you McHarg,' observed Arthur, smiling.

'It's my name.'

'Yes, but . . .'

'That's how she thinks of me, she says. She can't change it. And it's a usage that sounds well enough up here.'

'Yes, I can see how it would,' said the Prince. 'Another twenty years and they'll be calling you *The McHarg*.'

'Another twenty years and I'll maybe answer to it,' said McHarg. 'And you? How long will it take you to get used to not being a Prince?'

'Another couple of minutes should do it,' laughed Arthur. 'Not that I am entirely without titles, you know. They are there for the asking if I want them.'

'And do you?'

'Not really. But people want me to have them. Do you know, for instance, this very month I was scheduled to be inaugurated as the new Grand Master of the United Celtic Lodge of Welsh Freemasons at Caernarvon Castle. It's a family tradition, sort of. And the odd thing is, they still want me, despite everything. What do you think, McHarg? Should I let myself be initiated?'

And he was quite taken aback, even slightly offended, when McHarg gave himself over to a more wholehearted bout of laughter than anyone connected with the man could ever recall.

Other mysteries you'll enjoy from the Pantheon International Crime series include:

Peter Dickinson   *King & Joker*   71600
   The Last Houseparty   71601
   The Lively Dead   73317
   The Poison Oracle   71023

"Every new book of Dickinson's can be approached with anticipation."—Newgate Callendar, *The New York Times Book Review*

Reginald Hill   *A Killing Kindness*   71060
   Who Guards the Prince?   71337

"Hill's characters are clearly etched. The presence of a real writer makes itself felt."   —*The New York Times*

Norman Lewis   *Cuban Passage*   71420
"An unusually trim and plausible thriller."   —*The New Yorker*

Peter Lovesey   *The False Inspector Dew*   71338
"Irresistible…delightfully off-beat…wickedly clever."
   —*Washington Post Book World*

James McClure   *The Blood of an Englishman*   71019
   The Caterpillar Cop   71058
   The Gooseberry Fool   71059
   The Steam Pig   71021

"James McClure's are not only…first-rate procedurals, but they throw light on the human condition in the land of apartheid."
   —*The New York Times*

William McIlvanney   *Laidlaw*   73338
"It has been a long time since I have read a first mystery as good as this one."   —Robin W. Winks, *The New Republic*

Poul Ørum   *Scapegoat*   71335
"Not only a very good mystery, but also a highly literate novel."
   —*Maj Sjöwall*

Julian Rathbone   *The Euro-Killers*   71061
"Rathbone's new novel is quite exceptional…subtle yet straightforward and truthful."   —*Library Journal*

Per Wahlöö   *Murder on the Thirty-First Floor*   70840
"Something quite special and fascinating."—*The New York Times*

See next page for coupon.

Look for the **Pantheon International Crime** series at your local bookstore or use this coupon to order. *All titles in the series are $2.95.*

Quantity	Catalog #	Price
_____	_____	_____
_____	_____	_____
_____	_____	_____
_____	_____	_____
_____	_____	_____
_____	_____	_____
_____	_____	_____
_____	_____	_____
_____	_____	_____
_____	_____	_____

$1.00 basic charge for postage and handling $1.00

25¢ charge per additional book   _____

Please include applicable sales tax   _____

Total   [   ]

Prices shown are publisher's suggested retail price. Any reseller is free to charge whatever price he wishes for books listed. Prices are subject to change without notice.

Send orders to: **Pantheon Books, PIC 15-2, 201 East 50th St., New York, NY 10022.**

Please send me the books I have listed above. I am enclosing $_____which includes a postage and handling charge of $1.00 for the first book and 25¢ for each additional book, plus applicable sales tax. Please send check or money order in U.S. dollars only. No cash or C.O.D.s accepted. Orders delivered in U.S. only. Please allow 4 weeks for delivery. This offer expires 5/31/84.

Name_____

Address_____

City_____State_____Zip_____